Mardi Gras Madness

Mardi Gras Madness

Tales of Terror and Mayhem in New Orleans

Edited by Martin H. Greenberg
and Russell Davis

Cumberland House
Nashville, Tennessee

Published by Cumberland House Publishing, Inc.
431 Harding Industrial Drive, Nashville, TN 37211

Cover design by Bruce Gore, Gore Studios, Inc.

Library of Congress Cataloging-in-Publication Data
Mardi Gras madness : tales of terror and mayhem in New Orleans / edited by Martin H. Greenberg and Russell Davis.
    p. cm.
    Contents: Faces made of clay / Michelle West – King Corpus / Bruce Holland Rogers – Masking Indian / Charles de Lint –Sacrifice / Jane Lindskold – May oysters have legs / David Bischoff – Fat Tuesday / R. Davis – The invisible woman's clever disguise / Elizabeth Ann Scarbor- ough – Farewell to the flesh / John Helfers – Songs of leaving / Peter Crowther – Skeleton Krewe / Nancy Holder – Down in darkest Dixie where the dead don't dance / Gary A. Braunbeck.
    ISBN 1-58182-077-1 (alk. paper)
    1. Horror tales, American–Louisiana–New Orleans. 2. Detective and mystery stories, American–Louisiana–New Orleans. 3. Carnival–Louisiana- -New Orleans–Fiction. 4. Murder–Louisiana–New Orleans–Fiction. 5. New Orleans (La.)–Fiction. 6. Louisiana–Fiction. I. Greenberg, Martin Harry. II. Davis, Russell, 1970-

PS648.H6 M29 2000
813'.0872093276335–dc21

                                                                99-058601

Printed in the United States of America
1 2 3 4 5 6 7 8 9 — 04 03 02 01 00

Contents

INTRODUCTION

The festival of Mardi Gras is a tradition dating back more than two hundred years. Its roots can be traced back to the Latin *carnivale*, which means—roughly—"farewell to flesh." The premise was simple: a time of great feasting prior to the time of fasting that traditionally begins with Ash Wednesday. *Feasting . . . Fasting . . . Farewell to Flesh . . .*

I like the sound of that.

We've all seen it on television; perhaps some of you have even attended the massive celebration that is Mardi Gras in New Orleans. Mardi Gras is human excess in nearly every form imaginable. It is dark shadows amid alleyways and old cemeteries. It is fractured neon light patterns on feathered masks, strings of beads, and krewe coins. It is beautiful and ugly—frightening in its intensities. Women stand on balconies and bare their breasts to the crowd beast leering up at them from the streets below. Parades, clowns, drinking, dancing, sex, laughter, tears, children, adults, everyone disguised behind masks of any kind, costumes from every period . . . it is a chaotic carnival of human delights and debauchery.

Wonderful, isn't it?

How nice that as a species we are able to throw a party like this, a party that lasts for days on end, a party that provides all kinds of opportunities for . . . all kinds of things. How delicious. *Feasting . . . Fasting . . . Farewell to Flesh . . .*

As I write this, the year 2000 is upon us, and I wonder what that first Mardi Gras in the new millennium will be like . . . grander and more excessive, I suspect, than any other before. I'm assuming, of course, that the world won't end at midnight on December 31—but I could be wrong.

We posed some similar questions to some of today's best writers. Over the last two hundred years, what feasting has really occurred on the dark streets of New Orleans? What creatures have haunted the festival to end all festivals? Who haven't we seen in the nightly news or the papers that is saying farewell to flesh in a horribly unique way? What will the first Mardi Gras of the new millennium bring? And they have answered . . .

Michelle West spins a tale of loss gone too far, and Bruce Holland Rogers takes us on a journey between the extremes of feasting and fasting. Charles de Lint's offering is a ghost story of a completely different cloth, and Jane Lindskold's story delves into the murky waters of Mardi Gras history. David Bischoff's tale shows us how poorly Mardi Gras, organized crime, and voodoo mix. Elizabeth Ann Scarborough takes us to a dance where the masquerade is all too real. At the heart of John Helfers's story, a vampire mixes it up with a group of cultists whose intentions are anything but celebratory. Peter Crowther's tale explores that final Mardi Gras party, while Nancy Holder checks in with a story of true hunger. And our last offering, from Gary Braunbeck, combines the ghosts of the city of New Orleans' history with the fleshly desires of mortals.

In all, eleven stories of Mardi Gras that have never made the next day's headlines—for good reason.

Feasting . . . Fasting . . . Farewell to Flesh . . .
Enjoy yourself, and let the carnivale begin!

—Russell Davis

Mardi Gras Madness

Faces Made of Clay

Michelle West

This was the life she lived:

She woke up with the alarm clock, usually, but not always before dawn. She hit the snooze button three times, or if she was very self-indulgent, four, and then rose and dressed. Lunch was already made and sat in a brown bag substitute—something that could be washed and dried and reused—in the fridge.

She had short hair, wore glasses instead of the contact lenses that made her face feel naked, and never used nail polish.

She went to work in sensible shoes.

Work was the international documentation division of a large firm that shipped out technology parts to countries all over the world. A large corporation learned quickly that being a good corporate citizen was essential on the global stage, at least as far as dotting *i*'s and crossing *t*'s, and she had made a living of doing exactly that; learning which country required signatures in blue ink; which countries refused to accept any photocopies; learning which required certificates and which required personal statements of responsibility rather than corporate ones.

After a day neatly broken by lunch in the quiet corner of the office kitchen reserved for people who did not eat in the company cafeteria, she went home, pausing at the graveyard that separated her from the two halves of her existence. Geography.

Time.

Sometimes she would take flowers.

She had long since run out of the personal mementoes that she had left at the graveside during the first year of bereavement. Or rather, she had run out of those she was willing to part with. Absence had made her miserly, and as she had grown to realize that they were never, in fact, to return—not even in dreams, not in any reliable way—she hoarded anything that had a memory associated with it. Understood her dead mother's missive: *make memories. They may be all you'll have.* Such wisdom, her mother had, who had never lost anyone this way.

Here, between the safety of work and the safety of home was a bitter territory. Sometimes she took joy and comfort in the sight of their names carved in a stone that aged far less quickly than she had. This was a monument—to her grief, to their lives—that meant she was not crazy or deluded; they *had* existed. Her husband. Her son. What was left was *here.*

But at other times, she felt them as ballast, those names, chiselled into *V*-shaped grooves above their numbers. No matter; she came to pay respects because she had to pass the graveyard to get home; it had become ceremony, some private conviction, a personal rite that no day could end—or perhaps begin—without.

It was here that she met the man.

She noticed him first by the shadow he cast, although it was weak in the waning summer light.

Something about his face was familiar; it was striking; slender and elegant and not precisely beautiful beneath the frame of dark hair. That hair stretched past cheekbones, framing the whole. His nose was long, his eyes were clear. He was dressed for rain.

"Susan Fullerton?" He spoke only after her stare had had the time to grow awkwardly intent; to make of his face something of stone or clay, a monument, not a thing lived in and behind. Only his words broke the exploration; and she stood there, caught in the commission of some vague social crime, as if she had reached out with her hands to ascertain the shape and feel of his stranger's face; to explore the terrain by touch.

"You—I'm sorry—this is—I don't—" But he stood ten feet away, or more; well outside of the loose area that she defined as personal space.

"You don't often meet people here."

She shook her head. Something about his face. "Were you related to my husband?"

"Yes. Yes, I was."

The *how,* unasked, hung in the air a moment before it drifted away under her certain sense that he would offer no answer to the question. Only after no hint of a question remained did he continue. "I've been here before, but—I don't usually get out this late." His smile was warmer when he offered it again. "And I don't get out here nearly as often as you do."

She said, before she really thought about what she was saying, "Your life isn't here."

He laughed. "And yours is?"

She discovered that she didn't really like being laughed at by a significantly younger man. "I'm sorry, but I didn't catch your name."

"I didn't offer it."

"I know. And that was my tactful way of pointing out that you were being rude."

He shrugged. Smiled. The sun had reached that point on the horizon where yellow becomes a foreign color; where the sky is pink and purple with veins of deep blue. Shadows were still cast, although not dark ones, by its light. "I was waiting for you. I was sent to deliver this."

He held out a package that was wrapped not in paper and string, but in cloth. Hard to tell what its natural colors were; the sheen of the material caught light and reflected it, making a liquid blend of reflection and color. But she thought purple and blue, or perhaps purple and a deep green. It had been a long time since she'd accepted a package that looked like a gift from a man his age. Long time. Her teeth met through a fold of her lip.

"What is it?" she asked, looking up.

But he was gone; gone with the rest of the sunlight.

SHE SHOULD HAVE KNOWN better. She should have left the gift at the graveside. She thought of putting it down, but only briefly; she was standing in front of the graves, and it was a very, very inappropriate place to discard unwanted things. Nothing she had left here was unwanted or unplanned.

She tried to pick up the threads of routine. She went home. But just before she entered, she paused in the doorway to survey the apartment as if it belonged to a stranger. She was not comforted by what she saw: plain walls, beige carpet, austere shelves with only a few pictures that at a distance looked like pictures any home would have. Only the package in her hand seemed incongruous. Interesting.

She made dinner, in a manner of speaking; she had, store bought, a whole range of single meals in neat packages in a freezer whose inch and a half of white snow constantly reminded her it needed defrosting. While the microwave was humming its low, familiar monotone, she wandered into the living room, sat down on the worn armchair, got up, moved over to the equally worn couch. Thinking only that the colors of the fabric—in dim light, apartment light—were indeed purple and dark green, alternating in an interlocking diamond pattern that was held together by thick golden thread. Wrapped around the cloth, binding it in place, was a rough gold ribbon that was translucent and fine; she pulled at it, gently folding back a corner of soft cloth.

Inside was an envelope in cream and gold. Printed in gold foil in perfectly legible type was the name Susan Fullerton. No address. She opened the envelope, taking care not to tear it.

It contained two cards. The first was an invitation, in purple print with delicate green accents between each phrase of import, to a party. In a city that she had never visited, on a street that she had never heard of, given by a man whose name she didn't recognise. She turned it over; the back had a small map of intertwining cross streets with names in dark ink. The streets weren't laid out in a neat grid; they turned and banked in peculiar ways. But it was clear that they were city streets, they were so close together, and following the directions to the party—should she happen to find herself deposited at any of the streets that bore names—would be at least theoretically possible.

But as the invitation didn't come with a plane ticket, hotel reservations, or anything remotely similar, she grimaced the way one does when one receives a wedding invitation from a distant relative who lives in a geographically remote city. As she bent over, extending her hand to place the invitation carefully in the centre of a water-stained old coffee table, the rest of the bundle fell open, velvet chaffing against the grain of cotton, a spill of gold thread in her lap.

She stared down at the empty, perfect curves that hinted at large eyes in a blank face. A mask. Rimmed, as the package, in gold, enamelled in a pale purple, a pale green, the whole a ceramic wonder. She turned it over, and beneath the curve of each cheek was a single word. The two halves of a name. She touched the letters; they felt cool.

She looked at the invitation again. February. More than half a year away. But at least it was a good time to travel; no one travelled in February much, unless they were skiing.

SHE WAS QUITE SURPRISED at the travel agent's extended laughter. "New Orleans in February of *next* year is *not* the off-season. It's a damn good thing you're calling now; I can probably manage to find you *something* that's not too far away from the French Quarter. You said you were travelling without children?"

It didn't cost much to say, "No, I never travel with children anymore."

But after she hung up the phone, she cried for the first time in years, excluding birthdays, and when she slept, she dreamed of morgues and bodies on slabs behind a wall that looked to the unwary first-time visitor like an endless, terrifying bureaucracy of filing cabinets and labels.

THERE IS SOMETHING THAT sets a tourist apart from a native in almost any city, in any country. Although much is made of clothing, of weight, of the oblivious insularity that comes with knowing the small boundaries of a set life, the air of tourist that clings to a newcomer with no gentle roots in the homes of people born and wed to geography is not so easily pinned down. If it were; if it were, it might be expunged, eradicated.

And if it could be, there would be no strangers; there would be no outsiders looking in through glass, their hands asking for something just beyond their reach and receiving in reply to their varying requests the exact same sensation: the cold surface, the veneer, that can be seen through but cannot be traversed.

Susan Fullerton stood in the long taxi line at an airport. It was, as far as airports go, neither outstandingly ugly nor outstandingly welcoming; poured concrete and odd taxis did nothing to draw her attention away from people carrying hand-drawn signs. She stood staring at the crowd, reading faces, seeing in the geography of their lines some signpost, some marker—be it hair or glasses, nose, chin, age, or weight—that was somehow both familiar and unknown. Cousins meeting for the first time. Exchange students, maybe, although it was an odd time of year for them. People who had met through the ether, nervously seeking their own wrapped in the daily patina of the real.

"Ma'am?"

The first time someone had called her *ma'am* in that tone of voice, she hadn't heard him. Or rather, she had, but she had ignored the syllable and a half, assuming on some level that it was, that it *must* be, meant for someone else. Only his insistence, his dogged determination to actually catch her attention, forced her to acknowledge his label. She had invisibly become, with the passing of time, a faceless older woman, devoid of the possibility of romance or danger.

She had acknowledged it then, with no more than a pang at the loss, but she felt it keenly now, in this airport, at this time. The man at the head of the taxi line—the door to his booth half-open in the surprisingly humid cool—waved her forward as a man standing beside the hood of an empty trunk rolled his eyes. She picked up her bag. It was a single large suitcase, burgundy luggage plastic faded but not yet cracked by the wonders of modern baggage handling. The cab driver picked it up, deposited it in the trunk, and then ushered her into the back seat of his car. It was comfortable; smelled vaguely of stale smoke; was worn in places but not yet at the stage where it had to be patched or replaced.

Instead of watching the city go by in long stretches of highway that turned, by slow degree, into densely packed buildings, she chose to watch the numbers on the fare mount; she played guessing games as she compared the numbers with time and distance, miles melting into digital dollars. Only occasionally did her eye stray to the landscape moving beyond the windows; the highway's broad stretch slowly giving way to buildings, some new, some old.

The cab driver talked to fill the silence. "See those?" he said, as they drove past, the traffic now crawling as triple lanes were girdled into single ones, "those are slave houses. Well, they used to be. They're preserved, but they're on private land. There are places in the city where you can actually look at 'em." He lifted a hand from the wheel; his fingers, brown and cracked, ran in a line, like a disjointed arrow; she couldn't fail to see what he pointed at.

She looked at them, but in a perfunctory way, seeing their shape and size and noting them with a distant horror, a horror that words of faded outrage no longer touched or evoked; a woman interested in a history of vastly fewer years. She felt a pang of guilt, felt that she should be interested.

This was not what she came to the city for. Her silence was angry and mute when she at last arrived at the hotel in which she would be staying the week. There were things she didn't want to be reminded of, and once the memories started, they were hard to kill.

INSIDE, IT WAS *BUSY*. People in funny uniforms slowed to a run to see if she constituted an emergency or a guest who could safely be made to wait. She waited, curious; the hotel, unlike the streets and the airport, was crammed with people who also did not belong in this city. They had both—she and this mass of people—descended upon New Orleans in all the frightful glory of tourists with a thirst for the different who fail to see the similarities that bring that desire to fruition.

She had been told that gold and purple and green were the colors of the festival in this city; colors elsewhere were both more varied and less vibrant. There was a heart to the tradition here that had dug such deep roots the whole city seemed to be in thrall to the rhythm of the festival itself, and the colors that had been chosen, by someone at the festival's beginning, were those ones.

She did what she always did in situations like this: she made certain that she had, in abundance, clothing that matched the colors of the festival; not too gaudy—although from all advance publicity that hardly seemed possible (the truth was, at least three days before Mardi Gras, rather more mundane)—but not too plain. She brought sensible shoes for walking in and dress shoes on the off chance she decided she had the courage to actually go to the ball itself. She had been issued a secondary invitation, and it had been explained that it was an honor, a "call-out," although the travel agent, versed somewhat in New Orleans lore, also said quietly, "I've never heard of the krewe giving the ball; you should probably be a little bit careful about what they're charging you, if anything. Even the private krewes are a matter of public record; they just choose their own standards for exclusivity and stick with them."

After this, she had had to explain what a krewe was: a private club, dedicated in some way to the celebration of the carnival, and usually but not always involved in the public parades that led up to Mardi Gras itself. She'd gone on to give a list of established, public krewes who had offered Mardi Gras packages that had received no legitimate complaints.

That had put a sense of caution into her, if it ever left; but she did not cancel her reservations, and she carefully kept both invitations in a place where she would be certain not to lose them.

She had also brought warm clothing in case of cold and cool clothing in case of warmth; she brought sunscreen in three levels of protective covering, although she had no idea what the numbers on the bottle actually meant. She had chosen practical clothing to travel in, although she brought two costumes with her, both black and pseudoEdwardian, one with too much lace.

Her entire life was lived by contingencies.

As if, in the end, they had mattered.

And that was farther than she wanted to go. She bit her lower lip, kneading it between her teeth. Then she squared her shoulders, rolled up figurative sleeves—the suit jacket she'd travelled in would have been damaged by such a symbolic gesture—and retrieved the wallet from the depths of her purse.

It was alarmingly free of clutter. Bills, coins, one credit card, one bank card, and a medical emergency card with a series of numbers on it that essentially meant a large corporation would pay for whatever work was necessary and only leave her with a tiny deductible; other than that, it was empty. No slips of paper. No notes to herself, although she usually filled a billfold with them. She had left her driver's license behind, along with anything else that had her picture or her address, with the single exception of her passport.

She took the little map on the back of her invitation with her to the front desk and quietly asked where, in the city, she might find the streets mentioned. The woman wore a sober suit and a frazzled expression; she looked at the map, started to speak, frowned and handed it back. "Not in this city."

"But it says—"

The clerk turned the invitation over. "Says what?" She handed it back; it was blank. Purple and green and gold had faded into impersonal, untouched ivory.

"Ma'am?"

"It's—it's nothing. I'm sorry, I must have brought the wrong—the wrong map."

IN HER ROOM.

SHE sat for a long while, staring at the map, its back now devoid of words and address, of date. She considered throwing it out; decided against it. Instead, as if it were a note to herself, she slid it into the billfold of her wallet. She found the dance card; it, too, was just a card of pale, expensive stock. She kept it.

It was not in her nature to worry much about her sanity; she felt a pang of bitter disappointment, but worse, that scalding sense of shame one feels when, as an adult who should know better, you discover someone's taken advantage of your gullibility.

It would have been worse, but the mask was unchanged. She took it out and set it on her pillow. It wasn't as if she was going to sleep on the pillows here, given that they were made of feathers, so they might as well serve some purpose.

She had picked up a number of tourist brochures at the front desk before making her hasty retreat. They yielded very little information, although the pictures were slightly different in each variant. She read through them numbly, stumbling at last upon the parade schedule. Today was the Saturday before the Tuesday that signalled the end of carnival season. Tonight's parade was scheduled to be given by Endymion.

It was early enough in the day that she thought she might follow the instructions in the pamphlet and find a seat along the parade route. Choosing sensible clothing, sensible shoes, contingencies, she packed and deserted the room.

SIX O'CLOCK WAS NOT dark in the city streets; it was not precisely light either; it was that blend of both that is sometimes called dusk. The air was cool and damp. She had been warned that weather at this time of year was unpredictable, and was glad for the sweater, although wearing it made her feel unaccountably old; as if cowering from the elements was a thing she had learned only with age. It was; she could see the young men and women beside or on top of their coolers, or better, the ladders on the boulevard, their long legs smooth and uncluttered by veins or other signs of age, their clothing as light as their expressions, and as fey. The only sweaters there were over-sized sweatshirts, if there were any at all.

Susan had neither youth nor family. She had not thought to feel the lack of either so bitterly, not here, not outside of the city in which both were buried. But she brought her arms across her chest like a cross or a shield. She knew how to make do.

It was the one thing that she had.

The hours passed; the parade had, apparently, started, but like any parade it would sweep past the spot she had chosen only once, and only after it had passed by others closer to its start. She could wait. The numbers of people on ladders grew; the crowd unfolded like a giant rising from knees to feet; it roared, and the roar carried words that were both foreign and familiar. Hands flew up; some carrying signs, some carrying—of all things—nets; small children—and she was surprised to see how many of them there were, tucked between parents, carried on their shoulders— God, she *hated* that other people's joy could still cause her so much pain—raised their fleshy little palms to the night air, bopping adults on the head in their gleeful frenzy.

She thought she would go deaf.

She covered her ears with her palms, but it was a gesture so foreign to the carnival it actually drew attention away from the floats that now approached like colorful chimera in the distance, bringing night with them, bringing all of night.

It was funny; everything she read had indicated that there would be riders on the floats; that they would be costumed; that they would fit in with a theme chosen by the krewe for that year's extravagance. But the first float she saw was made of stars; not stars that were neon and bright, but cold, cold points of light in a black, distant sky that had somehow been taken and forced into the shape of a chair.

A throne. On it, a man, robes the color of dusk. A hood was drawn over his head; it hung low across his brow, hiding his face. She could see a hint of mouth, of nose, but the shadows released nothing else. He lifted his chin as the float drew near. The noise; the screaming; the cacophony; the raised hands and signs and nets, the flags, the banners held aloft by whole groups; these faded into a cold, bleak silence.

The float stopped. The parade, and all of its accou-
trements—people, bands, lights—came to a full and sudden
halt. She was deafened by silence, where a moment before she
had been deafened by sound. The extremes were frightening.

"Aren't you supposed to ask for something?" The figure
stood; robes fell like liquid darkness, and where its edges
touched starlight, the stars winked out. She was glad she was
wearing the sweater now; it smelled of the familiar: home. Safety.
She grabbed its edges in shaking hands; pulled tight. Tight.

He opened his great, pale hands, and in them, coins glit-
tered, although later she would wonder where the light came
from. *Doubloons*, she thought, stupidly, the word a hollow echo.
Her hands were fists; she had a feeling that she did not want to
catch anything he threw.

"Come, did you leave your life for the carnival in order to
watch it pass you by without ever touching any of it? Or maybe
you don't understand the rules? Or your own desires?" He lifted
his hands and tossed the contents wide; light scattered like dust,
borne by winds, tinkling as it hit the streets—what little of the
streets there were beneath people's feet.

She cried out and took a step back; another—

And the festival parade returned in all its glory, blinding
her. She covered her eyes a moment while the light forced water
from them. Someone beside her, his young voice full of concern, said simply, "Are you all right?"

And she turned her head to the side—she couldn't really
move anything else—to see a very familiar face, dark hair now
pulled back in a way that suggested its length, eyes darker than
she remembered.

"I—"

"I'm here to apologize for the invitation," he said, looking
genuinely contrite. "But we're an old organization, and the
krewe is a very private one. We don't generally participate in
parades; there are far, far too many laws that govern them now
for our tastes."

"But how—"

"We still hold our ball on the evening of Shrove Tuesday. The
end of Shrovetide, when the penitents confess and are forgiven

their sins." His smile was very slight. "If, of course, they can vow in good faith to forgo those sins in the future."

For just a moment she was young again, and the sins that she was being asked to forgo were before, and not behind, her.

"The invitation that you were sent is still good, but the mask is the only thing we require as proof of your membership."

"But I have no idea where the ball will be."

"No. But you will, when the time is right." His voice had grown louder and louder in keeping with the shouts and songs of people with a penchant for keepsakes. But it dropped again, giving up the fight; he spoke slowly, and she caught the words by the form they forced from his lips.

Beneath your feet.

Something she'd read in one of the tourist pamphlets came back to her—trampled fingers—and she did not bend or move until there was a lull in the ferocity of the voices directly around her. Then she knelt, furtive and almost childlike in her momentary intensity, and lifted first one shoe and then the other.

Beneath the balls of either foot was a single silver coin. She clutched them in the fists that she'd used to hold the jacket tight. There wasn't enough light to see by; they were cold and hard and heavy.

AFTER THE PARADE HAD passed, she returned to the safety of the hotel; the lights of the foyer seemed unnaturally bright, like surgical lights; she was happy to reach her room, where the lights were less intrusive. The mask was, as she left it, on the bed; she sat beside it, and only when she sat beside it did she unfurl her hands in just such a way that the coins would be completely visible to the light.

On one side of both coins, scuffed and worn, was something that looked much like a harlequin crest. But the two coins differed on their reverse sides; the head side. Although both faces were in profile, they either looked toward, or away from each other.

She recognized them both at once; they were different halves of the same face, and they could not—although the detail

work was very, very fine—have been embossed more permanently on silver than they were in places that only memory
reached. She whispered a name.

An eight-year-old-boy's name.

On the face of one coin, in cold relief, he was frowning. His
eyes were narrowed, his lips pursed in a thin line. He was on the
brink of an outburst; either a swearing streak, which was terrible, or a screaming fit, which was worse. Either way, he would
have landed behind the closed door of his room to "think"
about whatever it was he'd just said or done . . . but she had
never loved the expression, and while it was exact, it was not one
she would have ever chosen to commemorate. Funny, that she
would recognize it so completely when none of her pictures or
clear memories contained it.

Her eyes skimmed that surface and moved rapidly on to the
next coin. Because on the face of the next coin, he was smiling,
his lips parted, his cheeks dimpled. He had *just* started to hate
those dimples; to feel self-conscious about smiling because of
them. She felt a pang as she remembered the taunts of his school-
mates; at a remove of more than a decade she could pause to
wonder what taunts he offered in return. Children could be cruel.

But never so cruel as by dying.

She went to see his grave every day after work. It was Saturday, she was in a different city. But she felt his death as keenly
today as she had the day the earth had been newly turned. The
day she had quietly stood by and watched as, shovel by shovel,
they had filled his grave. She might have tried something histri-
onic; certainly everything beneath the frozen surface of her
expression screamed at her to do it: to jump into the open
grave; to tear back the coffin's lid; to throw her arms around
what she did not wish to let go of, to demand that they bury her
with him . . .

But her husband had left her as well, and there would be
no steadying hand, no companion in grief and loss, no one to
save the workmen from the outburst that, in the end, would
cause them pain and deliver her from none of her own, so she
had stood in quiet frenzy, beneath the surface of her own face.

She had hated life, then.

Now, she was simply indifferent to it.

There was danger in this city; danger in this place. These people had written to her in a language that could not be confined by mere words; her hands strobed the surface of silver in the silence.

She wanted to put the coins into her wallet, but she was almost afraid of losing these twin images; she chose at last to set them on the bedside table, and she lay down on the bed, the pillows stacked at as far a distance as they could be without falling over on the floor, a bright, three-colored mask staring at her from the depth of night.

But she didn't turn the light out; it went when the last of her awareness did, near dawn.

SIX HOURS WAS NOT enough to find a decent place on the parade route. She was ambivalent about the effects of her failure and decided, in the end, coins burning a hole in both memory and wallet, that she would retreat to the banks of the river. It felt strange to have a river like this accessible when the city hunkered just over her shoulder; in places the bank was covered with gravel, like an unfinished driveway, in others, rock or dirt. She had read that the city was a checkerboard city, meaning—she assumed—that it was impossible for a nonresident to divine correctly which areas of the city were actually dangerous.

She felt in no danger here, although the crowds seemed to melt at the edge of gravel, as if it were some sort of dividing line. The sun was setting; she faced the water, taking a comfort in the meaningless drone of its voice, the variations of current.

"Susan?"

Her hands were in her pockets; her purse slung over her shoulder. Her shoes were sensible shoes.

"Yes?"

She turned only as the sound of rolling stone over stone grew louder than the water. He smiled. "I always find you when its almost dark."

"I suppose you start looking too late."

He laughed. It was the first time she had heard his laughter, and it fell someplace in the register between the natural sound of moving water and moving stone. "Why aren't you at the parade? It's Bacchus, tonight. You really shouldn't miss it."

Her shrug was a half reply. "Why are the krewes named after Greek myths?"

He raised a brow. "I don't know. But if they are, it doesn't surprise me that you found room and time for Endymion, and none for Bacchus. You were never very interested in revelry and abandon."

"Abandon," she replied sharply, "has two meanings."

"Very well. You were never very interested in revelry and you are *far* too interested in abandonment." He reached out. She stepped back. "But find the time for Orpheus, and remember how he failed."

"What happened to him?"

"Happened?"

"After he failed. I never remember that part."

"I don't know."

It was quiet for a long time. Which meant, of course, that she was alone, on the banks of a river, on Shrove Sunday.

MONDAY SHE ROSE; MONDAY she dressed. She had brought with her two costumes, both black; both mock period dresses that fell from shoulder to ground and then some; she chose one of them after trying them both on in front of the full-length mirror that was the closet door. Almost no one wore costumes during the day, and she felt extraordinarily self-conscious doing so, but she had no one to hold her place upon the so-called neutral ground, and she was certain that later she would want it. She went and bought herself a paperback novel and retreated to the meridian that was called neutral ground, burying her awareness of her environment beneath the flow of another person's words. There was room; the room was chipped away as the pages passed and people took up their vigilant watch of the road.

There had long since ceased to be any comfort or escape in reading. Too many words had unexpected edges, so she could never read with her guard down; never get too close to the text. But if it wasn't comfort, it was distraction. Only two people stepped on her while she waited, and two people, worn into a sense of familiarity by the passage of time spent sharing nothing more than the waiting, asked her if she wanted something to drink as they readied themselves with plastic cups and the false warmth of alcohol. She accepted the plastic cup because she found warmth in the offer, but she neglected to drink the contents.

She rose when she heard music; by this time she had given up on the novel. It was too dark to make out the words, and the fear of being stepped on by someone in tall, pointed heels was quickly becoming reality. She wished for a moment that she'd chosen a bright, pale color, something visible, but she put it aside. Wishing, in her experience, was a waste of time.

Although it wasn't as if she had so much else to do with her time. Work. Home. Work. Home. And between them, history.

This time, she was in synch with the crowd; what they saw, she saw. She couldn't say whether or not this was disappointing; she clutched her drink to keep it safe as people pressed forward toward the barriers that kept the riders and the watchers separate. Words were allowed to cross it; throws were allowed in response. People, she'd been told, were more than likely to annoy the police officers who quietly lined the route, and lockup was not reputed to be the best way to enjoy carnival.

The floats came into view, and on them, riders with hands full of things that would in time become mementoes, taken out of the context of the moment and given life by memory. She had her hands full; she watched as people above her—the ladders again—became the end of arcs of light; doubloons, little trinkets, one paper airplane. Each catch occasioned a cry of encouragement—or triumph—and gave others a reason to continue their pursuit of obvious souvenir. She had hers; a cup.

But the young woman beside her smiled, hesitation gone, and said, "Aren't you going to ask for something?"

And she found herself responding, not to the desire for some proof that she'd been here, but to the girl. *Yes,* she thought, *I want to ask for something.*

She was not used to shouting; she had nothing clever to ask; nothing to say. Hard to make herself heard over younger, stronger voices. But she had the mask that she'd scooped up off the pillow, and she pulled it, with care, out of her bag. It was heavy, but it was beautiful, and if she held it just so by the corner, she could wave it like a flag.

She lifted it, turning to smile at the young woman, to gather strength from the smile's return.

And she found that she was staring at the face of a stranger. Not that the woman herself had not been a stranger, but the offer of food, the offer of tacit support for an absurd demand, was a common ground over which they had started to meet.

She looked around.

The cheering of the crowd had changed in tenor, but not in substance; the floats had changed substantially, although they still drove down the same street, passed by the same buildings. The man held out a hand; he was wearing a white glove. She stared at it for a long, awkward moment and it was withdrawn. He turned his back on her, and in a light suitable for spectacle, but not inspection, she noticed that he was wearing a tuxedo with full tails. He began to walk away, and the crowd parted as if it were the Red Sea and he were Moses. She understood why; there was something about him that was distinctly . . . unpleasant.

But she understood that he meant her to follow; did not, in fact, find it odd that he did not speak. She followed. She had been expecting something strange. Had dressed for it. She dropped her mask into the bag she carried, picked up the bag, and followed him before the path cleared by his presence closed behind him and she was lost.

HE LED HER TO a place that would have looked familiar had she been able to place a map against a geography that was made familiar by the fall of steps, the width of road, the facades of buildings which stood just behind the sidewalks. No grass, not here; no pretty trees. But the buildings were not in disrepair.

She could no longer hear the odd musicality of thousands of voices lifted in happy plea; even the music that accompanied the floats was gone. But as she followed her guide, a refrain of a different sort began to grow; a voiceless orchestration of notes. The notes pulled her round the corner, and as she crested the shadow of that final street, she saw a grand house. It was not out of place, although later she would remember that mixed in with the modern cars were cars of a vintage she saw in old movies and nowhere else, and among those, carriages attached to horses that seemed preternaturally calm. She was afraid that the dress she had chosen would be conspicuously inferior to the clothing on the men and women who came out of the vehicles in front of the house, but as she approached them, she realized that they were attired in every conceivable style.

She made her way to the door in odd company; an old man, a woman half her age, a boy the age of her—yes, acknowledge it—dead son. There was a man at the door who seemed to be checking invitations; he held out his hand for hers, and she held out the plastic cup. Burgundy caught the light in his gloved hand. She rummaged about in her purse and came up with the mask, which all of her silent compatriots were donning. She fitted it to her face; it was cool against the forehead and the cheeks, soothing. She tied it there, and on impulse told the man with the white gloves to keep the plastic cup and its contents.

Then she was ushered into the great room. It was sort of funny; she almost walked in when she was stopped. Her name, it seemed, had to be announced before she could step into the room itself. And even when she did, she was not to just join the growing crowd, as she had done upon neutral ground; she was to sit in a small section of floor with marbled benches that looked not unlike a juror's pen.

One of the young women sitting there said, "You don't understand, do you?" as Susan tucked herself into a bench and stared out at a crowd of people who were dancing in an oddly sombre way.

"No . . . I guess I don't."

"This is an honor. To sit here." Her hair was mounded in a soft pile that seemed to go on forever; it was pale, but gold.

"It is?"

"We've been chosen by the men of the hour; the men whose presence this year defines the ball. We're to dance with them. Don't you see? Everyone knows we're simply waiting our turn to be called out. Or do you think that just anyone can dance?"

"Can't they?"

The young woman rolled her pretty eyes; even with the mask across her face it was clear that they were a cool, crisp blue. "No. This is a very exclusive ball."

It was clear she was curious about Susan's pedigree, but as she did not offer her own, Susan felt no need—and a distinct lack of desire—to relieve that curiosity; she turned back to the floor, watching; wondering who it was who had invited her.

The answer was not long in coming, and not terribly surprising.

A young man dressed in exquisite formal attire made his way around the edge of the large dance floor and presented himself at the gate of the enclosure. "Susan Fullerton?" His voice was different, somehow; she wasn't sure whether it was the music, or the night, but there was a subtle nuance of menace that it had never contained before. She rose stiffly.

"Is everything all right?"

He raised a pale brow. "Why do you ask?"

"I had thought . . ." she faltered. "I no longer have the invitation, but I *thought* that the ball was tomorrow."

"Indeed," he said, after a long pause. "It was to be tomorrow. I have paid heavily to have it moved, but I have influence in the court at the moment."

"Why?"

"Why do I have influence?"

"Why did you have it moved?"

"Does it matter? The music will start, Susan, and we will dance." He offered her his hand; she took it. Hers was trembling.

"Is this very formal? I don't know how to waltz."

"It is very formal, but fortunately for you, I have learned how to lead. It took time."

"Then lead. But don't be surprised if I step on your toes."
"Very little surprises me."

HE WAS A VERY good dancer, or rather, he was a very good lead; she did not misstep because his grip was so firm at both arm and hand that she would have had to struggle to do so.

But she became increasingly self-conscious as the minutes passed; his gaze never left her face, and hers—hers was dragged to his. He was so very familiar it made her uncomfortable. The waltz grew in volume until she could hear nothing but the music; see nothing but his eyes, the cheekbones around them.

"Why aren't you wearing a mask?" she asked him, over the swell of the violins frantic pitch.

He laughed. "I am." After a long pause, he added, "Aren't you going to ask me to take it off?"

"No. Never."

"That's a pity. The dance—our dance—is ending." He led her off the floor and she looked toward the doors by which she'd entered. Peaked in the centre, they rose two stories and stopped short of a cathedral ceiling; they were closed and barred, their iron rings somehow incongruous with the room itself.

She turned to the man whose name she did not know and whose invitation she had so rashly accepted, donning a quiet dignity. "I will not be allowed to leave?"

"There is only one way out, and I believe you will find it closed to you."

"But—"

He shrugged. "Who will miss you? You've shut everyone out for so long there's no one looking in on you."

"My co-workers."

"True. A week from now, maybe two, when they've received no word at all and they've grown tired of leaving messages, they may call. But who? People are notoriously loath to interfere when it's been made clear that interference is not wanted. You are just another grieving widow; a woman whose family died and who didn't have the strength—quite—to be buried along with them.

"Not exactly the life of the party, were you?"

She was silent.

"Ah, here." He had led her to a small door; he opened it now. "This is not so bad a place; it is very like the one you live in now."

"It is nothing at all like the one I live in now." Her eyes stretched up the walls that seemed to go on forever, lined now with torches and now with glass globes and candles.

He laughed again. "It is very like the place you have made for me. Let me return the favor. Come, Susan. Let me show you to your rooms."

She nodded; his grip on her arm was numbing. The music had indeed changed as they evaded another's dance; she wondered, briefly, as the strains of the newer melody faded into the distance, what kind of a dance it was. It did not seem to be elegiac at all.

He stopped at a set of doors.

And she recognized them, and in spite of the grip on her arm, she froze. His hand tightened; she lifted her free hand and pried a finger loose. "Susan," he said, his voice as cold as the steel face plate; as cold as the glossy, easily cleaned paint; as cold, at *least* as cold, as the long, rectangular boxes just beyond, with their terrible, filing cabinet doors, that waited just beyond the doors.

"Why are you doing this?" she said, her voice breaking syllables into pathetic, small sounds that were almost like speech.

He offered her no answer. Instead, he pushed her through the doors; they swung on hinges, backward or forward, unless locked. She knew they weren't locked; not yet. Knew that they would be, when she was safely behind them. She was dragged, in a silence that was antiseptic and hollow, to the bank of bodies that comprised any hospital's morgue.

"This," he said, "is your place."

And, unusual in such a morgue was a small white nametag, set behind the steel frame of a more familiar cabinet. SUSAN FULLERTON. She might have screamed in terror as he pulled the drawer open, but beside it—beside it she saw another drawer, another name, and her fear snapped as if it were thin ice over a very, very deep lake. Things survived whole winters alive beneath a lake's surface. When the water was deep enough. When it was deep.

KEVIN FULLERTON.

His hand was on the handle. He started to pull it back. She stood, fifteen years younger, the fear now so terrible she literally could not breathe, could not imagine a life in which she could breathe. "*Don't!*"

"But you know what you'll see. You've seen it a hundred thousand times. You've let yourself see *nothing* else."

"Don't," she whispered. "I'll be good. I'll do whatever you want. Please. Just—don't."

"You don't understand," he told her, quietly, the ice of his voice breaking slightly as he disentangled his hand from hers. "This is *my* place."

He pulled the drawer back.

She screamed—but the scream was high and pathetic; hard to really scream when you can't breathe. There was no body. No body.

He pushed her gently out of the way, and with an ease that spoke of experience, pulled the white sheet back and lay down. Then, staring up at her face, he reached up with both hands, one to hair and one to chin, and he *pulled.*

His face came away. She saw it; the inside momentarily visible, the interior surface, like her own, of smooth ceramic, a name engraved in perfect small caps under the hole for each eye. It made her wonder how others had seen the mask that she wore, if they had seen it at all.

And then she didn't wonder at all.

The eyes that had been alive and clear were sockets; the skin, sallow and ancient, mummified now; ugly. Nothing there of the boy that she had lost, but she *knew* it was his body.

"Yes," he said, in a voice that was nothing at all like her son's voice, and everything like the voice of a corpse with no real vocal chords; dry as dust. Terrible. "You wanted to join me. Join me, Mom."

She nodded. Helped him pull the sheet up.

Sat down on her own, her black dress against white cloth. "Kevin?" she said softly.

"Yes?"

The sheets moved. What was left of his hands came up and pushed them aside.

"Have you been here all this time?"

"Yes."

"Do you—did I do this?"

He was silent. She wondered if he was capable of saying any-thing other than yes or no. She almost asked him to put the mask back, but it was gone, just as the mansion was gone, and the carnival.

"Did I do this to you?" she said again, her voice a mother's voice, the guilt in it something palpable.

Dead eye sockets turned toward her; she could not even pretend that there was expression in them. Then they turned away again; turned to face the ceiling.

"I loved you," she whispered. "I . . . loved you. Love doesn't forget. I couldn't bear to forget. I couldn't. It would have meant that you—that the memories—meant nothing."

"Yes."

"Love forgets?"

"It forgives," he said, and she heard a hint of the stranger's voice in this one, a melding, a blend.

She should have known the boy's face in the man's; was ashamed that she hadn't. "You would have looked like that. If you'd lived."

"Yes."

"If I stay here, will you ever leave?"

Silence. Then, "No."

"Do you want to?"

He laughed. The laugh was bitter; the voice fuller still. "Did you ever ask what I wanted?"

"I would have thought you wanted to live."

"I did. But I couldn't. This isn't a substitute."

"Is that why you invited me here?"

"You don't understand, Mom. I didn't invite you, not really. You never left."

She began to cry. Here, there was nothing left to do. Her tears were warm; they covered the whole of her face from her eyes to her chin and she didn't lift a hand to stop them because she still wore the mask. "It would have been easier if your father had lived," she said at last, when she could speak. She stood up.

"Yes. But you didn't hold on to him."

"No."

"Why?"

"Because, in a just world there's always a chance that we'll have to bury our husbands. But not our children. Not our children. Now hush."

She took the purse from her shoulder. Opened it, fished about for her wallet; it was easy to find. Except for a paperback novel and her sensible shoes, it was the only thing there. "Do you really have no idea why they name krewes after myths?"

"Really. We didn't cover that in grade three."

"All right, I'm sorry I asked." She wasn't. She swallowed, or tried to; her throat felt enormously glandular. All tonsil. In her hands were two doubloons; festival throws. Gifts from the dead. Her son's face. Her son's real face, caught in silver and light. She turned them over; saw the mask, her own face, she understood that now. Almost gently, she turned the coins over so that his profile faced down.

"Do you know where the dead go?" she asked him, in the smallest and quietest of voices.

He didn't answer.

"Do they go anywhere?"

No answer again. The silence was heavy with the things she wanted to say or do. Instead, she said, softly, "I loved you. Sleep well."

She placed one silver coin over either empty socket, taking care to make sure that the image that faced the light was her own. The doors flew open; a breeze that smelled of lilac and lavender, of wine and trees, of stone and sweat, swept in.

She closed her eyes. The wind's touch was sensuous, playful, demanding. Her hair leapt up in strands of black and white. Time, she knew, to go.

She walked to the doors, seeing the floor pass beneath her feet, linoleum in hospital grey. She paused once, in the door. *Remember Orpheus's mistake.*

But Orpheus was trying to bring the dead back.

No answer, of course. Not now, and perhaps not ever. She wanted to turn to see if a body remained in a morgue, or if some strange magic, some alchemical transformation, had taken place that had allowed these doors to open. She listened, and she heard the voice of a possibility speak one last time.

Death lasts forever. You'll get there. But when you do, the only luggage you get to bring with you is the life you led. Pack carefully, okay?

She laughed.

THERE WAS ONLY ONE minor problem. The halls led to the front door, bypassing the obvious merriment—she shivered at the thought—of the ball itself. But the doors were closed and barred, and a man stood in the centre of them with a large and not symbolic enough sword.

She would have turned away, but he beckoned her forward, with a furtive glance to either side, and she recognized the white gloves he wore, now so incongruous with the rest of his attire. The doorman.

He returned the cup she gave him with a quiet smile. It was empty, but she considered the gift well given, and when no one was looking, he opened the door a crack and let her out, placing the cup in her hand as he did so.

She turned to see the streets; they were crowded with people. The last of the floats was vanishing into the distance, and although it was strictly against etiquette, some of the paradegoers were now drifting in its direction. She reached up and touched her mask. It felt cool to the touch, but it was there, a certain reminder that it wasn't all just a dream.

She was tired. Was so very, very tired. She turned toward the hotel.

And the mask, secured by ribbon, slipped free somehow; slipped off. She felt it as a cool caress down the length of her face; didn't understand the significance of the touch until she heard it: the sound of shattering ceramic. Broken clay.

KING CORPUS

Bruce Holland Rogers

At first, Andy wasn't even sure it was a parade, there was so little to it. One float. One tiny band of jazz musicians. That wasn't enough to be a real parade, was it? But no other traffic flowed on Saint Charles Avenue.

For any other Carnival parade in New Orleans, for a *real* parade, the traffic would cease only when the police barricades held it back. For this parade, if it really was a parade, there weren't any barricades. The cars had just stopped coming on one of the city's busiest streets.

Andy watched the solitary float pass by. It was a flat-bed wagon decorated with a mildewed papier-mâché bull and pulled by six mules. An old man walked beside the lead mule, hand on the animal's bridle. One of the bull's papier-mâché horns was broken.

Three women in sequined dresses stood next to the bull. They, at least, were good looking. *They* looked like the Mardi Gras that Andy had imagined. The women threw bead necklaces, aluminum coins, and plastic cups to the people on the sidewalk, who seemed as surprised as Andy by this sorry little afternoon procession. Behind the wagon, came the band, just half a dozen seedy old musicians. They were more of a shuffling band than a marching band. Trailing them was one young, well-muscled man, naked above the waist. His skin was very black, and he waved a greasily smoking torch as he marched.

The sky was dense with clouds. The absence of traffic and the gray half-light both made this odd procession seem like something in a dream.

There hadn't been any notice of a parade today in the *Times-Picayune.* Andy had looked. He was planning to hit every parade and crash every party he could possibly crash for the whole of Carnival. That was what he had come for, the biggest party of his life, one last blowout between college and the working-stiff tedium he was sure would follow for the rest of his life.

Carnival had officially started the night before, but there wasn't much happening yet. Andy had figured on doing some bar crawling on his own this afternoon while his New Orleans friends were at work.

"Hey, hey!" a man called from the sidewalk. "String of beads!"

One of the women on the wagon threw the man a string of green beads. As the wagon rattled slowly along the street, other people overcame their surprise and shouted, "Hey, lady! Cup!" or just "Throw me something!"

Andy ran in the street to pass the torch bearer and the band. When he caught up with the wagon, he shouted, "Hey! String of beads!"

One of the women threw a string of amber beads. He caught it in the air, hung the strand around his neck, and trotted to catch up again.

"Coin!" someone else cried from the sidewalk, and one of the women threw a green metal disk that dropped onto the street short of the curb. Andy darted over and grabbed it. It had a bull on one face. The reverse was stamped: *The Mystick Krewe of Corpus.*

"Mister, that's mine!" said a child who had stepped into the street.

"Tawna, you get back here," said her mother. "There's plenty more coming. Mardi Gras just starting."

"Sorry, kid!" Andy said. He stuck the coin into his pocket, then trotted after the float again.

Just as the streets weren't blocked off, there were no sidewalk barriers along this parade route, as there would be for the real parades. Even so, only Andy had strayed into the street. Everyone else who shouted requests did so from the sidewalk.

"Beads!" Andy shouted again. He was close enough to the wagon to see that the woman who had thrown him his first strand was wearing a wig. Her auburn hair was crooked. "Throw me some beads!"

The woman threw a strand of amber beads over Andy's head, to the sidewalk, where someone else whooped over their prize.

"Come on!" Andy cried, grinning and tapping his chest. "Need some more beads here! Throw me some beads!"

The woman looked at the next strand she held. The beads were purple. She said something in French and tossed the beads into the air. Andy ran under them and snatched them, laughing.

"You, Sir!" boomed a voice from above and behind him. Andy turned. A masked man on horseback loomed over him. The black ostrich plumes in the man's helmet made him seem even bigger than he was. Andy thought maybe the man was about to tell him to get out of the street, but instead the man leaned forward in his saddle and said, "Your gifts, Sir. Golden beads. Purple beads. And the coin? Let me see the coin!"

The man's voice was compelling. Andy dug out the aluminum coin as the float and the musicians continued down the avenue.

"Yes, I thought so. Green!" the man cried. His lips were red and wet beneath the mask. "Gold, purple, and green! The colors of Carnival! You, Sir, are chosen! How would you like to see Carnival as few see it? How would you like to be the King of Corpus! Our guest! Our guest for all of Carnival!"

An old black woman in a black dress and a lace shawl had stopped to watch this from the sidewalk. She called out, "He probably got other plans, Mister!"

The masked man gave her a long, hard look. He said, "Do I know you, Madam?"

"I expect you know most everybody," she said, "or can, if you want to. But I guess I don't want you to know me any better than you already do." She turned and walked away.

The man watched her go, eyes narrowed, then returned his attention to Andy. "I'm offering you pleasures of the flesh, Sir, the true spirit of Carnival. All expenses paid, of course! Isn't that just the sort of thing you're here for!"

"What's the catch? What do I have to do?"

"Enjoy our generosity! Wear the crown! Let us take you to parties and balls where we introduce you as the king! What do you say? Will you accept the crown!" The man had a way of asking questions so that they weren't really questions.

"I don't know," Andy said. "Aren't some of those balls kind of stuffy? I'm looking for the wild side of Mardi Gras."

"And you shall have it! What is it you crave? Music? Food? Drink? Women? All yours!"

Andy grinned, not sure how seriously to take any of this. "You do make it sound pretty good."

"If it isn't all I promise, and more, you can renounce the crown. But you won't want to! Are you a man who loves a good time or not?" He reached toward Andy with a gloved hand. Andy hesitated, then clasped the offered hand. "That's the spirit! Wait here!"

The masked man rode ahead, turned the parade around, and brought the float back to Andy. As the three women in sequined dresses helped Andy climb onto the float, the masked man said to the band, "Coronation March!" The band played a spirited tune.

"Welcome, Your Highness," said one of the women. She had gray eyes. Her skin was the color of coffee with milk. Her hair fell in ringlets down to her shoulders. She gave Andy a fur-trimmed robe to wear over his T-shirt and jeans, and she kissed his cheek. "I'm Clytie."

"We don't get a king every year," said the second woman, a blonde. She was holding a red and gold crown. She kissed him, too. "I'm Pomona."

The third woman—the one whose hair had been crooked—gave Andy a third kiss and took his hand. Her hair looked fine, now. In fact, seeing her up close, he was sure it was her own; he'd been mistaken about the wig. "You can call me Sibyl."

"Sibyl!" said Clytie. "That's a depressing choice! You could choose a better name for Carnival than that!"

"It's my name," Sibyl insisted. Then she told Andy, "Come this way," and led him to a chair beneath the muzzle of the papier-mâché bull. "Sit here, in front of the *boeuf gras.*"

The masked man rode near as Andy said, "In front of the what?"

"*Le boeuf gras,* the bull!" the man said. "That ancient symbol. *Your* symbol, now that you are king!"

They put the crown on his head. "Hail, Rex!" the masked rider called out, and when he repeated the words the women chanted with him, "Hail, Rex! Hail, King Corpus!" The man saluted. The women curtsied. A few people on the sidewalk applauded, while others just stared.

"Your scepter," said Pomona. She handed Andy a roasted turkey leg.

"Can I eat it?" He hadn't realized before now how hungry he was.

"We'd be disappointed if you didn't."

He took a bite. It was wonderful.

"What else do you desire?" asked Clytie. The way she said *desire* made Andy think of all sorts of things she could do for him, but he thought to himself, *Down, boy!*

"How about a beer?" he said.

"What kind do you want?"

"What have you got?"

"Whatever the king desires."

"I like Black Butte Porter, but you can't get that here. Anything cold and foamy will be great."

The mules started the wagon with a jolt and turned it. The parade continued down Saint Charles. The band was still playing their Coronation March, but the tune became more and more raucous, as if at any moment the music might break out into a fight.

One of the women brought Andy a bottle with a familiar label. Black Butte. He tasted it. "Great! How did you happen to have this?"

"Hey!" a man called out from the sidewalk. "Throw me something!"

The women went back to throwing beads, cups, and coins.

"Do I do anything?" Andy asked Sibyl, who was closest to him. "Do I wave?"

"You do anything you like," she said. "You're King Corpus!"

Between bites, Andy waved his turkey leg at people on the sidewalk. When the leg was nothing but bone, the women brought him another one, and then another one after that, always with more beer to wash it down. He kept eating turkey legs and drinking beer all the way to Canal Street and the *Vieux Carré*. There, the wagon pulled to the side of the street. The music halted, and band members started to drift off, except for one white-haired horn player. Andy stood up to stretch his legs.

The torch had stopped burning somewhere along the way, and the young man who had carried it now laid it down between the legs of the papier-mâché bull. One of the women handed him a shirt. He put it on. The masked man rode close. In his gloved hand was a fan of twenty-dollar bills. These he offered to the young man, who reached out to accept them.

The horn player cleared his throat. He was looking at the young man. "All's I can say," the old musician said, "is if you take cash money from the captain, you better be prepared to spend it quick."

The young man seemed to consider this, then took the money and walked away. The horn player shook his head. "Well he can't say now I didn't warn him."

"You could mind your own business," the masked man said, glancing Andy's way.

"I'm too old to care, Captain. Besides, where you going to get another horn player good as me?"

The masked man laughed. "In this town?"

"Not like me. Can't nobody play like me." He started to walk away. "See you next year, Captain."

"Captain?" Andy said. "Captain of what?"

"As you are King Corpus, so am I captain of Corpus. A Krewe title. A Carnival name."

"I see," Andy said. "Well, captain. What now?"

"Dinner!" the captain said as a limousine pulled up next to the mule team. He dismounted. "I trust that you're still hungry?"

To his surprise, Andy found that he was.

WITH ITS PLUSH CARPETING, subdued lighting, and the fine china on the tables, the Pelican Club was not the sort of place Andy would have come if he were spending his own money. As Andy considered the menu, he said, "There aren't any prices."

"You're our guest," said the captain, who still wore his mask. "Hadn't I made that clear? It's on us. Everything your heart desires is on us for the whole of Carnival, Your Highness."

Andy ordered the pan-roasted venison with Port blueberry sauce. The captain ordered two bottles of wine, and kept refilling Andy's glass. Andy ate heartily, surprised at how much he could put away after all those turkey legs. For dessert he had cheesecake with a cherry sauce. Meanwhile, the captain and the three women picked at their food.

"More?" Clytie asked as Andy finished the last bite. She didn't wait for him to reply before she had called the waiter over to order him a second piece of cheesecake. Andy was about to say that he couldn't possibly have room for more, but in fact he was still hungry.

"You are a man of marvelous appetites!" the captain said.

"I'm sure he is," Pomona said, batting her eyelashes.

Clytie giggled.

"Don't give him the wrong impression," Sibyl said. "He can't have either of you!"

"Don't be so sure," Pomona said. She gave Andy a smile and hooked one finger over the front edge of her dress, between her breasts, inviting his gaze.

"If he had any idea . . ." Sibyl said.

"Oh, shut up," said Clytie. "Let us have a little fun. It *is* Carnival."

"You are having an effect on him," the captain said.

Andy felt the heat rise in his face. "Well, I . . ."

"Nothing to be ashamed of!" the captain told him. "We approve of your desires. That's the point. You're King Corpus. You should be hungry. You should be randy. Come on. I won't have these women tantalizing you for nothing!" He threw a stack of bills onto the check and stood up. "The king needs a consort, ladies. And I know just where to find one."

Clytie and Pomona sat on either side of Andy, with the captain and Sibyl across from him. In the interval between streetlights, it was dark in the limousine. Andy was pleasantly drunk. He rested one hand on Clytie's knee and the other on Pomona's. Clytie put her hand on his, and Pomona did the same.

Andy closed his eyes, enjoying the warmth, the feel of nylon stockings beneath his hands.

Clytie hissed. Andy pulled his hands into his lap and opened his eyes. In the darkness, he thought he saw a white-haired old woman, skeletally thin, sitting next to the captain. But as the limo approached the next streetlight, he saw that, no, it was Sibyl sitting there, and she looked anything but old. She was blinking, though, as if bewildered.

"You were sleeping!" Clytie told her.

"Ridiculous," Sibyl said.

"I saw you," said Clytie.

"So did I," Pomona said, and she looked at Andy.

"Wine," said the captain, "can play tricks with the eyes." He leaned forward and touched Andy's knee. "Are you well?"

"Tired, I guess," Andy said. "Maybe I should have you drop me off where I'm staying."

"Nonsense," the captain said. "The night is young, Your Highness!"

The limousine stopped in an alley. The captain got out and told Andy to wait. After he had gone, Clytie put Andy's hand back on her knee and said, "You *were* sleeping."

"Well," said Sibyl, but she didn't say anything more than that.

When the captain returned, he told Andy to come with him. The women stayed in the car while the two men went into a narrow corridor in one of the buildings, then up some stairs and down another corridor. The captain stopped and knocked on a door. The woman who answered was wearing black fishnet stockings and a vinyl skirt.

"All yours," the captain said, gesturing toward the woman. "Anything you want, paid for in advance."

The woman looked him up and down. "I suppose he's going to wear that crown the whole time."

Andy felt the heat rise in his face again. "Uh, maybe I should call my friends," he said, taking off his crown. "The people I'm staying with."

"Plenty of time for that later," said the captain. "Your consort awaits, Your Highness."

"What about . . ." Andy looked back in the direction they'd come.

"Those three aren't up for this much excitement, as much as they enjoy leading you on. If it's consummation you want, it has to be like this."

"No. I mean, will they . . ."

"Will they object? Will they think any less of you?" The captain laughed. "Your Highness, this is what they want for you! You're King Corpus!"

"You coming in or not?" said the woman.

"Go on, go on," the captain said, giving Andy a gentle push into the room. "Enjoy yourself! You *want* her, don't you?"

When the door closed behind him, Andy realized how much he did want her. To his surprise, and hers, he went on wanting her time after time after time. His lust renewed itself as constantly as his hunger had. It was nearly dawn when exhaustion claimed him.

WHEN ANDY WOKE UP, he was alone on the stained and rumpled sheets. His mouth felt pasty. The clock beside the bed read 3:23. Outside, it was another gray afternoon.

While Andy rinsed his mouth at the bathroom faucet, he heard the door open. The captain swept into the room, masked again today. He had some red and gold clothes draped over his arm. "Shower! Shave! Dress!" he said, laying the royal costume across the bed. "More revels await!"

Behind him came Clytie, Pomona, and Sibyl. "Did you have a good time?" Clytie asked.

"Made her earn her money, I'm sure," said Pomona. She thrust manfully with her hips and said, "Make way for the king!"

Clytie laughed. The captain picked the crown up from the floor.

"He's blushing again," Sibyl said.

"Oh, come on!" Clytie said. "Don't be embarrassed, Your Highness. We've been around. We know what men like."

They took him in the limousine to a late lunch and immediately after that, to another expensive restaurant where Andy had great slabs of prime rib, glass after glass of wine, and three desserts. After dinner, they drove around the city, and the women told Andy about what New Orleans used to be like, about the casinos and brothels in Storyville, about the older French architecture that had been lost to fires. They spoke as if they had been around to gamble in Storyville or even to see the original city, which was absurd. They probably weren't that much older than Andy.

Later, the captain brought him to another prostitute, and Andy's energy with her was as limitless as it had been with the first. In the morning, he woke up alone again just before the arrival of the captain and the women.

By the fourth day, it had become a routine, except that the captain brought Andy a tuxedo and a mask instead of his usual royal costume, and instead of dinner at a restaurant, the five of them attended a ball.

At the door of the ballroom, two men stood inspecting the invitations. The captain stood near them, watching, then reached into the breast pocket of his tuxedo and produced five invitations.

Sibyl looked at hers. "I could have done this," she said.

"Yes," Clytie said, "but yours don't last as long, do they?"

"Ladies!" the captain scolded, but he was looking at Andy. "Shall we go in?"

They presented their invitations and were admitted. When Andy's invitation was returned to him, he took a closer look at it. It was elegantly engraved and hand-painted—something worth keeping, he decided. He folded it and put it in his pocket. Then he followed the others to a table near the dance floor with a numbered placard. Table 17, it said. They sat down.

All the men in the ballroom wore masks. None of the women did.

"Ah!" said a bald man who strolled up to the captain. "It's you, if you are who I think you are!"

"Yes, I think I do know you," the captain said.

"But I didn't know you were a member!"

"I'm a member of all the clubs," said the captain.

"All the clubs!" The man chuckled. "Now that would be a feat! But really, I know you're *not* a member, and I'm surprised that I don't recall your name coming up in the discussion of invitations."

"I was here last year. I come every year."

"Yes, but I don't recall . . ."

"You're thinking I would be blackballed for some reason?" The captain smiled a charming smile.

"Actually—"

"Have you met this gentleman?" the captain said as if to change the subject. He stood and motioned for Andy to stand as well. "This is King Corpus."

The man did not shake Andy's hand, but said, "Corpus? Is that a krewe?"

"Indeed. A very ancient one."

"Not older than Comus, however. They were the first. I have friends in Comus."

"Latecomers. Imitators. But so are they all. That bull of Rex's? They got that from Corpus."

"You're having me on. I never heard of Corpus."

Andy felt in his pocket for the green coin. "Here," he said. "A throw from the Corpus parade."

The man took it, then chuckled. "Well, no wonder I never heard of them." He handed the coin back to Andy. It was blank.

"Hardly anyone ever remembers us, Your Highness," the captain said with a smile. "At least not clearly. That's how we prefer it."

"Excuse me," said a white-haired man, stepping close to where the captain was seated. "I believe you're sitting at our table." A woman, his wife probably, stood behind him, along with two younger men and their wives.

"And what table did you think this was?" asked the captain.

"What it says there." The man pointed at the placard. "Table seventeen."

The captain picked up the placard and showed it to the man. "Thirteen, you mean." And the printed placard did say, Table 13.

"It said seventeen," the man said. He asked his wife, "Didn't it say seventeen?"

"There's never any table thirteen," said the bald man. "It would be bad luck."

"There is *always* a table thirteen," said the captain, "and we always sit at it. Every year." He looked at the man whose invitation said Table 17. "There are plenty of unreserved tables at the back. And the food is the same, after all."

The white-haired man opened his mouth, but his wife said, "Look, the waiters are coming out. Let's just go find a table." They and their retinue left, but the bald man wasn't satisfied.

"Something's wrong here," he said. "I'm going to go get the seating list. For that matter, I'm going to go get the master guest list!"

"By the time you've crossed the room," said the captain, "you won't remember what it is you have gone to do."

The bald man gave the captain a sharp look. "We'll see about that." He strode away, a man with a mission. He didn't come back.

"We won't stay for the dancing," said Pomona.

"No," Clytie said as a waiter set a salad before her. "We don't come to these silly balls because we like them. We just come because we *can*."

"You must be starving, Your Highness," said the captain.

As usual, Andy was indeed very hungry.

That night was the same as the other nights, a different woman in a rundown hotel. As Andy was taking his tuxedo jacket off, he found his invitation. On a hunch, he took it out and unfolded it. It was a blank piece of paper.

But the woman was real enough. The dinner and wine at the ball had been splendid. If the captain and his ladies were con artists of some sort, at least Andy couldn't see any way in which *he* was being conned.

DAY AFTER DAY, NIGHT after night, Andy's Carnival partying stuck to the same pattern: Lots of eating and drinking in the evening, lots of sex into the wee hours and slumber into the afternoon. The Krewe of Corpus took him to parades, to black-tie balls, and to costume balls. He was gaining weight. They brought him a succession of larger and larger tuxedos and royal costumes for the various occasions. It seemed to him, even though he was a little uncomfortable with his rapidly acquired fat, that he was having the Carnival of his dreams, that he had nothing at all to complain about.

Weeks went by. Late in the Carnival season, on the Monday before Fat Tuesday, Andy found himself at a costume ball in an immense ballroom that was packed from wall to wall with costumed revelers. He wore a cape trimmed with black-tipped white fur—Clytie insisted that it was real ermine—and his crown. One minute, he was standing right next to the captain, who wore his usual mask, and then he was alone. Alone, but for the crowd of total strangers on all sides. The press of all those bodies made the room very hot. Andy made his way out into a corridor, which was at least a little less crowded.

"Look at you," said a voice. "Look at how they fattening you up."

Andy turned. Sitting at a card table with Tarot cards arrayed before her was a woman whom he didn't quite recognize. She was wearing a lace shawl.

"I been wondering if you left them by now. But here you is. You don't know what you in for, do you?" she said. She wasn't looking at him as she spoke. She could have been talking to herself. "I knew you didn't know what you was getting into."

Ah. Now he knew her. This was the old woman who had been there on the sidewalk when the captain had first offered Andy the crown of Corpus.

"Don't look at me," she said to the air. "You and me lock eyeballs, and they will be able to feel it. They already feeling something, I bet."

"What are you talking about?" Andy said.

"Don't look at me," she said again, calmly, looking at her cards. "You got until the end of Mardi Gras to tell them you don't want to be no king. You only got until then."

"Why would I do that? I'm having fun!"

"What about your people? Your friends? Your family? Haven't given a thought to them, have you?"

That was right. Andy had friends in town. He had been staying with them. He had meant to call. They must be wondering what had happened to him.

What *had* happened to him? Mardi Gras time had swept him up, that was what. Maybe, knowing him, his friends would understand after all.

"They got the glamour working all around you. I can feel it. Mardi Gras come tomorrow, and the glamour only get stronger then. And look at you," the old woman went on. "You all swelled up like a toad. You all fatted up like that bull of theirs. Won't always be that way. If you don't—"

The captain's voice boomed, "There you are! For a moment, I feared we had lost our merry king!"

"Just needed some air, Captain," Andy said.

"It's time we proceeded to dinner, anyway," the captain said. He was looking at the old woman. "You are hungry, I trust?"

"Always," Andy said.

The old woman shook her head, but she said nothing as she gathered up her cards. Her hands trembled. The captain was still looking at her as he said, "You enjoy being King Corpus, don't you Andy?"

"You know I do."

"Have we misled you?" The captain's eyes never left the old woman. "In any way, have we failed you?"

"It's been just like you said. Everything I want is mine."

"Good!" The captain gave Andy's belly a pat. "Good to know that our generosity is *appreciated.*"

The old woman stood and said, "Excuse me," as she shouldered her way past Andy. The captain watched her go. Then he looked at Andy. "We're sparing no expense to keep you happy," he said.

"Easy for you," Andy said, lowering his voice. "You can give people scraps of newspaper, and they think it's money."

"It *is* money," the captain said. "What is money ever but paper wedded to belief?"

"So I'm right," Andy said. "How do you do it?"

"Dinner," the captain said. "Dinner, and then a night of fleshly pleasures! Who cares what currency feeds your hungers, Your Highness! What matters is that they be fed!"

Later, as he undressed for that night's prostitute, Andy felt something in one of his pockets. A tarot card. The Devil.

THE MYSTICK KREWE OF Corpus woke Andy at noon on Tuesday— early by their standards, but there was a lot to see. They helped him into his royal costume and took him into the French Quarter again, where the streets were packed with lasciviously costumed celebrants. Andy saw men dressed as cowboys and Indians. The front of their costumes looked normal, but their butts were bare. One cowboy wore only chaps, pistols, and a hat. Other men were in drag in real evening gowns, in rhinestone-and-dyed-feather parodies, or even in stagily erotic streetwalker costumes. There were some women dressing the same way.

There were other sorts of costumes, too. Andy saw giant crayons in various hues, a pair of goldfish, a band of hook-handed pirates that waved to a cluster of old men in chartreuse diapers and baby bonnets.

The balconies above the street were almost as crowded as the streets below. Andy heard someone shout, "Show us your tits!" followed a moment later by wild cheering. One of the women on a balcony was flashing the crowd below.

"Tits are the order of the day," Clytie said when she saw a family—mom, dad, and nine-year-old son—wearing papier-mâché breasts on the outside of their clothes.

"The *body* is the order of the day," said Sibyl.

"Indeed," said the captain. "And the body of King Corpus needs feeding!"

Andy touched the tarot card in his pocket. "I've been thinking," he said.

"Yes?" said the captain.

For a moment, Andy let the sentence form in his head: *Maybe I don't want to be King Corpus any more. Maybe I've had enough.*

"Let me guess," said the captain. "You've been thinking of what to eat and drink today, yes?" He lowered his voice. "You've been thinking of other pleasures of the flesh as well, no doubt. It *is* Mardi Gras today. You *are* King Corpus. What about two women at once this afternoon? Would that please Your Highness?"

Andy was hungry, and once he had eaten, he knew he'd have other appetites to satisfy.

"Come on," said Pomona. "Let's see if we can find a strip club that serves decent sandwiches. You can whet two appetites at once." She winked at Andy.

He spent the rest of the day eating, drinking, and gawking. The Krewe of Corpus was always with him, except for the hours that he spent with two women that the captain found for him. The captain came and collected him for dinner, and Clytie, Pomona, and Sibyl greeted him like a conquering hero. "Hail the king of flesh!" said Clytie. They gave him wine, and he drank it with gusto until he was light-headed.

"You've grown enormous," Sibyl said. She seemed both delighted and disgusted by this. "Have you noticed? Have you seen how fat you are?"

"*Le boeuf gras*," said Pomona. "You have really become the king!"

"Back into the street!" the captain announced. "It's getting late, and we have someplace to be!"

"Where?" Andy said.

"Consecrated ground!" said the captain. "Come on, Your Highness!"

They wandered the streets some more. It *was* late. Mounted police with bullhorns were announcing the approach of midnight. "Mardi Gras is over in fifteen minutes," one of them blared out. "Time to start going home. It's all over in fifteen minutes."

The crowds had already thinned out. The streets were littered with garbage and, here and there, parts and props from abandoned costumes. An oversized cardboard baby bottle lay on its side in the gutter.

"Here," said Clytie. She pressed something into Andy's hand. It was a turkey leg. "Your scepter for the final moments of your reign."

Andy hesitated, then bit into it. It was as delicious as the first one they had given him, all those weeks ago.

The captain stopped before a wrought-iron gate. It squeaked as he opened it. On the other side, Andy could see tombs in the dim light. "Follow me, King Corpus!"

"Why?" Andy said.

"It's nearly time," said Sibyl.

"Come on, Your Highness," Pomona half sang. She tugged up the hem of her skirt, exposing more leg. "Like what you see? Come on!"

He took another bite from the turkey leg and followed the Krewe of Corpus into the cemetery.

"Here," said the captain. He took something from his pocket. A tiny box.

In the distance, the police were announcing the end of Mardi Gras. Midnight had come. Andy stopped chewing. The bite of turkey was unpleasantly greasy in his mouth. He spit it out.

"It's Ash Wednesday," the captain said. "Your Highness, if you would be so good as to remove your crown."

"I don't feel so good," Andy said. His belly ached. His head throbbed. All the overeating, and the drinking and debauchery were catching up to him with the stroke of midnight. He made his way to one of the tombs and leaned against the side.

"This won't take but a moment," the captain said. "Turn around. Just a little ritual for Ash Wednesday."

"I'm not Catholic."

"Neither are we," said the captain. "Our allegiances lie in another direction altogether. It doesn't matter. It's true no matter what you believe." He looked at the three women. "It's true no matter how much power we gather unto ourselves in this life. It's true no matter how long we may live."

"What's true?" Andy grabbed the rolls of fat on his belly, disgusted with himself. His bowels rumbled.

The captain stepped closer, turned Andy to face him, and sprinkled some of the box's contents on Andy's head. "Ashes." He dabbed ashes onto his finger and marked Andy's forehead with an *X*.

"What's true?" Andy said again.

"*Pulvis es, in pulverem reverteris,*" said the captain. "That is true. For you, and eventually even for us. Thank you, Your Highness. Thank you for serving to remind us of that."

The women curtsied to him.

"Remind you of what?" Andy started to say, but then he turned and vomited against the side of the tomb. He dropped to his knees. He vomited again. He retched.

When he could stand up, he was alone.

EXCEPT FOR THE STREET sweepers with their flashing yellow lights and the occasional mounted policeman, the streets were empty. Just an hour after midnight, and the party really was over.

And that was fine with Andy. For once, he'd had his fill of partying. He didn't think he'd want to eat another bite, take another drink, sleep late, or even think about sex again for weeks and weeks.

And as he thought that, he felt a little tremor of truth and terror that he didn't yet understand.

He should call his friends, the people he'd been staying with here in New Orleans. He should try to explain.

If he could remember who they were. He laughed a short, bitter laugh. Oh, he had really done a number on himself. He couldn't remember their names! But he was sick, exhausted. He just needed to find someplace to crawl where he could sleep it off. He'd be fine in the morning.

WEEKS LATER, ANDY FOUND the storefront. A sign in the window said, "Madame Baptiste," and "Palm Reading & Divinations." He put his skeletal hand on the door and opened it. Bells on the door jingled.

The old woman emerged from the back room and started to say, "What can I do for—"

Then she stopped cold and stared.

"Oh, child," she said. "You gone and went through with it! Look at you!"

Andy considered himself. The Salvation Army clothes that hung loosely from his skin-and-bones body. The blue veins showing in the pale skin of his hands.

"But didn't I try to warn you off?" she said. "Didn't I tell you that you had until the end of Mardi Gras?"

"I knew you would remember me," Andy said. "You could have told me more clearly what was in store. You could have made it *clear.*"

"Child, I could not." She shook her head. "Do you know what a risk it was to interfere with them at all? To have words with you at all? I couldn't draw them down on me. I couldn't have their wrath. I got some talent, honey, but I'm nothing to *them.* Now they won't care what I tell you or what you understand. Too late for you to change your mind."

"Who are they?" Andy said. "*What* are they?"

"They old," she said. She clutched at her lace shawl. "They been here since New Orleans wasn't hardly nothing at all. And when they put the glamour on, they can make you see things. Or not see things. When you was king of their krewe, they was probably there watching you when you thought they wasn't. Might be they following you now, into this room." She made a sign with her hands. "They like to see it all, how they fatten up their *boeuf gras*. How it all end."

"But why?"

"They make you king, and you remind them that everything going to pass away. Even them, someday."

"What will happen to me?" Andy said. "I can't eat. I don't sleep. I don't remember people, and people who should remember me, don't."

"That's the glamour. They wasting you away now."

"Why?"

"King Corpus, he revel in the flesh and then the flesh leave him. That's what Mardi Gras mean to them." She shook her head again. "Nothing you can do."

"You could have warned me!" Andy insisted.

But she shook her head sadly. "You took their gift," she said. "I done give you all the warning I could."

ON EASTER MORNING, PEOPLE walked past the rumpled bundle of clothes in the gutter on Royal Street. It was a dry husk curled up so tight, shrunken down so small, that no one who passed it imagined that it might have once been a human being. No one imagined that it had once been a king.

MASKING INDIAN

Charles de Lint

It's the last thing I expect to find hanging on the wall of my apartment when I get home. I haven't seen that costume in ten years, not since I left New Orleans. Back then it was hooked up in a place of honor on another wall, the one in Lawrence Boudreaux's front room.

Larry died last year. I would've made it back for the funeral, but I only heard about it afterward, when it was too late to go.

I drop my jacket and purse on the sofa now and slowly walk up to where that plumed extravaganza hangs. The colors are so bright they dull everything in my living room and I'm not exactly known for my good taste. The lime-green bust of Elvis sitting on top of my TV is perhaps the subtlest thing I own. What can I say? I like kitsch.

But this costume . . .

When I lift a hand to touch one of the plumes, the whole thing fades away before my fingers can make contact. It figures. I've been looking for years for a miracle to clear up the mess of my life, but when the impossible does come my way, this is what I get: a moment of special effects.

I stare at the wall where the costume was hanging. Thinking of it, of Chief Larry, wakes a flood of old memories that take me back to when I was a runaway, a little white girl looking for her black roots among the Black Indian tribes that rule the Mardi Gras.

"YOU'LL LIKE THIS," Wendy said. "Marley says she's got a ghost in her apartment."

Jilly looked up from her canvas to where Wendy sat on the Murphy bed at the other end of the studio, her blonde curls pressed up against the headboard, legs splayed out in front of her on the comforter.

"Who's Marley?" Jilly asked.

"The art director's new assistant at *In the City*. You met her at that party at Alan's a couple of weeks ago."

"I remember. She was the one with the bright red buzz cut and the pierced eyebrow, right?"

"That's her."

"But she's not exactly the happiest camper, is she?" Jilly went on. "I remember being struck by how she seemed so outgoing, but there was all this other stuff going on behind her eyes."

"Sounds like you're describing yourself," Wendy said.

Jilly laughed, but Wendy caught the momentary empathy that flickered in her friend's pale blue eyes.

"So what kind of ghost does she have?" Jilly asked.

Wendy had to grin. "The ghost of a Big Chief's Mardi Gras costume."

Jilly put down her brush and came over to the bed.

"A what?" she asked.

"You know, one of those huge feather and sparkle affairs they wear in the parades."

"Except it's the *ghost* of it?"

"Mmhmm," Wendy said. "Except, how can an inanimate object even have a ghost? You'd think it'd have to be alive first . . . so that it could die and become a ghost, I mean."

Jilly shook her head. "Everything has spirit."

"Even a costume?"

"Maybe especially a costume. It's already made to be a secret, isn't it?"

"Or to hide one."

Jilly got a dreamy look in her eyes. "The ghost of costume. I love it. Do you think she'd let us see it?"

"I'll have to ask."

"A LONG TIME AGO," the old black man says. "Back when we were slaves. The only ones who welcomed us here were the Indians. That's why we respect them like we do, why we call up their spirits with the drumming and parades."

He was brought up in one of those Black Indian tribes in New Orleans: a Flagboy, running information from the Spyboys to the Second Chiefs; a Wildman with the buffalo horns poking out of his headdress, scattering the crowds when they got too close to the chiefs and could maybe mess up the ornate costumes; finally a Big Chief, Chief Larry of the Wild Eagles, squaring off against the other chiefs, spasm band setting up a polyrhythmic racket at his back while he strutted his stuff.

I can't keep my gaze off the outfit where it's hooked up on the wall of his home—a spirit guide, he tells me. An altar and a personal shield, a reflection of his soul.

It boggles my mind. I can't imagine how much it cost to put that fantastic explosion of flash and thunder together. It's a masterpiece of dyed plumes, papier-mâché and broken glass, peacock and turkey feathers, glass beads, egg shells, sequins and fish scales, velvet and sparkles and Lord knows what else. The headdress rises three feet above the top of his head when he puts it on, and the whole costume has to weigh a hundred or so pounds, but he can carry it like it has no weight at all.

Tired as he was last night, he didn't let that stop him. He was up the whole night before, sewing and helping others in the tribe with their suits. He marched twenty or thirty miles through the city yesterday, carried his tribe through over a dozen confrontations with other tribes, drank straight vinegar to cut the cramps; but he was still so swollen when he got home last night that they had to cut him out of his suit.

Yeah, he's something, Chief Larry, but he's still got time to talk to a street kid like me.

"Thing is," he says, "people forget this wasn't always a show. Time was we governed the neighborhoods. We kept the music and spirit alive—hell, we were priest and police, all in one. Masking Indian was just a little piece of what the tribes were all about. We were like the Spiritual Churches then—we looked after the souls of our people."

"What happened?" I ask.

He shrugs. "Progress happened."

He says the word "progress" like it's an epithet. I guess for him it is.

I don't know why he ever took to me. Maybe he felt sorry for me. Maybe he just liked the idea of helping a little white runaway connect with the black blood that she got from her great-grandpa, blood so thin, it doesn't show any more than the winter coat of a hare against a snowdrift. But he lets me hang around the Wild Eagles' practices. I sit in the back and bang away on a cowbell, adding my own little clangs to the throbbing, primal rhythm of bass and snare drums, tambourines, congas, percussion sticks, pebble gourds, bucket drums, and anything that can make a noise and fill out the beat.

The tempo just keeps building until everything seems like total pandemonium, but Chief Larry's actually exercising a strict spiritual and physical control over the proceedings. Comes a moment when everything feels transcendent, like we're plugging straight into the heart of some deep, old, primal magic. When we're one, all the Wild Eagles, everybody in that room.

It's better than crack, but just as addictive.

"Sometimes," he tells me, "people ought to just leave well enough alone. Everything's moving too fast these days. We're so busy, we can't see what's in front of our noses anymore. We don't need to know everything that's happening, every place in the world, every damn second of the day."

He pauses to look at me, to make sure he's got my attention.

"What we need," he goes on, "is to connect to what's around us and the spirit that moves through it. Our families, our neighbours, the neighborhood."

"The tribe," I say.

"Same difference."

MARLEY BUTLER WAS ON the computer when Wendy arrived at the *In the City* offices the next morning. She was working on a collage to illustrate an article on the upcoming festivities organized by the Good Serpent Club at the end of Lent. Every year they put on a kind of a mini-Mardi Gras, more block party than parade. A half-dozen streets in Upper Foxville were closed off and people from all over the city gathered to listen to live bands, sample Cajun and other Louisiana-styled cooking, and march around in costumes and masks. The only gathering as colorful was in July when the Gay Pride Parade finished up a week of celebrations, but for that they closed off Williamson Street all the way from Kelly Street to the lake.

Marley was using scans from photos taken during previous years' Mardi Gras festivals, combining them in such a manner that the individual photos were still recognizable, but taken as a whole, they became a masked face.

"That's pretty cool," Wendy said, looking over Marley's shoulder.

"Thanks."

Wendy slid into a seat beside the computer desk and popped the lid on her coffee.

"So do you still have your ghost?" she asked and took a sip.

Marley gave her a wary look. "Why?"

"Well, I was telling Jilly about it last night and she was wondering if we could come over and see it."

"You're making fun of me."

Wendy shook her head. "No, really. I swear I'm not. We just like weird stuff."

"Weird stuff," Marley repeated, obviously dubious.

"Look, I've told you about Jilly—how she's really into this kind of thing."

Marley gave a slow nod. "And you?"

"I just like a good story."

"You're not telling me something," Marley said.

Wendy hesitated. How did she explain this without coming off as a complete flake?

But, "Okay," she said. "Fair's fair. See, I've got this tree that grows on stories. I raised it from an acorn and ever since it's been the tiniest thing, I've given it stories. It's huge now—way bigger than it could possibly be if it wasn't a magical tree—but I still give it new stories whenever I can."

Marley said nothing. Her gaze held Wendy's, but Wendy couldn't figure out what the other woman was thinking.

Wendy tried on a smile. "So now you can make fun of me," she added.

"You've got a tree that grows on stories," Marley finally said.

Wendy nodded. "A Tree of Tales."

"Where is it?"

"I transplanted it to Fitzhenry Park when it got too big for the pot I was keeping it in. You should see it. It's already huge."

"So do you find it cathartic, feeding it your stories?"

Wendy shrugged. "I guess. Depends on the story. Why do you ask?"

"Because I've got a story I'd like to tell it."

"I REMEMBER A TIME," Chief Larry tells me one day, "when things really meant something. Everything had a meaning. The difference now is, things only seem to have a meaning if we give it to them. But it shouldn't be that way. Is the crawdad any less of a crawdad if we're not there to acknowledge it?"

I like that he tells me this kind of stuff. Growing up, all I ever heard was, "Shut up. No one's talking to you."

"It's like a Zen thing, right?" I say.

I read about this once when I was hiding out in the public library from the truant officer. Let me tell you, that's the last place they'll come looking for you. I've learned about more stuff skipping school than I ever did in the classroom.

"You know," I add by way of explanation, "does a tree falling in the forest make a sound if no one's there to hear it?"

" 'Course it makes a sound. That's the whole point of what I'm telling you."

"But what about quantum physics and this whole business about observable phenomena that scientists are studying now? They're saying that things like quarks only take on a discernible identity when they're being observed."

"I don't know quarks from farts," Larry says. "I just know the world doesn't need us to give it meaning. Just like nothing was put here for our use. If we're caretakers, it's only to leave things a little better than when we got here. Me, I think we're just one more animal, messier and more mean-spirited than most."

"IT'S NOT ALWAYS HERE," Marley said as she unlocked the door of her apartment.

She's worried we're going to think she made it all up, Wendy thought, but Jilly was nodding beside her.

"That's the way these things work," Jilly said. "If they were predictable, they wouldn't be very mysterious, would they?"

Marley gave her a grateful look.

"It's funny," she said as she ushered them in. "I never once stopped to wonder if I was crazy. I just knew it was really there, even if it fades away whenever I try to touch it."

Her guests made no reply. Marley's hallway led straight into her living room and there, hooked up on the wall, was the costume, an extravaganza of reds and pinks so vibrant that it seemed to pulse. Jilly moved forward, Wendy trailing behind her, until they were both standing directly in front of it.

"Oh my," Jilly said.

Neither of them tried to touch it, though Wendy was sorely tempted.

"What's it doing here?" she said.

"Just being gorgeous," Jilly told her. "It doesn't have to be doing anything. That's what I like best about this sort of thing. It just is."

"No, I meant why would it appear here?"

"I used to know the guy who owned it," Marley told them. "It showed up about a week or so after I found out he'd died."

"Were you close to him?" Jilly asked.

Marley nodded. "Once upon a time. It was years ago, back in New Orleans."

"I'm sorry."

"Me, too. I should've gone back to see him, but I always thought, there'll be time. But there never is, is there?"

"Never as much as we'd like," Jilly said.

Marley said nothing for a long moment, gaze locked on the costume, then she blinked and turned to her guests.

"You guys want a beer or something?"

"Beer is always good," Jilly said.

"So did he ever wear it?" Wendy asked when they returned from the kitchen with their drinks.

Marley nodded. "You bet. He looked amazing in it. Some of the tribes, they saw those red and pink plumes coming towards them on Mardi Gras night, they'd just head down another street so they wouldn't lose a confrontation to Chief Larry and his Wild Eagles." She smiled at the blank looks on the faces of her guests. "Do you know anything about the Black Indian tribes down in New Orleans?"

When they shook their heads, she started to tell them. Not about how she ended up on the street, or the simple gift that Chief Larry had given her by treating her as a human being, but describing the tribes and their influence, how it all came together on Mardi Gras night in a pageant of wonder and noisy magic.

Just before they left, Marley walked up to the costume and reached out a hand. Wendy gasped when it vanished. Innocuous as a ghostly costume might be, there was still something disquieting about the fact that it even existed in the first place. Turning, she saw that Jilly was only smiling, her sapphire blue eyes shining bright with pleasure.

THIS NIGHT AFTER THE Mardi Gras, Larry tells me it's his last year of leading the Wild Eagles.

"I'm getting too old to carry the weight," he tells me.

I wonder if he means the costume, or his responsibility as Big Chief. Probably both.

Like me, he's got no blood family. The difference is, his people died; they didn't turn their backs on him. Two sons were shipped home in coffins from Vietnam. His wife was killed in a car crash by a drunk driver. That left him with the Wild Eagles. Just like me now. My great-grandpa on my mother's side used to run with his dad, back in the old days. That's how come I ended up on his doorstep in the first place, wanting to know about that part of my family. I already knew too much about the Jordan side of the family tree.

"So what are you going to do?" I ask.

"I don't know," he tells me.

There's something different in his voice. Like all the strength has gone out of it.

"You'll still have the Wild Eagles," I say.

He nods. "But it won't be the same. I was the Big Chief. Now I'll just be another guy, banging a drum."

I don't want to say, that's more than I've got. I'm just a hanger-on.

But it sort of comes out anyway.

"But you're still part of the tribe," I say. "You don't have to be alone."

He nods again, but his gaze changes. I can tell he's no longer feeling sorry for himself. He's feeling sorry for me.

"That family of yours," he says. "They must've hurt you pretty bad. Other people, too, I'm guessing."

I shrug.

"But you never gave in to anybody, did you?"

Once, I think. But that was enough.

"No," I tell him. "I just ran away."

"Sometimes that's all you can do," he says.

I can only look at him. Bad as things were, I still feel kind of ashamed for running. In all the books I read, people stand up for themselves when things get bad. But I wasn't brave enough.

"Sometimes it's not just the smart thing to do," he adds. "Sometimes it's the brave thing, too."

It's like he's reading my mind.

"Doesn't seem so brave to me," I say.

He shakes his head. "You just don't know enough yet to make that kind of a pronouncement. Wait'll some time goes by."

"It's going to have to be a lot of time."

"Could be," he says. "If that's what it takes . . ."

WENDY FELT A LITTLE awkward taking Marley to where she'd planted the Tree of Tales in Fitzhenry Park. The tree was a miracle, but you wouldn't know that from looking at it, and she was afraid Marley wouldn't understand. She'd grown it from an acorn, nourished it through a winter, then transplanted the sapling here in the Silenus Gardens, that part of the park that was dedicated to the poet Joshua Stanhold. And it had grown . . . how it had grown. But while a botanist might be surprised to find such a large and healthy example of *Quercus robur*—the common oak of Europe—growing here among a handful of native oaks, most people wouldn't give it a second glance except to admire its lines.

As they approached the tree, walking along the concrete path and keeping out of the way of the in-line skaters and joggers who seemed to think they owned the park, Wendy could see a man sitting under it, talking, except he was alone there under the boughs.

She smiled. There was proof, though she didn't need it, that she wasn't alone in sharing her stories with the tree.

He got up as they arrived and gave them a friendly nod before walking away.

"*This* is it?" Marley said.

Wendy nodded.

Marley craned her neck, staring up into the sweeping canopy that spread above them.

"But this tree looks like it's . . ."

"I know," Wendy said. "A hundred years old."

Marley shook her head. "But if it grew so fast . . ." She looked to Wendy. "How could nobody have noticed?"

"People don't pay attention to things that are impossible," Wendy said. "At least that's what Jilly and Christy are always saying. That's why all these improbable things like a Tree of Tales—or the ghost of a costume—can exist with hardly anybody noticing. They don't want to see them."

"And we did?"

"I didn't think so in the beginning," Wendy said. "When John Windle—the crazy old guy who got me involved with taking care of the tree—first approached me, I didn't want to know about it for a minute."

"What changed your mind?"

Wendy shrugged. "I don't really know. Jilly was always telling me about these wonderful magical things that happened to her, but I thought they sounded more scary than exhilarating. But once I gave in and started taking care of the tree, I came to understand what she meant. Everything seemed bigger and more in focus. Everything seemed to have meaning—not necessarily meaning to me, but to itself. I guess what was most important was when I realized that. Everything's here for its own purpose, not for how it relates to me. I'm a part of it, but just that. A part."

"You remind me of Chief Larry," Marley said. "He used to tell me stuff like that."

Wendy smiled. "Of course, the intensity of what I felt didn't last. Which is probably just as well, since I've also got to live in the world that everyone else inhabits, and it's kind of hard to interact with people when you're always looking to see if they've got an elf sitting on their shoulder or something."

Wendy shook her head as Marley's eyes widened.

"No," she added. "I don't see that kind of thing. That's more up Jilly's alley. But I do have this." She lifted her arms to encompass the oak boughs spreading above them. "And it's magic enough for me."

"And you really planted it?" Marley asked.

"Yup. Eight years or so ago, it was wintering in a pot on the windowsill of my kitchen."

"Wow."

"Mmm," Wendy said, a dreamy look in her eyes. "Whenever Jilly tells me some really improbable story, I come here and I'm reminded that the world is bigger and stranger and more wonderful than it sometimes seems to be. And I don't think I'm alone. Remember that guy who was sitting under the tree when we arrived?"

Marley nodded.

"I'll bet he was telling the tree a story. I find lots of people come to sit here and talk to it. Most of them probably don't even know why they do it, except it makes them feel good. But they're nourishing the tree all the same."

"I . . ." Marley began, but then her voice trailed off.

"I understand," Wendy told her. "You want to tell it your story, but you want to do it in private."

"I don't mean to be rude."

Wendy smiled. "You're not. Want me to wait for you by the memorial?"

"I might be awhile."

"That's okay. I don't mind waiting." Wendy patted her shoulder bag. "I've got a book and, well, maybe you'll want some company when you're done."

Before Marley could protest, Wendy gave her a jaunty wave and headed back the way they'd come.

So HERE I AM, talking to a tree. To tell you the truth, I don't feel any magic in it. Even with a ghost in my own apartment, Wendy's claims just seem like too much . . . I don't know. Wishful thinking. But I talk all the same. I tell my story. There's nothing particularly original about it, and what does that say about this world we live in? Too many kids grow up just like I did, unwanted, unloved, never knowing a kind word or even a kiss until, in my case, I hit puberty, started to get some curves on my skinny-ass frame, and the guy in the trailer park who used to babysit kids for whoever was stupid enough to trust the freak with their children "made me a woman," as he put it.

But that wasn't the worst of it. The worst was when I told my parents. I don't know why I did; I already knew they wouldn't care. But the old man goes ballistic. Starts screaming about my "goddamned nigger blood" and beats the crap out of both me and my mother. I'd have more sympathy for her, living with such a monster, but she wasn't ever that much better. That night she just spat on me and then hauled herself to her feet and staggered out of the kitchen to leave me lying there on the cracked linoleum.

I ran away that night.

I'd already known that my great-grandpa on my mother's side was black, or partly black, though you wouldn't know it from looking at me. I'm so fair-skinned that just thinking of going out into the sun gives me a burn. The funny thing is my old man's darker-skinned than I am—got some Seminole blood a few generations back, Creole, who knows what else. Mostly meanness.

Anyway, I decide to go find out about the ancestors on my mother's side. She's no saint herself, but I already know the Jordan side of the family is made up of these mean-spirited sons-abitches, so what have I got to lose? I knew the Butlers came from the city, so I head up to New Orleans and ask around about my great-grandpa Gilbert Butler, did anybody know him? and that's how I finally ran into Larry Boudreaux.

Life gets a little better. I'm still living on the street when I connect with the Wild Eagles, scraping by the best I can, but I find what I'm looking for. My great-grandpa was a good man; it turns out that the blood didn't turn bad until it came around to my mother and who knows how much marrying into the Jordan family had to do with that. But better still, I find a friend in Larry. I learn that there are people here in the world who'll treat me like a human being instead of just the family's ugly pet, or street trash.

But the thing is, it's still hard. No matter how far away I get from it, I still feel like the kid in the trailer park who had to run away. The kid who lived on the street like a feral cat, never quite trusting the hand held out to it. I can only go so far with people, only look over the wall I've got built up inside me, instead of coming around or letting them in. Maybe that kind of thing never goes away.

It did when I was with Larry, but once I moved, all the doubts came back again. I guess I could've gone back, but I had my pride. I wanted to make it on my own, prove how I could be a real success, before I went back. But now it's too late. Larry's dead and I know he's the only one who wouldn't have cared one way or the other, only that I was happy.

I tell the tree all of that and then I lie back on the grass and stare up into its boughs. I don't feel cleansed or relieved or like I've touched any kind of magic. Wendy's Tree of Tales is a piece of work all right, but there's more mystery in why the ghost of Larry's Mardi Gras costume likes to hang on the wall of my apartment.

But thinking of that costume gives me an idea.

WENDY WASN'T MUCH HELP as they worked on the costume in Marley's living room, trying to copy the ghost of Chief Larry's suit that was still hooked up on the wall, but Jilly threw herself into it with cheerful enthusiasm. Even when Marley and Wendy had to go to the office, Jilly left her own work unattended in her studio and spent long hours at Marley's apartment, pasting and gluing and stitching. But then, that was Jilly, always ready for an adventure, always ready to drop everything and lend a hand.

Still, Wendy helped out where she could, and if she was klutzy with the detail work, she was good at sorting beads and dyeing feathers and putting together meals. The other two would get so caught up in what they were doing that they wouldn't even have thought of eating if it hadn't been for her.

She also liked to see how Marley was loosening up, not just with Jilly, but at work, too. Mostly Marley kept to herself—it was only because of Wendy that they'd hung out, eaten lunches together, relaxed enough so that, while Marley didn't talk about her past, she'd talk about other things. Like the ghost of a Mardi Gras suit hanging on her living room wall.

There wasn't much they had to go out and buy. Marley had a surprising amount of the raw materials they needed for the project, as though she'd been planning to make a costume like this for years. She pulled out boxes and tins and plastic bags filled with sequins and glass beads, fabric remnants, rhinestones, seashells, colored glass, and the like.

"I'm just a packrat," she explained with a shrug.

Jilly grinned. "With ever such conservative tastes."

They dyed bundles of ostrich, turkey, and peacock feathers, made a frame for the headdress with wire and covered it with papier-mâché, constantly using the ghost costume for a reference. But while they started out copying, before too long their costume took on a life of its own.

"Which is the way it should be," Jilly said. "Don't you think?"

Marley nodded. "Larry wouldn't want a tribute—he'd want this suit to have a life of its own."

Not to mention an afterlife, Wendy thought, looking at the ghost hanging on the wall.

I LEAVE NEW ORLEANS not long after Chief Larry steps down from his leadership of the Wild Eagles. By this time I've got a room in a boarding house and between a couple of part-time jobs, I've been taking night school to get my high school diploma. The diploma gets me into a one-year computer arts program at Butler University, so I make the move. I can't afford my own equipment, but the labs there are really impressive and as a student I can use them whenever I want. I'm in there a lot.

I don't know when I realized I wanted to be an artist. It's not like I grew up, always drawing or anything. I guess it came from doing posters advertising gigs for groups that people I knew were in. It was something I liked and was actually good at. Eventually I discovered that I enjoyed collage work the most, which is what drew me to the computer studies. If you've got the material on your hard drive, you can manipulate and play with it forever. And with the quality of printers these days, and if you're using the right kind of inks and paper, every print you run off is archival quality.

But I never make more than one print of a piece.

That's something I learned from Chief Larry and the Wild Eagle practices. Anything really good, is always different. Unique. You might start out aiming to copy something, but if it's got any heart, if it's got any real spirit, it'll be something else again when it's done.

It'll be its own thing.

Works for people, too.

It took them the better part of a week and a half to get the costume finished. Finally, Marley lifted it up on its hanger. She looked at Wendy and Jilly, then carried the suit over to the wall where the ghost of Chief Larry's hung. When she hung it up, the ghost didn't so much fade away as fade into the costume they'd made.

For a long moment, none of them spoke. A tingle ran up Wendy's spine and she saw Jilly wearing that contented smile of hers again, the one that always came when some piece of the big mystery underlying the world manifested itself for a moment.

"What are you going to do with it?" Wendy finally asked.

Marley grinned. "What do you think? I'm going to wear it to the Mardi Gras that the Good Serpent Club's putting on."

"Can we come?" Jilly asked. "We could bang the drums and stuff."

"You want to join the new tribe?"

"You bet."

Wendy nodded as well, though she wasn't sure how well she'd do, gallivanting around on the street, dancing, and banging a drum. She didn't have quite the abandon Jilly did for this sort of thing. "There are no public spectacles," Jilly liked to say. "There's only fun."

"What are you going to call your tribe?" Wendy asked.

Marley thought about that for a moment. "I don't know. Maybe the Unforgotten Ones."

"KEEP IN MIND," CHIEF LARRY says another time when we're talking about Mardi Gras costumes. "Masking Indian's not about hiding yourself. It's about revealing yourself. It's about remembering the ones who went before and the spirit that's in everything, and honoring both. Your suit's a shield against hurt, but it's also an altar of belief and faith and hope."

"I'll remember."

He smiles. "I know the world can be a hard and wicked place, and sometimes it's all we can do not to want to just check out and leave it behind. But it's our job—people like you and me who care—to fight those wrongs best we can and offer up a hope of something better. Every time we do a good thing, the spirits smile and the world's that much better. I know it's no big deal. It's not going to change the whole world. But it's a start.

"See, the people watching and laughing and having themselves a party . . . it doesn't matter if they understand; it only matters that we do. Because masking Indian's not just a reminder of the good spirits that share the world with us, it's a celebration of them, of us, and how we can all get along if we just make an effort."

And thanks to Larry, and his ghostly costume, that's something I'm not likely to forget again.

SACRIFICE

Jane Lindskold

River god. Broad and long and wide. Muddy. Rubbing against the city of New Orleans like a vast boa constrictor getting a feel for his meal.

Oh, the Mississippi River is held back by levees, tamed by those high walls and sturdy embankments. That's what the engineers think, anyhow. Those who know better know that Old Man River is constrained as much by custom as by those walls.

Sleeping river god, but sometimes he wakes. He's waking now and even though he's still drowsy, he knows it's about time he was fed.

Somewhere, dimly, he recalls that once upon a time he was wed.

It's an odd city, New Orleans. A city where the dead return to earth without touching the ground and the living breathe air though under water. It's an odd city, as full of contradictions as a nut is of meat.

New Orleans is built on a bog on a soggy crescent of land between a vast, temperamental river and a lake that could be called a sea. The Frenchmen who built the city there saw the location's potential as a center for trade. Others saw its potential as city to rival Atlantis when it came to drowning.

These were the ones who made the deal with the river god, a deal that has been pushed to its limits but never quite forgotten. That's a good thing, too, 'cause without that pact with the Father of Rivers, New Orleans would go back to being a bog, no matter what the Army Corps of Engineers likes to boast.

HER NAME IS MIRABELLE and she is indeed beautiful: beautiful, proud, and slightly arrogant. In an older time, folks would have termed her an octoroon, for her great-grandmother had been a black woman from Haiti, and in those days just how much black blood a body carried made all the difference in issues of slave and free.

These days people say those things don't matter. Mirabelle knows that they are wrong. Without her Haitian blood, it's unlikely that her temper would shatter glass and crystal, that she would catch glimpses of the dead folk walking about the city streets late at night, that she would hear the thumping of distant drums or the voices that whisper from the mouths of rum bottles.

Mirabelle has sorcery in her blood, sorcery that she credits to her Haitian great-grandmama, though maybe she should give a bit more credit to her red-haired Irish grandmother who has the second sight or her half-French, all-American father who tells the future from the way the wind ripples through the treetops.

But Mirabelle is young, just eighteen, and she's clinging to the most exotic elements of her heritage. That's pretty natural, because Mirabelle is getting ready to die.

BROKEN PIECES OF GLASS and bits of fractured mirror decorate the surface of the mask. Interstices between these irregular pieces have been filled with swirling abstract curves in lurid green, purple, or gold paint—the type that puffs and holds a three-dimensional shape. The effect is rather like cabled veins on an old man's arm or an over-flowing river coursing through city streets.

Only the mask's elongated oval eyeholes are picked out in anything resembling a regular pattern. These are outlined with a tightly fitting border of diamond-shaped Austrian crystal. The delicately faceted stones capture the light and cast it back in a shower of rainbows.

The mask's lips are softly smiling, like those of an Archaic statue or a satisfied lover, and are dusted with a glitter of crushed rubies or crystallized blood.

To accompany the mask, Mirabelle will wear a sweeping, multitiered gown worked from scraps of green, gold, and purple satin. Not one segment of fabric is precisely the same size and shape as any other. Only the fact that all the scraps are cut in straight lines and angles had made it possible for Mirabelle to fit the garment together at all.

The similarities in color between the sinuous curves of paint on the face of the mask and the identically shaded patchwork of the gown force the eye to seek a symmetry that is suggested but wholly illusory. The effect draws the gaze and forces it away again almost immediately. It is disquieting and unsettling.

Mirabelle is rather pleased. Just as the mirrors on the face of the mask give back broken images of the viewer rather than an image of the wearer, her costume is designed to distort and redirect. She doesn't know what effect that will have, but she hopes it might save her life.

Mirabelle might be getting ready to die, but that doesn't mean she particularly wants to do so.

UNTIL IT BURNED DOWN in 1919, the old French Opera House was the location of many prestigious debutante balls. It still hosts one, a ball held on irregular notice when the stars are right and the Mississippi runs high and the moon is a drawn bow— roughly every twenty years. On this occasion, the descendants of those who made a pact with the river god gather to make their offering. Invitations are issued by ghosts wearing the formal attire of the eighteenth century.

Nobody who receives one of these invitations ever refuses it. They know the consequences reach far beyond their own lives to the lives of everyone in New Orleans. What good would it be to survive the ball to die in the flood?

"Why can't we simply move away?"

That's the question generations of young women and young men have asked when an initiated family member tells them about the responsibility they have inherited.

"Try," comes the answer.

The strongest-willed last about a year away from New Orleans, but they're never the same afterwards. The nightmares that start when they leave the city for more than a week sear channels in their brains. Even when they're awake they can sense the waters surrounding the city. On a good day, New Orleans is just thirty-five feet above the sea. On a day when the river is high, the waters rise to fifteen or more feet above street level. It's not good for a person to realize how close the god is dwelling. It's easier to give in.

Mirabelle doesn't think of herself as giving in. Instead, she has cultivated pride in her heritage. She's a savior of the innocent, a voluntary sacrifice. Sometimes she feels a real kinship with Jesus on his cross. Nonetheless, when the night of the ball arrives and she enters the carriage that will carry her to the old French Opera House, Mirabelle feels that confidence draining away.

She's glad she's wearing her defiant mask with its fragments of mirrors and broken glass. That way no one can see how terrified she really is.

NEW ORLEANS IS NOT completely unaware of the sacrifice made for her survival. Indeed, when the city was little more than a few men living in shacks in a swamp, a Carnival revel was held.

There are many theories why Carnival has been celebrated in New Orleans pretty much without interruption since the city's founding. These theories usually discuss New Orleans' continental heritage and suggest that the French and Spanish culture of New Orleans made the importation of the celebration inevitable. It did, but only because other forces were at work—otherwise every other American city founded by the French or Spanish would have its Mardi Gras and, quite simply, they don't.

Unknown to themselves, those early Mardi Gras revellers were dancing to unheard music eddying out from a ball held to choose the woman who would sacrifice herself to keep Old Man River in his bed. Early on the signatories of the pact had drawn straws or rolled dice; but as the agreement evolved into sacred duty, their self-respect demanded more of a send-off for the doomed woman—and a celebration for the survivors.

The first Mardi Gras parades didn't hit the streets of New Orleans until 1857—about a century after the first Bride's Ball—but it takes a while for resonances to penetrate, especially when their sources are being deliberately muted.

Once the parades evolved past their faltering start, Mardi Gras grew fast and wild. Although it was held every year, rather than intermittently like the sacrifice to the Father of Rivers, echoes of the original sacrifice kept popping up. More than one social ball was reigned over by a god, echoing how the river god ruled over the sacrifice and the city. The Krewe of Proteus came close when they named their event after the Old Man of the Sea. The Krewe of Rex, in spontaneously creating a king for Mardi Gras in 1872, paid unconscious tribute to the real king of the event.

There are many other echoes. The king cake that is used to choose the queen of the Twelfth Night Revellers. The Baby Dolls who strut through the streets shouting, "Hey, hey, I'm gonna quit my job." The colors of the Mardi Gras flag and streamers: green, purple, and gold. Whatever else folks say that those colors stand for, green is the color of the water god's hair; purple is reserved for royalty; gold recalls the cost.

Protest. Say that Carnival is an old tradition—older than Mardi Gras in New Orleans. Then remember.

The commonest derivation of the word *carnival* is from the Latin *carne vale* or "Farewell to the Flesh." The festival has been explained as a farewell to the eating of meat before the long Lenten fast. It is curious, however, that the places where

Carnival has survived most powerfully—even though Lent now requires no more than a token sacrifice—is where living water is powerful: Rio de Janeiro, Venice, Havana, New Orleans.

Farewell to the flesh. Farewell to the body of the girl who will give herself to the water so the water god will not take the city. Farewell.

PROUD-STEPPING WHITE HORSES with plumes in their headstalls draw the carriage carrying Mirabelle through the riotous finale of Carnival season in New Orleans—Fat Tuesday itself. The carousers along Canal Street neither see nor hear nor even scent the carriage's passage. Their unawareness makes Mirabelle feel as if she is already a ghost. She shivers.

To distract herself, she lifts the curtain at the window with a purple-gloved hand and stares hungrily at a lively chaos that only a year or so before she would have dismissed with the native's disgust for tourist excess. Men and women in T-shirts and jeans, some wearing face paint, fewer wearing masks, crowd their way along the banquettes, fish in a human stream.

Many wear ropes of gaudy plastic beads, relics of parades earlier in the day. Others clasp large plastic glasses holding vividly colored drinks. Although the evening is yet young, the humid air reeks with the smell of alcohol tinged with that of vomit. Jazz from a dozen competing sources—some live, some recorded—bombards the ears.

Mirabelle drops the curtain, her heart aching for a life she had scorned without ever experiencing.

If I have a chance, she thinks, *I'll dance in the streets. Shout at the krewe's parades. "Mister, throw me something!" Too late. Too late . . .*

Directed by their ghostly coachman, the white horses turn onto Bourbon Street. Here the rowdy excess is, if anything, more frantic. Mirabelle can sense the cyclic insanity growing in intensity like some perverted philosophical syllogism: Mardi Gras is fun; Mardi Gras is wild; I'm here at Mardi Gras, therefore I'm fun, I'm wild.

Coming from all directions down the grid of the French Quarter's streets, Mirabelle can see other carriages similar to the one that bears her. Like her own coach, they move unconcerned through the boiling pot of humanity, all converging on the increasingly solid Romanesque ghost of the old French Opera House.

Arriving at their destination, some of the coaches discharge groups of men and women, all masked and in costume. Mirabelle wonders if her father or grandmother—both inheritors of the pact, though their own debut balls are long past—are among those politely offering their invitations to the doormen and passing into the hall.

She'll never know. Secrecy is the right and privilege of the signatories. The ball itself is only spoken of once, at the time when the new initiate is told of his or her inherited responsibility. After that the ghosts take over, arranging everything as they have for over two hundred years.

Mirabelle suspects that the only reason that there is any mention of the pact by living person to living person is so that the newcomer will not mistake the ghosts for dreams or for the advent of insanity.

One by one the debutantes dismount from their carriages—swan, fairy, angel, princess—visions in white and lace, silver and sequins. Each stands tall in a costume from dream or nightmare, quiveringly aware that she is a prospective offering to the river god.

Oh, let it be one of them! Mirabelle prays silently, unworthily, and hates herself for her fear.

When Mirabelle's carriage stops and she is handed out by a footman, she realizes that Mardi Gras in the "real" world has vanished to nothing but a stray note of jazz or a bleat of raucous laughter. Even these are faintly heard and easily ignored.

She accepts the footman's guidance and then steps proudly to the door, her invitation in her hand. Determined to leave fear behind, she tosses her head and sees sparkling stars of reflected light twinkle from the face of her mask.

"Debutantes, come this way," a gentle yet strong feminine voice is saying as Mirabelle enters the Opera House and joins the flock of girls moving to obey.

The woman who takes charge of the twenty or so debutantes is dressed in a magnificent lavender gown; a wig with tight, silver corkscrew curls just touches her shoulders. Her features are covered by a full-face mask. A three-dimensional gauze butterfly, wings outspread, flutters over her eyes. Her sculptured lips are neutral and expressionless.

Mirabelle wonders who the woman is; if they know each other in the world outside of this life. She wonders if the woman is alive at all. Just as the floors of the ghost of the French Opera House are solid beneath her feet and the walls unyielding, so the human spirits are no longer insubstantial ghosts.

How many young women have you conducted to their doom? Mirabelle thinks, but she doesn't voice the question aloud.

"I am called Madame Papilio." Their guide introduces herself as she leads them into a spacious room off to one side of the Opera House's wide, central theater. "My role is to instruct you in the ritual of tonight's ball. In addition, I will answer any of your questions as best I can, but I remind you that it is forbidden to pass on the information to any who have not yet made their debut."

Masked heads nod all around.

"The program is simple," Madame Papilio continues. "When all the guests are seated, you young women will make a grand procession into the room. There will be a first dance with the young men of your generation."

A young woman dressed like an angel with wings of spangled gold mutters, "The fellows get off easy, don't they?"

Her question could have been dismissed, for it had not been actually addressed to Madame Papilio, but their guide chooses to acknowledge it.

"Actually, they do not," she says. "Since the Father of Rivers is male, the sacrifice must be female. That is defined by the laws of symmetry. However, whereas only one female initiate is actually chosen to act as the sacrifice, each male is destined to father at least one daughter and one son to continue the line. A female initiate may escape passing on the duty. She may choose not to have children—though most do—but a male may not."

"What if he doesn't get married?" the golden angel asks, her tones showing she still doesn't believe this is balance enough.

"Come now, dear," says Madame Papilio, her tones just a trace haughty. "Surely you know that marriage is not a prerequisite for children. Only if a man dies a virgin is he free of this charge, and virginity is a sacrifice in itself."

From the set of the golden angel's shoulders, Mirabelle thinks she is inclined to argue further, but Madame Papilio sweeps on with her explanation of the ball:

"After the initial dance, you will next be called out by a member of the older generation. Since, quite obviously, your names cannot be used, each of you will draw a number from a box. Incidentally, those numbers will be used to select the order in which you will process into the room as well."

Her gaze, concealed but not completely hidden behind her mask, sweeps over them as if considering how well they will present themselves. Mirabelle blushes slightly as Madame Papilio's dark, violet eyes dwell slightly longer than usual on her own costume. Already she is aware that the brilliant blending of purple, gold, and green in her gown—while completely appropriate for modern Mardi Gras—rather stands out among the demure, almost bridal, costumes of the other debutantes.

Mirabelle forces herself to meet Madame Papilio's gaze and feels, with a certain degree of shock, that she recognizes approval in them.

"When those two introductory dances are ended," Madame Papilio pauses and adds parenthetical fashion, "which symbolize the introduction of the new generation and the continuity of the old with the new—you will form a semicircle. Order is not important, but I'll assign two of you . . ." she glances around and nods toward the golden angel and then to Mirabelle and says, "you two young ladies to look for my signal and stand at opposite ends of the crescent. The rest of you distribute yourselves evenly. Shall we have a quick rehearsal?"

Under her direction, the debutantes find their places along the curve of a rather ragged arc. Madame Papilio shakes her head in despair and runs them through it again.

"You can tell that dancing has gone out of fashion," she says despairingly. "No grace, no natural sense of spacing and order . . ."

The third time she is more satisfied.

"Better." The praise is grudging. "You—Miss Golden Wings and Miss Patches . . ."

Her nod makes clear that the second *nom de guerre* applies to Mirabelle, "You did very well indeed. Now, ladies, after the crescent is formed, a footman will collect your numbered tiles—during the dancing tuck them in your glove if you didn't think to provide yourself with a purse. The tiles will be placed in a clear crystal bowl so everyone can see them. Then you will each draw again. This will supply the order in which you will accept slices from the cake. Does everyone understand?"

Twenty-four elaborately coiffed heads nod. Mirabelle feels the beads in her own headpiece cold against the back of her neck and shivers, imagining bony fingers caressing her. She bites the inside of her lip, impatient with her own cowardice.

Madame Papilio goes on, explaining the ritual of the cake eating, what they should do thereafter, concluding:

"At that point, we'll know who is the chosen queen. The ball will continue until eleven-thirty and mind that there be no sulking or inappropriate behavior."

You mean like raw panic? Mirabelle thinks wryly.

"Then the company will escort the queen to the king. Each female debutante will be escorted by a male, but the queen walks alone."

She looks at them and, despite her elaborate costume and old-fashioned wig, Mirabelle receives an impression of business-like efficiency.

"Any questions?"

A delicate girl in fluffy white, her lacy skirts evoking a snowflake or a swan, raises her hand.

"Madame Papilio, after the . . . the queen has been chosen, do we maintain our masks?"

"Yes. No one must know exactly who is the queen. Symbolically she is all of us, you see. Not just all of us here, but all of New Orleans. To personalize her would be to reduce our joint participation in her . . . union with the river god."

"And afterwards?" This comes from a tall, slim young woman whose gown, though fully as formal as the rest, suggests something American Indian in the style of its beadwork. "Does no one ever know who . . . did so much?"

"Not formally. Of course, there is the process of elimination."

Madame Papilio's tone is dreadfully practical. "Someone will be missing. If your family associates with other pact families, it may not be hard to deduce. Even so, it is considered bad form to discuss it. Is that all?"

Mirabelle catches a slight noise, less like speech then like twenty-four mouths opening, then closing again.

"Very good." Madame Papilio holds up a box containing pale ivory tiles about the size of dominoes, though much thinner. "Draw a tile, then get in line. I'll signal the captain that we are ready."

MIRABELLE IS FIFTH IN line, directly after a rather stout girl whose seed pearl encrusted white satin gown is echoed in the patterns on the face of her mask.

I wonder how long ago she learned that she would make her debut here? Mirabelle wonders. *Or did she plan that dress for a more traditional coming out?*

Heart pounding, she schools herself to walk with slow and measured steps, remembering all the weddings in which she had done her part as flower girl and, later, bridesmaid.

Always a bridesmaid, never a bride, she thinks, swallowing a nervous giggle. *Of course, today I don't really want to be a bride. Do I ever? Even if I'm not chosen—if I'm not pitched by loving family and friends into the river to drown so that no one else needs to drown—do I ever want to be a bride? Do I want to be a mother to a daughter who will someday make her debut in this horrid place?*

For a moment, Mirabelle understands how the fate of the men is somehow as terrible as that of the women. She thinks of her own father with his greying brown hair and kind eyes watching the procession and wondering which of the masked figures below is his own little Miri. She thinks of her grandmother and imagines her terror when realizing that her granddaughter might be chosen. She could imagine the upright old lady's self-condemnation:

"If I'd only kept my knees together. If I'd only had better sense, Mirabelle wouldn't be down there. Mama, Mama, why didn't we have better sense?"

Oddly enough, thinking of the reactions of the people she loves best—and of her uninitiated mother at home with the younger boys, believing that Mirabelle is merely out with a few friends, of her older brother who must be among the throng of male debutantes (funny how she'd forgotten Tod until Madame Papilio had mentioned that men shared the price of the pact with the women)—thinking of them, Mirabelle again finds her pride and her courage.

She tosses back her head and the beads touching her neck are no longer deadmen's bones but sparkling spheres of glass. All around the tiers rising high around the Opera House floor, men and women take note of the firmness of her measured tread and see their own reflections in the fragmented mirrors on her mask. Then their fear and dread leave them for a moment and they recall how they are part of a proud tradition, a sacrifice willingly given for the good of all.

Mirabelle is almost sorry when the procession ends and the dancing begins, but not because time is running out. She simply doesn't want to stop glorying in the gathered initiates. Nevertheless, she takes the gloved hand of the young man who calls out her number and lets him sweep her through the intricate steps of the first dance.

There must be some magic at work, for the young women who had been so clumsy when practicing forming a simple crescent a few minutes before now glide about the polished dance floor like angels through the clouds. The transition to their second partner goes as smoothly as if it had been choreographed in advance.

Her own heart glowing with a curious surety, Mirabelle wonders if each of the other debutantes has reached a similar acceptance of her possible fate, but here and there a muffled sniffle or a tear-stained glove reveals that more than one of the prospective queens is close to breaking down.

Then the music ends and the debutantes form their crescent as directed, Mirabelle at one end and Miss Golden Wings at the other. The room falls completely silent, so silent that the slight squeaking of a wheel on the cart when the king cake is brought into the room is clearly audible.

Someone high up in the tiers giggles nervously and is hushed. Mirabelle feels a trace of her earlier terror return and struggles to banish it.

The pride I felt is as real as the fear, she reminds herself firmly. *And the pride is so much more pleasant.*

For so very important a confection, the king cake really isn't very large. Mirabelle has seen many bigger wedding cakes. Indeed, this flat sheet cake is almost disappointingly pedestrian, like something made for a grammar school birthday party. Its only oddity is that the white frosted exterior is divided into a neat grid consisting of twenty-four squares, each neatly numbered with blue icing.

I wonder what they do when the number of debutantes isn't neatly divisible by something. Does some girl get a larger piece than everyone else or do they make a special pan?

Mirabelle recognizes that her mood is veering from fear to nervous hysteria and seeks desperately to regain her tranquillity. It isn't easy given that she knows perfectly well that one of those pieces of cake contains a little figure of a baby and if she receives that piece she will be the new queen—and drowned in the river at midnight.

She holds up her chin and when the footman comes around to collect the thin ivory tiles she is pleased to see that her hand doesn't shake at all. When the box returns to her a few minutes later, she draws out a new tile with easy composure.

Seventeen.

Her birthday is the seventeenth of August. She wonders if the coincidence means anything. As from a great distance she hears one of the debutantes gasp when she draws the tile bearing the number thirteen. The girl to her right—the fluffy swan—is inaudibly sobbing. Only the slight shaking of her shoulder where it touches Mirabelle's gives her away.

Oh! Mirabelle thinks in impulsive dismay. *Let it be me. I'm not afraid—not really afraid. I don't want to die, but I'm not afraid. Listen to me, Old Man River. If there's any fairness in this, don't pick someone who's so scared.*

There isn't an answer and she doesn't really expect one. Indeed, Mirabelle hates herself for the silent request as soon as she makes it. What is she putting on her mother? Her father?

Her grandmother? She might not be afraid, not this minute at least, but could she wish such sorrow on them?

She knows that seems arrogant, but surely there is some woman among those here who wouldn't be missed. Wouldn't she be a better choice?

Mirabelle's hand is trembling when she puts it out to accept her small square of cake. Light caught by the mirrors in her mask shoots out at odd angles, scattering stars on the simple curves of the blue seventeen. She wants to rip the cake open, squash it with her fork, anything to prove to herself that the little confectionery baby isn't inside. Just barely she manages to restrain herself and when the signal comes she does as Madame Papilio had coached them.

Lifting an antique silver fork, Mirabelle cuts the square of cake neatly down the center. She feels a slight resistance then, almost in synchrony with twenty-three others, she hears a faint "ping" as silver meets china.

She looks down at her plate. Protruding from the rich chocolate cake is a rounded piece of pink confection shaped like an infant. Her fork has removed its head, but still it is unmistakable.

As coached, Mirabelle calls out into the silent room, amazed at the clarity and coolness of her own voice:

"Madame Papilio, I believe it's here. I would like to declare myself the queen."

Beside Mirabelle, the swan girl collapses in a heap, her china plate clattering to the floor and shattering. Mirabelle doesn't blame her. Her own knees feel rather weak as the captain of the ball, a man dressed in eighteenth-century formal wear embroidered with seashells, leads her forth and she accepts the homage of her people.

The captain crowns Mirabelle with a simple, silver diadem ornamented with a pearl-encrusted crescent that glows from within with a soft, nacreous light. As he settles the crown onto her head, the captain recites what is clearly a prepared speech.

"When our pact was made, the river god sent this crown as his mark and seal. The crescent upon the crown is a reminder that New Orleans—long called the Crescent City for where it is cradled within the waters of the Mississippi—exists only at the sufferance of the Father of Rivers. The crown's return is our most certain sign that he desires a new woman be given to him."

Mirabelle wishes she could see what she looks like as a crowned queen, but the orchestra begins playing something lush and regal and she is called upon to dance with her subjects. She dances for hours without needing rest or refreshment, buoyed by a sense of unreality.

It's like I'm dead already. I'm not thirsty or hungry or tired. My feet are light and my soul at rest.

At the end of every dance Mirabelle whispers in her partner's ear:

"I'm going to be all right. Don't worry about me. Tell Mama and Grandma and the boys that I love them."

That way, despite masks and costumes, she's certain that she gets her message to her father and brother. If her words reach ears they aren't meant for, somehow she's certain that the mystique of the queen will keep them from being trivialized.

A few minutes before eleven-thirty the orchestra completes the final dance number. The piece they strike up next has something in it of a wedding march, something of "Pomp and Circumstance." Mirabelle has never heard it before, but the music sounds absolutely and completely right.

The newly designated Maids of the Queen's Court offer gloved hands to the young men of their year. Mirabelle takes her place at their head and leads the entire file out into the night.

Outside, the air is humid as if the river god is rising from his bed, eager to claim his prize. Ghosts, recognizable as such now, direct the assembled signatories of the pact into a seemingly infinite file of elegant open carriages. Mirabelle rides in one alone, as is only fitting for a queen. She doesn't even have a driver. The elegant matched four who draw her carriage need no guidance.

The procession down to the waterfront is through empty streets, though Mirabelle is certain Mardi Gras revelry in New Orleans is far from over, that the streets are littered with glitter and confetti, with discarded plastic cups and crushed beads, that bunting and crepe streamers hang limp and wasted in the thick night air.

Here, however, every element of the city gleams pristine in the moonlight. Twisted wrought-iron balconies are freshly painted, streets are clean, vines in flower, and carved stone sharp and accented with perfect shadows.

Mirabelle struggles to solidify a fey understanding—crippled by her own exhaustion and sudden conviction that none of this is real, that tomorrow she will awaken in her own bed, this nothing more than a very vivid dream.

It's archetypal, she thinks, dredging the word from some nearly forgotten book. *I'm not seeing New Orleans, but some ultimate form of New Orleans. New Orleans as it never was but always is. I belong to that city now, not to the other one. I guess I won't even belong to this one very long, except maybe as a ghost.*

At the riverside, none of the malls and walkways that clutter the banks of the modern Mississippi are present. Not even the French Market is there. The rocks that protect the bulkheads are gone, as are the bulkheads themselves. The bridges that straddle the wide Mississippi are nothing but memories. In this place out of time, Old Man River pulses wild and untrammeled through the city that exists by his sufferance.

Aware that her time has come, Mirabelle shakes herself from an almost hypnotic examination of these waters that will end her life. Peripherally, she is aware that a small cortege of very large men has dismounted from the carriages behind and has come to stand quietly around her own conveyance.

They're the enforcers, she realizes. *The ones who have to pitch me in if I back out.*

One of the men offers her a hand down and she accepts it. The rest bow to her and those remaining in the carriages follow suit. The effect recalls smooth water rippling beneath a chance gust of wind.

"Do you have anything you need to say or do?" Mirabelle asks the nearest man. "Any summoning or something?"

He shakes his head. "No, Your Majesty. We're just here to help you along if needed."

"You're too polite," she says and she can't help it if a certain degree of sarcasm creeps into her voice, "but I will handle this on my own."

Waving lightly to the host in the carriages, Mirabelle walks steadily down the riverbank. The ground underfoot is smooth and gently slanting. When she reaches the water, she resists an impulse to poke her toe in to test the temperature, deciding that would be undignified. Then, without a backward look, she steps into the water.

Immediately Mirabelle can feel the Mississippi dragging at the hem of her heavy skirts. Without any move on her part, she is pulled out into the current. For a moment, she is billowed up on a cushion of air trapped beneath her skirts. Then a lapping wavelet tilts her and the air escapes. Almost immediately, the weight of the sodden satin drags her under.

Behind her mask, Mirabelle gasps as the sudden cold and gritty water fills her mouth. Suddenly, the mask seems constraining, like being trapped within an aquarium. She tears it violently off, ignoring sharp pain where the mask's strings are tangled with her hair. As the mask drifts away from her toward the bottom of the river, Mirabelle glimpses a final, multifaceted, fragmented image of herself illuminated by the glow from her crown.

There she is, over and over again in the broken bits of mirror, her cheeks puffed out to hold her last breath, her hair floating around her head and shoulders, constrained only by the queen's crescent crown.

In sudden desperate revelation, Mirabelle recognizes the ornament on the crown for what it is. It isn't the crescent of the Crescent City. It is the Horned Moon, ageless symbol of the Moon Goddess. It is the same Moon that crowned Hathor, the same graceful curve in which the ancient Greeks saw Artemis's bow.

And knowing this, Mirabelle realizes what her ancestors have forgotten—if they had ever truly understood. The woman sacrificed isn't simply fed to the river, she is put there to rule it. One force and one force alone truly dominates living water and that is the Moon who makes even the oceans dance beneath the pull of her tides.

Mirabelle impales her palms on the points of the crescent moon. As if replacing her blood, cold white light flows through her, easing the pain in her lungs, and letting her control her descent. Although no longer alive, properly speaking, Mirabelle is certain that she is not dead.

She fans out her fingers and scripts an invitation in light to Old Man River. Instantly, he takes form out of the muddy waters, leaving the area around them crystal clear so that Mirabelle's moonlight illuminates an insubstantial palace.

Protean and supple, the river god shifts through various shapes as if seeking one that will best suit them both. Finally, he resolves into a handsome, dark-skinned man neither old nor young, whose long, green hair and beard move with the current.

No royal robes are needed to grant the Father of Rivers dignity or majesty. He wears worn dungarees rolled up to below his knees and a loose button-down shirt open to the waist. His broad, almost splayed feet are bare. Instead of a scepter or trident, he carries a fishing pole: a simple rod and line like those used by a dozen generations of youngsters going after catfish and river bass.

"I thought," Old Man River says, his voice the rough rumble of raging water, "that no one remembered."

"No one did," Mirabelle admits, "but I saw my face and knew the truth of who I was to be."

"My queen," he says, extending a hand.

"And ruler," she replies, placing her own daintily within it.

"But of course." The river god laughs, appreciation for Mirabelle's dark, lustrous beauty—and for her courage—in his storm-grey eyes. "I might not even ask for another bride if you please me."

Mirabelle smiles, filled with the Moon's glowing strength and with confidence in her ability to be queen to this king.

"Well, I did come here to keep Old Man River in his bed," she says softly. "I must see that I keep my part of the bargain."

He draws her to him then. For a brief moment on the streets of New Orleans every woman is crowned in silver light and every man knows himself a king.

MAY OYSTERS HAVE LEGS

David Bischoff

There wasn't supposed to be a funeral at Mardi Gras. Yeah, sure somebody was slated to be dead, but that hadn't happened yet, thought Tony Viti.

But then this Tuesday was fat with the dead.

Tuesday was wobbly-hobbly with Dixie beer, obese with gumbo, chunky with bougainvillea floating like seaweed in the French Quarter.

Tuesday was overweight with bubbling bayou and accordion, with the strong good coffee choked with chicory and that friendly drunk's smile from oblivion, with horn.

Mardi Gras. Fat Tuesday.

Tomorrow your Wednesday was Ash.

Lent's a long time, friend.

Have an oyster and a splash of Louisiana hot sauce.

Good eatin'.

THE WORDS RAN THROUGH Tony Viti's head with the heated excitement of the Mardi Gras floats, churning through the crowds—garish boats on waves. Although it was only March,

93

the humidity and heat seemed high as he made his way
through the bumping crowd. He wore a linen jacket and white
slacks and a tie. He felt like Sidney Greenstreet after a year of
the Pritikin diet.

He would have taken the jacket off, except for the gun
underneath.

Damned New Orleans. Damned Mardi Gras. Damned business, he thought as he made his way through the mould and the
sweat and the drunkenness. It was like being in the stomach of a
fat man who'd eaten too much pasta carbonara, baked ziti, chi-
anti, and Louisiana hot links and then overdosed on LSD.

But when you were just an underling with the mob, and
your specialty was poppin' people, the boss said jump and you
got your Brooklyn butt on da plane.

Why the hell they couldn't get a mechanic to fix their own
gears down here was beyond Tony. Some of these criminals, he
heard, could go snout to snout with Jaws. But what Jackie
Bologna said was that the heat was on the mobs down here, and
they needed an outsider. A hop on a jet, an air-conditioned hotel
room, a nice crawfish dinner—then a quick run down an alley in
the crowd, a thwip of a silenced gun, and out. You'd be swallowed
up in that massive beast of the crowd and on the other side of the
city by the time anyone knew that old Willie the Numbers was
leaking motor oil from his brain. Then a snooze, a massage, and
a romp with some Louisiana Cosa Nostra cousins—and back to
LaGuardia in time for the card game with the boys.

Willie the Numbers. Willie the Numbers.

He's been in New Orleans before, of course. He wasn't like
one of those pathetic New Jersey goombahs—whose idea of a trip
was to visit Mulberry Street for some vino at the bar where Joey
Gallo got shot, and whose vacations were at Wildwood eating saltwater taffy under some god-dammed creaky boardwalk.

No way.

Tony had been to plenty of places. He'd been to Vegas,
he'd been to L.A. Hell, he'd been all over the country. His big
goal in life, in fact, was to go to Hawaii; Honolulu to be exact. Sit
in a bar with a mai tai, let the Pacific breeze blow through those
cool shirts.

The boss, he'd been back to the old country, but Tony—Tony couldn't see that. What the hell! You could get good wop chow all over the New York area. This country, it had all the scenery you could possibly want. And people, they talked American—well, most of them, anyway.

Sure, he'd been to New Orleans. He'd even been to Mardi Gras. He'd even met Willie the Numbers. He'd eaten blackened shrimp with him. He'd talked shop. Wise guys, they were fun. Willie was from the Bronx, but he'd taken a trip down South, liked the action, liked the food, the women, the hot sauce. He'd stayed. But then he'd stepped on a few toes down here in the past years, and now they'd called on a New York family to take him.

Not take him back, though.

Just take him out.

The miasma of Mardi Gras enveloped the gangster. The jiggy rhythms, the flashes of flesh. Oh, oh, if he could only ditch this job, snort some blow, down some beer, and join the revelers. How he would dance! How he would cavort! Tony Viti knew how to have a good time, yes indeedy. And once he got a nice stash in the bank, he was going to quit this business and open his own gun shop or something (well, unless he got to be a made man somehow, in which case he'd hang on a while to lord it over some of the goons he had to work with).

Amidst the hubbub, the hullabaloo, here it was:

A funeral, for Christ sakes.

It moved forward like time and destiny, a black coach with tassels and finery, rolling-almost-strolling on wood wheels. Upon this coach was a walnut coffin, shiny and new, almost too shiny to throw dirt over. This coffin was decked with flowers. Splendid lilies, pretty posies—a wealth of color over black, black, black. At the reins behind the big quarter-horse was an old, old man, wrinkle upon wrinkle.

But it was the Dixieland band behind this parade within a parade that caught Tony's attention the hardest.

They were all black men, this group. All black men, dressed in tuxedos and caps with tails. They didn't so much follow the wheeled death cart as they flowed behind it. Tooting their horns and clarinets, they wound a sinuous dance. Flowing, showing the whites of their eyes, they were like streamers behind a kite.

They were playing "When the Saints Come Marching In," of course, but somehow, with the edge and syncopation of Dixieland jazz . . . and something more, something else . . .

And sheesh, it gave him the creeps. Shivers ran through his slender body, and they sure weren't the sweet ones like when Sylvia dragged those long painted nails over his back.

The last member of this parade was an old black man, holding a long pole decked with colorful ribbons, topped with a hook. He danced and pranced like Fred Astaire blended with Sammy Davis, Jr. Though he sported wrinkles upon wrinkles and age hung upon him like a shroud, his eyes were bright as newly minted pennies.

THE BLACK MAN SWIRLED and whirled—

And the next thing Tony knew, the old guy was right up next to him. He smelled of Brut Cologne, sweat, and whiskey.

"You sir, you sir, you sir," he said, eyes rolling, a gleam of dark delight showing in them. "Yessir, yessir, yessir!"

Suddenly, that hook was around Tony's neck and he was being dragged over toward the rolling coffin. Only the coffin wasn't rolling anymore. It had stopped and the crowd swirled about it, oblivious to the thing. The trumpets were still tooting. They seemed to be blaring right in Tony's ear.

They were playing the Godfather theme.

"What the—" cried Tony. Reflexively, he went for the Barretta parked in its shoulder holster under the linen jacket.

He pulled his black beauty out, but before he could do a damned thing, it got knocked from his hand. It skittered away along the cobbles.

"Mister Mister Mister," said the black man. "Lookee here! Got some nice gumbo for you."

The hook pulled him up to the coffin.

The coffin's lid began to slowly open, and somehow all those flowers stayed affixed on top. Pitch dark swirled within the coffin and a rotting floral smell—and something more.

Voices and hands rushed up and Tony felt himself lifted and lifted. Then he was falling and falling, somehow wrapped in a filmy gauze. He fought and struggled, but there was a cloth around his mouth and a choking stench that slammed through his mouth and his nostrils, ramming straight up into his brain.

Vague sensations of being lifted, and weak reflexive struggle with his highly trained body—

And then roughly he clumped onto hard wood.

And woody darkness thumped over him.

TONY VITI AWOKE.

ALL about was a medicinal miasma, but even through this he smelled the rich scent of dirt.

Opening his eyes, he could see that he was in total darkness. Darkness unlike he'd ever seen before. He lay prone upon his back.

"Jesus!" he said.

Tony Viti reached up. Less than a foot above him his hand ran into padded velvet. It could go no further.

Trying to keep calm, he reached to the sides.

Padded velvet.

"Jesus Christ!" he said.

Stay calm, man. Stay calm. You don't know what's going on . . .

But even as he tried to turn on his killer's trained mind, that smell of dirt combined with the scent of rot—

And the memory of that old black man and the Mardi Gras parade rushed back in a musky swirl.

Tony pushed up hard. Nothing happened. He took double handfuls of velvet and ripped. Ripped so hard the cloth came off in strips. But his fingernails hit walnut (pine? teak? oak?) and went no further.

Oh God! He was buried alive.

At first pure panic drove through him. He pushed again, then drove his knees up, pushing, pushing, pushing with every ounce of his breath. Then, expended, gasping, he lay down and tried to get control.

Think. Think!

Crap! Willie the Numbers must have known he was coming. He'd sent out a strange posse after him and put him in here . . .

He could feel sweat dripping down off his face in globules. He could smell his greasy guinea self, and it didn't smell real good.

Okay. Okay, he was in that coffin, sure. But it didn't mean that he was necessarily *buried.* Shit, Willie was probably goofing on him.

Tony checked his holster again.

Yep. Gun was still gone. He stretched but couldn't reach down where he kept his stiletto strapped. The ceiling of his tomb was too high, the sides too low.

Steady there, fellow. Don't want to take too many breaths. Don't want to use up the oxygen. Use the old noodle, the old pasta factory. You've been through bad stuff and worse stuff. And you didn't do that by panicking.

If he could just scrunch up just so . . . He could push up with his knees, get some leverage and . . .

Even as these thoughts went through his head there was a scratching at the top of the casket. There was a thumping sound—and he realized it was his own heart, hammering in its rib cage.

Some kind of chant seemed to vibrate the wood and his flesh.

Then, the casket lid started to open. It lifted by increments, first letting in a slant of smoky light. Tony smelled candles and incense. He heard a shuffling sound, and then, as his eyes adjusted (Jeez! Thank God he wasn't buried alive!), he smelled that damp, earthy smell again through the mix. And also something more—something distinct, yet not identifiable.

A man with a scar stood by the coffin. He held an automatic handgun. "Get out."

Tony was stiff and cramped, but he did as requested. As soon as he lifted himself up he could see where he was. It was some kind of grotto. Well, that explained it. He was below the ground all right—but in a cave. The coffin was on the cave floor.

"Out," said the man wearing the J. Crew T-shirt. He motioned with his gun, and Tony scrambled up and out.

There was a group of men in the room. It looked like something out of a Batman comic.

They were in fancy old chairs. There was artwork hung on the side of the walls. There was an armoire and a fancy antique table where bottles of wine and plates of food sat. There were also dolls and small canvas bags scattered about . . .

And that strange smell. Spicy Cajun food—and something more, something weird.

Tony's eyes immediately fastened on the man sitting in the biggest chair—a chair like something out of Disneyland's Pirates of the Caribbean ride.

It was Willie the Numbers. His mark.

"Well, well, well," said Willie. "Welcome to New Orleans. Welcome to Mardi Gras."

Tony said nothing. He pushed himself out of the casket and tilted over the table. Sitting there, smack in the middle was a bottle of Johnny Walker Red. Tony opened it up and didn't bother with a glass. He just knocked back a swallow. His eyes smarted and his throat burned. He took another blast, then another . . . and finally he started feeling a touch better. He wiped his mouth on his sleeve.

"Make yourself at home," said Willie.

"What's going on? I don't understand. Guy comes down for Mardi Gras, gets himself shanghaied."

"Let's cut the crap, Tony," said Willie. "I know why you're here. Hey look—you're just doing your job, right."

Tony squinted at him. "I don't know what you're talking about."

Tony figured, hell he wasn't dead. If Willie wanted him dead, then that's what he would be—out of the picture. There was something more the guy wanted.

As the alcohol sifted through him, and he relaxed, he looked around. He saw that the items laying here and there were masks and vials of material. A dead bat hung from the ceiling. He looked up and he saw that the bottom of an ancient casket hung down. A skeleton arm hung down.

"I see you notice where we are, Tony."

Tony took another blast of whiskey. "Under some god-dammed cemetery?"

"A very old one, Tony. This is a place of power . . . of great *gris-gris*. Are you familiar with that term, Tony?"

"What? Like in Dr. John the Night Tripper. Magic stuff?"

"That's right Tony. And I'm way into Dr. John now, too."

"What—jeez, Willie. You're not telling me you believe in that crap."

"How do you think I knew my old bud Tony Viti was coming down to whack me."

"I told you. Mardi Gras. I'm just down for Mardi Gras."

"Look, Tone," the big-boned, raw-face wagged a finger at his colleague. "Let's save our breaths here. I got a deal for you."

His eyes were adjusting to this place, so Tony found himself looking around. There was a tunnel off to the side that dropped into murky darkness. Forms moved within and Tony thought he heard the sounds of skitterings and clackings.

"I know why you've come. My dear friends in the area want me gone." The man's flesh hung from his face slackly, like some deflated mask. It looked as though he'd just lost a great deal of weight. When Willie the Numbers shrugged eloquently, his jowls wagged. His eyes seemed like tiny specks of hard black against startling white. "And they are too damned scared to do it them-selves—for good reason."

A kind of yolky mist moiled in the side corridor. A hissing escaped and Tony smelled a sulphury smell, mixed with old sweet wine.

"Reason? What are you talking about?" Tony didn't show an ounce of fear, even though his spine had turned to saltwater taffy. You show fear, the bastards owned you.

"Okay. So look around you, fool. You think this is bowling night on Bourbon Stree?. I'm into *gris-gris,* man. Black magic. Power! It works. The puissance between my fingers is real."

The guy held up his hand. Sparks flew between the tips of his fingers and a greasy smoke rose up, coagulating on the ceil-ing. Suddenly, a snake leered down, its slithery tongue flailing about, dripping ooze. The man's fingers wavered and with a "thwip" the snake melted away.

It was Tony's turn to shrug. "I see better acts when I go to Vegas."

"Lots of Caribbean heritage here too, Tone," said Willie. "Certain tradition." He took up one of the crude dolls that lay by the side. He pulled out a long needle and jabbed right through the thing.

A terrible pain cut through Tony. It felt like a fist had pushed through his viscera and then out his back—gooey with saltwater taffy.

He groaned and fell to his knees.

"Kidney stone acting up, Tone?"

"Oh, jeez —"

"It's a little tributary of the *gris-gris* gone on a Caribbean cruise, Tony. It's called voodoo."

The pain was unrelenting. Tony found himself screaming despite himself. "Okay. Okay. Stop."

"Will you help us out? I warn you, if you don't, Tony Viti, I'll happily kill you. But it will take a good long while."

"Sure. Sure. Shit . . . I'll do it. Oh man, just cut this crap out!"

The agony stopped, and there was no after-sting. It was as though it had never been there, ever.

The men who stood by Willie's side opened their eyes.

They had no pupils.

"Oh, Christ. You're not going to tell me you've got zombies. I thought only the Bronx boys had zombies."

Willie guffawed. "Tony, Tony, Tony. Always the guy with the yawks." He leaned forward. "Now this is what I want you to do!"

WAX JACKIE BOLOGNA?

No way!

"Airport," Tony Viti told the cabdriver, then threw his small valises into the back seat and got in himself.

He'd woken up in an alley, soiled and with a headache, but otherwise okay. Beyond him, in the darkness, he could still hear the revelers of Mardi Gras. The music, the jazz, the total hullabaloo . . .

What the hell kind of job had Jackie sent him on, anyway? he wondered. Then he'd hurried to his hotel, called the airport, and got himself a reservation for the first plane out of this hole. What was he going to tell Jackie? He'd figure that out on the plane.

"Crazy day, huh Mister," said the driver in a Cajun accent.

"You don't know half of it."

"People come here for Mardi Gras . . . Some don't know some of the dark stuff about N'Orleans."

"You're tellin' me."

"You like the food anyway?"

"Yeah. Sure. But I'll tell ya . . . I'll take a nice slice of Ray's Original Pizza any day."

Tony sat back and tried to relax. God, his head was throbbing! Whatever the hell had happened to him here, he wanted nothing more to do with Louisiana or any of its citizens.

"Simple. Just go out and kill your captain," Willie had told him. "That's all I want you to do."

Sure, Tony had said. Sure, no problem.

Willie had told him where to go to do the job, and that was it.

But of course he couldn't whack Jackie. Christ, he'd be in enough hot clam sauce for not getting Willie. Of course, everyone would understand that . . . of course. Yeah, maybe he'd have to pay some restitution . . . but that would be better than being dead in New Orleans!

Right. Just get out. Drinks and bad chicken on the plane, pal.

Tony opened his eyes and looked up as he felt the cab slowing down. They were in some sort of old section of town, headed into town.

"Hey! This isn't the way to the airport!"

The cabbie turned around. He had no pupils in his eyes. "The airport is not where you're going, pal."

In his hand was a silenced pistol.

THE IMPACT OF THE bullet rang in his ears . . . resonated through his dreams . . .

He struggled, half-conscious, through a parade of images.

Blood. Mardi Gras. Blood. Nausea. Flashes of streamered light. Rolling, rolling lights. The smell of beer and the dancing, dancing, dancing of the parade. Color, color . . .

Dimness.

He awoke for a moment, and he thought he was in a hospital. There was some kind of bottle hanging on the bed . . . A tube coming down into his arm.

"Drink this," someone said.

And Tony drank.

Color, color, color . . .

Darkness.

Tony Viti woke up.

Darkness was still upon him, but he was awake.

There was no more pain, but only because he could feel nothing but numbness, flowing all over his body.

Tony Viti lay flat upon his back, arms to his side.

He did not feel panic, but only because he could not feel much of anything. When he finally collected himself, he tried to get up.

His head hit the top of his little room.

A padded top.

His hands reached out and found the sides.

Somehow, Tony Viti remained calm.

Jeez. A coffin again. Buried alive.

He took a deep breath. The air was already musky and foul, with very little of value in it. Still Tony somehow remained calm.

Well, that was it. He'd suffocate. He'd screwed up yet again. The oxygen would run out and he'd die. But at least he'd die and then that would be that. It would be all over. *Fini.*

Not much of a life, but then whose was, really.

Never should have come to Mardi Gras. Never should have showed his face in New Orleans.

Tony patiently waited for the end, grateful that somehow he was drugged and calm and accepting. It would be dark and peaceful and sweet . . . Unending rest.

Then, he heard a sound.

It sounded like digging. What the—

Was he going to get dug up? Despite himself Tony Viti felt a flutter of hope. Where there was life, there was hope, right?

There was a scraping on the coffin.

But then Tony's eyes shot wide open in the dark.

The scraping was not from the top where the lid of the coffin was.

It came from below the coffin.

Tony Viti did not remain calm.

FAT TUESDAY

R. Davis

I'm writing it down now. Before night comes and the celebration begins in earnest. Right now, this moment, there's a dog barking in the alley outside and he sounds half-rabid. The high notes from his throaty bark vibrate in the cheap glass of my window. I won't look down at him. I had an uncle who went mad. Stark, raving, mad. When they carted him away he sounded like that dog. I'm writing this down now because just waiting would surely cause me to end up like him, frothing at the mouth and barking at the moon. Still, I suppose if I were going to go mad, I'd have done it by now. But I can see my hands shaking as I type . . . and I've been drinking steadily since I last saw him. Wait! I'm getting ahead of myself, and I need to go slow enough to get it right. I will finish this tale though my mouth tastes of rotten flesh and ash, and darkness will come soon enough.

Tonight is Fat Tuesday. You know about Fat Tuesday, don't you? The Mardi Gras? A grand party where the whole city of New Orleans goes stark raving mad? Just like my uncle, only worse, because very few get carted away. Very few. I'm a writer, Martin Grant is the name, and I've done my homework. Depending on who you ask, Mardi Gras has been around just about forever. The curious, the rich, the simply bored all come here for the carnival season that begins with the feast of Epiphany on January 6, and ends on Fat Tuesday with a city-wide celebration. I looked it up, and the whole point of it origi-nally was to party like mad right up until Lent—when fasting replaces feasting. And that's it, you know. Feasting. The word *carnival* come from the Latin: *carnivale*. I'm no linguist, but from what I've been able to determine, the word *carnivale* means "farewell to flesh."

I ARRIVED IN NEW ORLEANS on the afternoon of January 6. I changed clothes, ate dinner at a café outside the French Quarter, and returned to my cheap room. I was pleased with myself. I'd gotten an assignment to write an article about the carnival season and all the strange things that occur during that time. I was living on a relatively decent per diem that covered my expenses. Since good food was my weakness, I took a cheap room until the end of February, figuring on spending most of my money in restaurants. I slept well that night and arose refreshed in the morning. I left the news on while I showered, and the lead story was about a murder victim discovered in an alley outside a jazz bar. I shut off the water long enough to listen to the on-site report:

"*Thanks, Chip. I'm down here near the site where the victim was found. Of course, the alley itself is cordoned off by police tape, and no statements have yet been issued. Wait, here comes the county coroner and an investigator—*"

A brief pause followed and then I heard a man's voice.

"*OK, folks, we're going to make this quick and we're not answer-ing questions at this time. What we've got is one dead male, approxi-mately twenty-eight years old. His identity is unknown at this time. As of now we are calling it a homicide. It appears that the victim died of massive blood loss, but we'll have to do an autopsy to confirm that. That's all for now.*"

A babble of voices arose as the detective walked away, and then the reporter's voice cut back in.

"Chip, that was Detective Jake Soames of the New Orleans Police Department. As you heard, they are ruling it a homicide, but eyewitnesses first on the scene have been saying that it's worse than that. According to them, the victim's throat has been ripped out, much like the killings that started last year at this same time."

Chip broke back in.

"Kris, the murders you're referring to are the unsolved 'Vampire John' killings that started during last year's carnival and mysteriously ended on Fat Tuesday, correct? Have the police or any of the witnesses indicated that there might be a connection?"

"No, Chip, as you heard, the police aren't saying much. And the four eyewitnesses were taken by police a short time ago for questioning. . ."

I turned back on the water. "Vampire John" killings? I didn't recall hearing about them, but it might be an interesting place to start. I prided myself on writing about the underside of public events. People are sometimes blind to what's going on around them, especially in the midst of a party or social occasion. Killings during Mardi Gras? It was perfect.

After I finished dressing, and had a wonderful breakfast of croissants and jam, I made my way to the library. What I found there got me really excited about this particular story. The essence of it was this: During last year's carnival celebration, a serial killer had been wandering the streets. Because of his rather gruesome method of slaughter a local disc jockey had dubbed him "Vampire John." Vampire because all the victims had died of massive blood loss sustained when their throats had been torn out, and John because he was unknown. The name stuck.

The killer was never caught, leaving his last victim's body in a city park filled with revelers on the night of Fat Tuesday, and then disappearing. He killed eight people. I was stunned. This should have made national news, and I'd never heard of it. But then again, New Orleans was the "murder capital of the U.S., " so maybe people just didn't get riled up about it. Some citizens interviewed in the articles expressed concern, but most assumed it was just another nutcase loose during carnival. They also thought the police would catch him. I checked just to be certain that my hunch was correct, and it was. The detective who worked the Vampire John killings last year was none other than Jake Soames. He was one, I decided, that I needed to talk to. But first, I needed to visit the county coroner's office and have a chat with Will Baker, the chief forensic pathologist.

WILL BAKER WAS A short, rotund man, who wore coke bottle lenses in his glasses. At first he was tough, acting like he didn't want to talk, but instinct told me to stay with him, and I was right. Given the chance to speak "off the record" he'd tell me his life story. He was also familiar with the whole history, at least the medical side of it, of the Vampire John killings. Once he loosened up, he told me enough to know that this was the story I was going to write.

I asked him about the victim found this morning. "So, the guy died of massive blood loss, right?"

"Yes, from a wound to his throat."

"What kind of a wound?"

"It was," he paused, "well, it appears that his throat was chewed out."

"You mean like the killings last year."

"Exactly like them. I'd hoped the monster who was responsible had left forever, but evidence indicates that it's the same man."

"Which evidence is that?"

He gestured. "Come on, and I'll show you. That is, if you don't get sick easily?"

"Not really," I replied as I followed him down the stairs into the room where he performed autopsies. When we entered, the victim was still laid out on the examination table.

"How long are you gonna keep him there?" I asked.

"Not long. Detective Soames is due by shortly, and I knew he'd want to see the body, so I left it out. Besides," he chuckled, "this fellow here doesn't really mind." He patted the body on the shoulder.

"So what is it you wanted to show me?"

"OK, first you've got to understand something. While we've been saying massive blood loss, what we really meant was the victim had no blood."

"No blood?"

"None whatsoever except what had spilled down the front, and that was very little. Usually, in cases where there's a major tissue injury, loss of a limb, cut throat, that type of thing, quite a bit of blood actually remains in the body. You don't have to lose it all to bleed to death, you know."

"No blood at all?" I repeated, a little suspicious that maybe Will was having me on.

"None. Now, for the really strange part." He pulled back the sheet. "Come take a look at something."

"The strange part?" I mumbled to myself as I walked over. "What?"

"There's not a lot of tissue remaining here, but under a magnifying glass you can see it," he said, pointing to the victim's neck.

"See what?" I asked.

He handed me a magnifying glass, which I aimed at the area he pointed to, the very base of the neck. "You see those little swirls in the bloodstains on the skin surface?"

"Yeah, so?"

"Well, unless I'm mistaken, those are tongue swirls. The perp licked the blood off his victim."

I jerked back suddenly. "Are you shitting me?!"

"I don't know, did I eat you?" Will cackled. I was beginning to realize that forensic people had rather bizarre senses of humor. "No way," he said when he saw my look. "I'm as serious as the dead."

"And that's pretty serious," said a voice from the doorway.

I jumped. "Jesus! Are you trying to scare me to death?"

The man laughed. "No, but unless I miss my guess, you're a reporter and my friend Will here is giving away our secrets."

Will blanched a bit. "Not really, Jake. He's cool, off the record and all." He sounded a bit plaintive.

Jake shook his head. "That's what they all say." He turned to me. "So, which rag do you work for, and how long till I'm gonna see this in the paper?"

I took in Jake's appearance now that my heart had stopped racing. He was a fairly tall man, maybe six-one or so. He wore khakis and a blue shirt. His hair was mussed and brown, and looked like it hadn't seen the good side of a comb all day. His eyes were brown and didn't leave my face. "No," I said, realizing that I was taking too long in giving him an answer. "You're not gonna see this in the paper anytime soon."

"Oh really?" he asked with kind of a sardonic twist of his head.

"Two reasons," I replied. "One, I'm a freelance writer and so I don't write the story until it's finished, and two, the story isn't finished. Good enough?"

"I suppose," he said. "What choice do I have?"

"You don't," I said, "But I mean what I say. I won't write the story until it's over. OK?"

"Alright," he said.

We exchanged names and a bit more information. I realized that I liked Jake quite a bit. He was a straight shooter, and he played fair with me. You don't find that too often in police officers when you're a writer. I asked him if we could get together again to talk some more, and he agreed, reminding me of my promise to keep quiet. "Besides," he said, "maybe an outside perspective will shed some light on this thing. God knows it's dark enough now."

"Not a lot of leads, huh?"

"We've got the same thing we had last year at this time."

"What's that?"

"A bucket full of nothing."

"Well," I said, "maybe I can dig up something. Do you have anything at all?"

He turned to Will. "Give him the rundown, Will. Unless you've got anything for me that I wasn't expecting, you can slab this guy." He pointed at the body on the table.

"No," Will said. "Nothing new here." He sighed. "I wish there was."

"Me, too," said Jake, as he turned to walk out. "Catch you later?" he asked.

I nodded. "Yep. I'll call you later." I turned and looked expectantly at Will. "Well?"

"Oh yes," he said. "Here's what we've got but it isn't much. Our suspect is quite tall, say six-seven or better, and exceptionally strong—"

"Wait," I said. "How do you know that?"

"Well, last year, one of the victims was a pretty heavy guy, about 250 pounds. Based on the bruise marks we found under his armpits, we deduced that his attacker had picked him up. The victim was about five feet, six inches tall, and that means that in order to pick him up, our killer would have to be substantially taller and stronger. I'd guess he weighs more than that, too, but that's a guess."

"What else?"

"OK, let's see. We think he's either bald, or he wears a hair net, because we haven't yet found any hair at a crime scene. Probably, he's bald because even with a hair net, some hair escapes. He's also got very sharp teeth, like they've been filed." He paused. "I guess that's about it. Doesn't seem like a lot for nine murders does it?"

"No, but it's a start," I said. "Thanks for your time, Will. We'll talk again, I'm sure."

He smiled. "No problem, Martin. Just keep a lid on it will you?"

"Sure thing," I said. "Besides, if I wrote a story about a vampire in New Orleans, no one would believe me anyway—"

I turned and left, determined to find this Vampire John before I left New Orleans. And I knew the truth. What we had here was a case of someone who'd gone off the deep end and actually decided he was a vampire. I'd heard about it before. With those thoughts firmly in my mind, I headed out to find some lunch.

THE PROBLEM WITH EATING is that when there's time to enjoy it (as I dearly love to do), it's great. Otherwise, it's just something we have to do in order to stay alive. When I'm really busy, that's how I view it: a necessity and no more. So I ate what should have been a good lunch, and then continued my search. My first visit was to all the crime scenes. This consisted of visits to three alleys in the French Quarter, two warehouses where they stored floats for the parade held on Fat Tuesday, one city park, two downtown retro dance clubs, and one apartment building. All in all, I spent the day looking and waiting for inspiration.

I didn't find much. But I was hoping that when I talked with Jake Soames, I'd get something more than maybe what he'd even told his rather loose-lipped friend Will. I called him, and we agreed to meet at a bar near the station that night. Over cocktails, he told me a bit more. It was then that I began to realize why Soames appeared so disheveled.

I asked, "Is there anything more you could tell me than Will did?"

"Yes, there is," he said. "But you've got to promise to never use it. Ever."

"Now wait a minute," I said, "I can't even put it in once the case is solved?"

"No," he said. "Not ever."

"Then why tell me?"

"I have to tell somebody. It's been eating at me for a year." He sipped his scotch, and stared at a point just over the top of my head.

"All right, I guess I can promise to keep it out." (Yes, I've decided to put it in now, because it doesn't matter anymore. No one will be able to take retribution on me after tonight anyway.)

Soames talked and drank steadily for some time while he told me his tale. I'm quoting directly from my recorder here:

I'd called it a night. It was two days before Fat Tuesday, last year, and I still didn't have any real solid leads. I didn't used to drink as much, but now, well, it's all I can really do to keep myself sane. I went to a bar, this bar in fact. I like it here because it's a dim, smoky, quiet place. I ordered my favorite, the same as I'm drinking tonight with you: scotch rocks. It burned going down. I'd been here maybe fifteen minutes or so, just thinking, when a well-dressed guy sat down next to me at the bar. He wore black jeans, and a cream-colored, raw silk shirt. He had on an embroidered vest with a blue and silver pattern on it. He nodded pleasantly to me as he sat and motioned to the bartender. He ordered benedictine, straight up. Once he got his drink, he sipped it, and leaned back with a sigh. He turned to me and said, "A welcome break, is it not?"

I nodded. "Yes, though I personally can't imagine drinking straight benedictine."

He smiled slightly. "It reminds me somewhat of home. It is painful to drink, because it stings the vocal cords. I do not mind because it also warms the stomach." His voice was deep, melodious, but very soft. It held the slightest hint of an accent which I couldn't place.

"Well," I said, "to each their own."

"Always," he replied, and then we raised our glasses to that informal toast.

We said nothing for a few minutes, just sat and watched CNN on the television over the bar. Deciding that watching the news wasn't going to help me any, I turned to the stranger and asked, "So, what do you do?"

He looked closely at me, and replied, "It's not important, friend. What you do, that is important."

"What I do?" I said in some confusion.

"Yes," he said. "You are a hunter of sorts. Right now, you are hunting Vampire John."

I stared at him. "Yeah, I suppose you could say that. After all, it's been in the papers. So what?"

He sipped his drink and I saw his jaw muscles clench slightly when he tasted the liquor. "It will end, you know. At least for this year."

"What will end?" I asked.

"The killings. They will end on Fat Tuesday, and not a night before."

"Wait a second, who the hell are you? And how could you know that?"

"An interested party, let us say. All that should matter to you is that the killings will end."

My cop instinct kicked in. "First, you didn't answer my question. How could you know that? And second, of course it matters to me! We've got some lunatic running around the city who thinks he's a vampire."

He was staring at me compassionately. His eyes were gray. I began to relax a little. It's funny, I was thinking to myself I'd almost started to believe that this guy was the killer.

"Listen carefully to me, Jake Soames. I have watched you agonize over each victim, each lead that went nowhere. You will be unable to catch the killer because I know him."

"You know him?" I exclaimed.

"Yes, I know him well. I know that the killings will end on Fat Tuesday because I am him."

I tensed, started to rise and go for my gun at the same time. His eyes never left mine, and then his voice hit me. No higher than a whisper but it slapped into me with the force of a baseball bat. "Sit down!"

I couldn't stop myself. I sat. "How, wha—"

"Poor Detective Soames. I'd explain it all to you, if I had the time. But I don't. Already the hunger that claims me at this time of year is growing. Here is the crux of it: There are many kinds of so-called vampires in the world. But all are cursed in some fashion. My curse began so long ago that I doubt you could even comprehend it. You see, when I became a vampire, I was a priest serving in a large church in France. When offered the chance at everlasting life on Earth, I found the temptation too great to resist. God called down his vengeance upon me, as he must all creatures of darkness and evil. My curse is that I must still abide by the rules of Christianity as much as I am able. So, when the feast of Epiphany begins, a frenzy comes upon me. And I must feast. I must drink each night, wholly slaking my thirst. Normally, we are far more reserved than that. This is the truth: I am here, and the frenzy is here. But at midnight, on Fat Tuesday, Lent begins. Then it will be over. Do you understand?"

I nodded, knowing that Lent was a time for fasting. Somewhere, deep inside me, I was screaming for release from his eyes. But he continued.

"I want you to stop hunting me. Go away. Take a vacation. I am told you are a good detective. Eventually, you might succeed in finding me. I do not wish to kill you because you serve a valuable purpose to society. I do not wish to kill anyone, but I must. The frenzy, the hunger, compels me like the voice of an angel. I will do what I must to survive, and no more. But if it means killing you, I will. Am I clear?"

I nodded again, and felt control return to my limbs. "So that's it then? I'm just supposed to let you walk out of here?"

"Yes," he said, "if you wish to live." His lips parted slightly, and I could see his pointed canines jutting down from the top of his mouth.

"Why warn me at all?"

"Check your facts again, Detective Soames, about the victims. They all deserved to die."

"I'll think about it, how's that?"

"Do what you must, as I shall. For now, I must go. The hunger calls."

"Wait!" I said.

"Be quick, I must leave," he said.

"What's your name, if it's not Vampire John?"

"Roland," he said "Roland DuMaurier." Then he turned and left the bar. I haven't seen him since.

I ORDERED ANOTHER ROUND of drinks and just sat there. Thinking. Soames looked at me. "I know what's going through your mind right now," he said.

"Oh yeah?" I asked.

"You're wondering why I didn't stop him, right then. I wish I knew, but I don't. I could tell you that I didn't believe him, that I thought he was just some nut. And that might be the truth. I could tell you that there was a rational explanation for everything that happened that night: He was a hypnotist, I was tired, the lights were dim, whatever. That might also be truth. But the truth is, I just don't know.

"The killings stopped, as he promised on Fat Tuesday. I hoped, then, that he'd leave. He'd find a new hunting ground, and I could just bury it in the unsolved case file and let it go. But he's still here. The frenzy, as he called it, is back. I must stop him this time. I must." Soames shuddered and I realized what a terrible burden of guilt he must be carrying.

"Well, you've certainly got your work cut out for you," I said. "Maybe I can help."

He turned to me and said, "There is no help for me anymore. I must find him and kill him. Do I believe he's a vampire? I don't know. But I've got to try."

I gulped the last of my drink. "Look, Soames, I've got to spend a little time thinking on all this, do some more digging. Why don't we meet again in a couple of days?"

He shrugged. "Whatever. You know where to find me."

I nodded. "Yeah. And in the meantime, you've got my number. Call me if anything comes up, OK?"

"Sure," he said. "I checked you out, you know."

I smiled. "I was sure you would."

"You're the same Martin Grant who uncovered the Times Square murders, right?"

I grinned at him, remembering how I'd tracked down the Times Square killer. "The same," I said.

"What did people say that guy was?" he asked.

"A werewolf, if you can believe it," I said. "He used resin-cast teeth to chew on his victims. He'd been a special effects artist before he went nuts. He was quite good at creating a monster."

Soames looked at me, and then said quietly, "And?"

"And," I said, "he was a man. A psycho for sure, but just a man."

"Maybe," Soames said, standing to leave, "maybe our vampire is the same kind of thing?" He sounded hopeful, almost desperate.

I stood also. "Maybe," I said. Then I grinned at him, trying to lighten the mood. "Or maybe he's a real vampire."

Soames didn't smile. "That's not funny, at all."

"Yeah, I suppose you're right. Call me later, will you?"

"Sure thing," he said. And with that, he left the bar. It was the last time I saw him. The next day, they found his body on the steps leading to his front door. His throat had been torn out, he had no blood left in him. The only difference between Soames and the other victims was how he looked in death. Instead of appearing horrified, he was smiling. Knowing what I know now, I can't really blame him.

I COULD TELL YOU the details of the next four killings but it wouldn't matter. I could explain in detail how the police found the bodies like they had the year before. How I talked with Will Baker, and lots of other people trying to track down the killer.

But no one knew anything. There were no clues. Just bodies drained of blood. I did find out that our mysterious Roland DuMaurier had told the truth about one thing. With the exception of Soames, every person who died had deserved it in some way. They weren't all criminals, but they should have been. They were abusers and molesters who'd gone uncaught. Some of them were connected to drugs. It doesn't matter except to illustrate that our killer had spoken at least some truth that night.

I wouldn't have found him, though I suspect he knew I was looking, except for one small thing. Luck. Pure random chance. I'd started spending my nights in dark dance clubs. My only thought was that because of the noise, and the crowds, and the ever-present costumes, that he might choose to strike again in that type of place. On the night of the fifth killing, now two days ago, I was leaning against a railing that overlooked the dance floor. I saw him then, or at least, what I thought might be him. He looked exactly as Soames described, right down to the vest. But I couldn't see his eyes. I watched him as he danced with a young woman. He seemed out of place to me, his dance moves appearing strange and out of sync with the times. Still, the woman was obviously having a good time. At the end of the song, he leaned close to her, and whispered something in her ear. She giggled and nodded. He pointed to a door leading outside, and they began moving toward it.

I began to push through the crowd, trying not to lose sight of them. If this was the guy, I thought, then I wanted to get to him quick, preferably before he killed the girl. The crowd surged against me and I lost sight of them as they went out the door. The lights began to flash again as the music started to pound. It took what seemed forever to reach the stairs leading to the dance floor. The crowd worked against me. While I'm not certain, I think it took me maybe ten or so minutes to make my way from my vantage point where I had seen them go through the door to reach it myself. I pushed it open.

It lead into an alley that was littered with dumpsters and trash. I paused for my eyes to adjust to the dim lights, trying to listen for the sounds of a struggle over the music. I heard nothing, but turned right and began walking down the alley, deeper into the darkness. Suddenly, he was beside me.

I jumped when he laid a hand upon my shoulder.

"You were searching for something?" he asked.

No point in lying I decided. "Yes," I said. "Actually, you."

"Then you have found me," he said. "What is it you want?"

"I knew Soames. He told me about the bar, you, every-thing."

"That is unfortunate," he replied. He stepped away from me slightly and released my shoulder. "I had hoped that Detec-tive Soames could have kept quiet. I gave him mercy, you know."

"Mercy?" I croaked. "You killed him!"

"Oh yes," he said. "I did indeed. But he was a tortured spirit. I thought to give him a release from pain."

"Tortured, all right! By you."

"You are incorrect. Detective Soames, though a good police-man, was not a good husband. I have watched him this past year. I hoped he would seek help—for all his burdens. He did not. He beat his wife, and death was the only mercy I could give him."

"What a deal," I said. "I suppose now, that you're going to try to kill me?"

He took another step backwards, and the light from the street illuminated his face for the first time. "No," he said, "I have already fed for this night."

I could see he was telling the truth. The area around his lips was covered in blood. "Great, how convenient for me!"

"You do not understand," he said.

"What's that, Roland?"

"I will feed once more before Lent begins. On the night of Fat Tuesday. I will come for you because you are a parasite. A man who feeds on the pain of others. You are a leech on society, no more. It will be a mercy."

"Me?" I said. "I'm a leech? What about you? You're the bloodsucker here!"

"I have no choice. I am compelled by a hunger I cannot control. You could have chosen."

I looked at him and realized how serious he was. In my mind, I began to plan. I'd keep him talking and then just jump him. He wasn't that much bigger than me. "Well," I said, "I've got to tell you that I'm not feeling tortured in spirit really. I feel fine. Let's just call it good at that, OK?"

I saw him smile, saw his pointed teeth. It occurred to me that his looked really good compared to my friend's in Times Square. He said, "Once again, you misunderstand your predicament. Right now, you are not bothered by me, because you doubt my reality. When you come to realize, as Detective Soames did, that I am real, that I'm not just a, how do you say, a 'psycho,' then you will be disturbed."

"So," I said, "You're a real vampire, huh?"

"As real as midnight, as real as God, as real as death."

"Why don't we find out!" And as I spoke I leapt upon him.

He caught me with just one hand. Looking down into his face, I could see he was smiling. "Foolish man! I do not doubt the strength of your disbelief!" And with that he hurled me across the alley where I slammed into the wall, and fell stunned to the ground.

"I give you your life until midnight on Fat Tuesday. Enjoy it if you can." And with that he disappeared by turning toward the unseeing crowd at the mouth of the alley and melting away.

I heard his voice in my head then. "You'll find the girl's body behind the dumpster next to you. Look at it as a reminder if you still harbor doubt."

I got up, found the girl's body, but did not call the police. It occurred to me as I walked back to my room that Will Baker had been all wrong in some of his guesses. He wasn't all that tall, just strong. He didn't leave hair behind because the dead don't lose hair. I replayed the whole event over in my head while I walked, trying to find the holes, trying to look for something that would change my mind and make me believe that he was a phony. All I found was more proof that he wasn't.

So now, I am sitting here. It's almost midnight on Fat Tuesday. I can feel him coming. I can almost taste him in the air. The party on the streets below has grown progressively louder. They are uncaring, lost in their world of revelry and drunkenness. They are feasting before Lent comes upon them once again. And somewhere in that crowd is a vampire named Roland, who was once a priest. And he's hunting me.

He hungers for blood, my blood. And yet, I am not afraid. I could be wrong. It might have been a dream. I might wake up in the morning, my neck intact, my blood still warm and flowing through my veins. I will end the tale here, as it is finished either way. I will lay down on my bed and try to sleep. I will make what peace I can with myself and God. I will say farewell to my flesh before I sleep. The booze doesn't seem to be helping any. My hands are still shaking even now, but I am not afraid. I wonder if my uncle is somewhere tonight, howling up at the moon through the bars of his cage.

This story is finished now. It is time for sleep. I will transmit it to my editor via e-mail, and then I will rest. I am not afraid. Dear God, I am not afraid.

THE INVISIBLE WOMAN'S CLEVER DISGUISE

Elizabeth Ann Scarborough

The invisible woman opened the envelope with a thrill of anticipation. There was no question of it being a bill, or a fake check made out to her if only she would change her long-distance service. It was oversized for one thing, and bright turquoise, for another. It might have been an offbeat wedding invitation, though it was too big and not pastel enough for a birth announcement. Some time after she had become invisible to the world at large, she continued to hear from distant relatives and friends who had not seen or spoken to her in years but who now had children, even grandchildren of marriageable age. It had occurred to her to notify these people of her new status by sending them checks written in invisible ink.

However, this could not be from any of those people, because now not even they knew where she was. The turquoise object had been slipped under the door of the deluxe hotel suite she currently occupied. The suite was far too expensive for

most people and now, at Mardi Gras, was probably the only
room in New Orleans still unrented. She did not have to rent it.
The maid service left much to be desired since nobody knew she
was here, but the price was quite affordable for an invisible
woman.

She had not become invisible all at once, of course. It was
more of a gradual fading that happened over the years. She had
been married once, because it was time to be married. She was
invisible most of the time then to her husband, who worked at a
traveling sort of job and eventually found someone who suited
him better. They did not have children.

Her parents died, and as she had only one sister who lived
very far away and with whom she had never been very close, her
past faded into oblivion with no one to remind her of what she
had been like as a child.

She had to work very hard after the divorce to maintain herself, to pay bills she had foolishly run up, and as she never made
time to see her few friends, she was soon invisible to them, too.

As slowly but surely as a stalking mummy, age crept upon
her and she was no longer twenty-something, thirty-something,
and soon would not be forty-something either. Much more
quickly, her absorption in her desk work and her rapid con-
sumption of empty calories to fuel herself during both work and
lonely hours caused her to become invisible to men.

She first realized this when men she met socially did not
seem to hear what she said and looked over her head or right
through her to some younger and more attractive woman or
another man. It was not that she was particularly boring. They
had never found her so before at least. But somehow, she truly
became invisible. At last she was even invisible at work to the
men and then, finally, she showed up one day to find someone
else—a younger, better-educated woman—at her desk. The
woman looked right through her, too, and at that point, the
invisible woman bolted for the bathroom mirror and found
that except for a somewhat shapeless and rather tasteless pants
and top set, bulging more than she liked to think she bulged,
there was nothing of who she was, who she had been, reflected.
She was glad the chic young thing who had her job had not

seemed to see the clothing any more than she had seen the invisible woman.

That day, she took off her clothes and went home to her apartment.

At first, finding that she was totally invisible depressed her terribly, but gradually it occurred to her that there was a sort of freedom about it that appealed to her sense of humor.

She could go where she liked and do what she wanted. It wasn't as if she could walk through walls or anything like that, of course. She wasn't a ghost, merely invisible. But she could slip through doors unnoticed along with other people. She could snatch food when they were not looking at it, snatch money if she liked, but she didn't like to do that most of the time. She wasn't a dishonest person at heart. But there was so much in the world for an invisible person with her eyes open, that there was no need really to take too much.

She could snatch a book and leave everyone scratching their heads when alarms sounded as she left the store. She would read it and return it in very nice condition as soon as she was able. She couldn't get served in restaurants of course, but she could take bites from other peoples' plates or help herself in the kitchen. After seeing the condition of some of those kitchens, however, she thought of applying for a job as a health inspector—by mail, of course—and informing the public health officials that they could have protected public health much more efficiently had they employed invisible people all along.

At first she spent a great deal of time playing with clothing and jewels—she had enjoyed looking at them so much when she was younger and more visible, though she never could afford what she liked. Now she could have anything at all that she desired, but somehow it wasn't much fun to see her body's over-ample contours in chic designer clothing without a face above them, no face to be set off by a collar, no wrist or arms to be flattered by a certain sleeve length, no feet to enjoy the priciest shoes. Boots were nice. They gave the illusion of feet and legs at least.

But she could hardly wear them in public unless she swathed herself in bandages, which rather defeated the purpose. Once or twice she went out wearing a lot of makeup with the clothes, but she always worried that people would notice she was wearing something she hadn't paid for. After awhile, she gave up and returned most of the clothes and jewels and shoes.

At least, as an invisible woman, she could go out and hear interesting conversations people didn't want her to hear, and that gave her something to think about and for a while relieved her isolation and loneliness. She quickly decided that if she was going to revel in invisibility, she needed to move from Portland to a warmer climate. Running around nude in the rain made her want to steal nothing more than indoor warmth and a cup of coffee.

Thus, here she was in New Orleans, home of Mardi Gras, voodoo, and of the Anne Rice books she had always enjoyed. She was feeling greater and greater kinship with the main characters all the time—although she, unlike many of them, did not need the cover of darkness to do her business. She found that she liked to go out after dark, nevertheless. The town was more interesting after dark. The smells were sharper, not such a jumble, and the noises clearer. She even fancied that from time to time she had seen some of Rice's eldritch friends lurking elegantly near the shadows. Besides, for most of her life she had been afraid to go out alone in a city on foot after dark. Then she realized that while she might need to be extra careful crossing streets, muggers didn't target invisible people.

Besides, she didn't carry a purse. Mostly what she took could fit into her hands. Otherwise she had to be fairly stealthy about moving it around. Disembodied floating objects might possibly attract unwanted attention. In darkness, at least, she could filch dark-colored objects without too much bother.

Even before Carnival began, she enjoyed prowling the darkness. There was violence at times, and all of the things one normally read about in the morning paper. But she could pass by unnoticed and after awhile, there was very little she feared.

Now that the season and the parades had begun, it was wonderful to pass through the crowds unnoticed.

She had always thought of Mardi Gras as one big parade; but actually there were two weeks' worth of parades put on by, this year, fifty-three different organizations right there in New Orleans. Surrounding areas had their own parades.

She had made the mistake of attending a parade while *totally* invisible only once. Her feet were so bruised and bleeding from being trod on by the time she extracted herself from the surging crowds that she was sure she had left bloody tracks. She had finally taken to wearing running shoes. The crowds were so thick that nobody noticed an extra pair of shoes milling with the shoes that had legs attached. It was too hard on her feet to do all that walking without arch support. To protect the rest of her hide against such intrusions from elbows and other painful and damaging objects, she walked down the street with the revelers, beyond the barrier separating the parades from the spectators.

It was fun! She could dance with the music, a blend of jazz, Caribbean mambo, blues, heavy with piano, ethnic drums of indeterminate origin, trombones and saxophones and other instruments she associated with jazz or big band music. There was a sort of jingling percussion instrument, too, that contributed heavily to the wild feel of the music.

She loved catching the "throws" or trinkets thrown by the people on the floats. The items were mostly cheap and gaudy long strings of plastic beads, cups, doubloons (fake coins with the names of the clubs or krewes that put on the parades), even lace panties and gilt or sequined tiaras. Some of the stuff had collector value, but most of it was right up there with what you might give for favors at a New Year's or children's party. Most of them she gave to people she spotted at the back of the crowd, looking disappointed, children sometimes but even other adults—including other lone middle-aged women she thought were beginning to look a bit see-throughish themselves.

A few of the trinkets she took back to the hotel to drape over the lamps and spread out on the bed and television. To take full advantage of her invisibility, she had to travel light. She had pretty much abandoned her own things when she left home. She even hid the trinkets behind the furniture or under the mattress when she left the room, in case the maid come in or the room was rented while she was away.

She was still lonely a lot, but sometimes now she enjoyed herself. Like last night. There was a wonderful night parade along the river. Some of the maskers in feathers and sequins and very little else danced on the shore; some were aboard boats decorated to look like sea serpents and Atlantis complete with a whole squad of long-tailed mermaids. The music had been darker and more mysterious than usual—the same festive beat but with a lot of the Indian undertones some of it had, and more drums and jingles.

Unlike most of the parades, this one was entirely lit with torches or flambeaux. Even the street lamps had been turned off for the parade, and a whole phalanx of robed figures, whom she had at first feared might be some branch of the Ku Klux Klan that wore only black, formed a torchlit barrier between the crowd and the floats, boats, and maskers. Hell for the fire marshals, she thought, wincing a little. She was surprised they permitted it. Most of the parades she had seen featured the torches only as fiery atmospheric touches provided by a few of the parade participants—not as a primary source of lighting. In the firelight the shadows were long and grotesque and seemed to caper demonically independent of the fantastic creatures who cast them.

The throws were marvelous, too—heavy crystal beads that sparkled in the torchlight instead of plastic ones, and bracelets and necklaces of marcasite and garnets, hard to see in the dark, but really quite beautiful. Something she would have been proud to wear back when she had a self to wear it on. The doubloons they threw made heavy clanking sounds as they hit the street. She picked up two, though she could not make out inscriptions in the feeble torchlight. She held onto the coins, but had passed the jewelry on to some of the women in the back of the crowd who looked like they needed some luck.

The parade wound past the French Quarter, where some of the women, not all of them young and firm either, flashed their breasts from the balconies. Well, so did some of the women in the crowd. This mildly shocked the invisible woman until she realized that she was at least marginally barer than even the most scantily clad of them. Only nobody could see her. Or so she thought.

When she read her name on the envelope, she felt herself blush. Deeply. Apparently someone *had* seen her. All of her. And they knew who she was. She felt a distinct chill, although the temperature was already, in early March, in the mid-seventies with humidity of about the same percent.

"Mlle Vanessa Lightfoot" was elegantly calligraphed on the envelope. No one knew her name here. No one. How had they found out?

From the envelope she pulled an elegantly die-cut, embossed, and gilt-edged card, a fan shape with a shell design containing a mermaid with an elongated tail in a symphony of purple, green, and gold, the Mardi Gras colors.

She knew what this was, she thought. She had seen similar things in the Mardi Gras guides and magazines. And she had seen the mermaid design last night. It depicted the same character as the costume worn by the maskers on the Atlantis float.

Yes. Written in gold ink across the green sea in which the mermaid swam was the invitation: *"Krewe of Melusine 2000 commands your presence at her Melusinseranade on the evening of Mardi Gras the seventh day of March, year of two thousand, from seven of the clock until two-thirty."* Added to the bottom in an elegant hand, this time in green ink on a golden shell, *"Come as a character from your favorite folk or fairy tale."*

It further listed an address in the French Quarter.

She was already hearing some of the Mardi Gras terms on local television. The Krewe of Melusine, the krewe responsible for last night's extravagantly macabre parade, was oddly absent from the television stories that had been running steadily since Carnival began.

She stepped back out long enough to go to the hotel lobby newsstand and grab a copy of the ubiquitous Mardi Gras Guide.

Through the big glass windows, festooned with gilt banners and plastic beads, she saw the glitter and heard the music of a parade two blocks away.

She returned with the guide to her suite. It showed the parade route of the Krewe of Melusine, the parade she had followed last night, but there was little else about them in there, except that their organization had entered into the festivities for the first time this year. Well, perhaps that explained why they were recruiting new blood, if not why they could see her. Perhaps, she thought, they were simply more observant than most people. Wouldn't that be nice? Maybe there were people out there who were interested in whatever particular group of characteristics made her unique and saw her because of them. A bit daunting that she would be stark naked when they did. However, in the course of Carnival so far, she had already seen a great many people wearing very little more than she did. Perhaps down here nudity was viewed differently. Maybe Krewe Melusine was made up of middle-aged nudists, for all she knew.

But they expected her to show up in costume for their ball, so she would have to get busy. She smiled as she considered that she quite literally hadn't a thing to wear.

Who would she go as? She was a bit long in the tooth for the heroines, but then again, nobody could see her so she could get the appropriate disguise and be Rapunzel with yards of blonde hair if she wished! She felt like a cross between Cinderella and the fly invited into the spider's web.

Costume shops were all over the city, but she couldn't find a costume she liked, that fitted, anywhere. With the season so well underway, the selection was well picked over and she was not the petite size that most designers fondly imagined their customers would be. For two days she hunted the racks and the temperature rose into the eighties. Even though she risked wearing her running shoes in the daytime, she was growing footsore. Her invisible skin prickled with heat rash and was rubbed raw from chafing. Unused to even mild heat during this season, she was so terribly hot and dripping with perspiration she was surprised people did not try to elude the moving vertical lake she felt she had become. And her search was fruitless. Except for kiddy Halloween costumes, little remained in the city.

Why on earth hadn't the people throwing the party issued their invitations earlier? Probably because they had only spotted her, maybe even recognized her from someplace else, at their parade the night before the invitation arrived. Whoever they were, whatever their reason for inviting her, she desperately wanted to discover.

Perhaps she should just go as she was after all, drape a length of cloth over her arm and be the emperor wearing his new clothes if anyone *did* see her and asked. But the emperor (or empress, as anyone who could see her would be quite aware), though naked while wearing "invisible" new clothes, was not himself invisible.

For a fancy masked ball you really needed to wear something unlike yourself. For her, that would be someone visible.

Someone normal. Or almost. Character from a favorite fairy tale?

She found a mask in one of the shops that reminded her of something, something she had a hard time remembering for a time. The mask was covered with holographic film that bounced reflections from its surface. It was trimmed with gilt and sequins. The main part of the mask covered the upper part of the face, but it also featured a cascading veil of crystal and gold beads to cover the lower face. She also found a gold gilt wig with carefully arranged curls such as the white ones a judge might have worn in the old days. Both of these items appealed to her and she took them without quite knowing what she was going to do with them.

She saw the black robe crumpled in a box of discarded costumes in the back of one of the shops. It had a hood. Probably featured a skull mask and a scythe too, but it had black spangles on it so that it would sparkle. She took it too.

Still, she didn't know which fairy tale character she had in mind with that odd assortment until she returned to the hotel room and saw the ornately framed and gilded dressing table mirror. One more foray to a hardware shop and a sporting goods store, and she began assembling her costume.

SHE DITHERED A LITTLE about whether to arrive early or be fashionably late. She didn't really know the protocol. Finally, because she couldn't stand the wait, because it had been so long since her presence or absence made a difference to anyone, and because she didn't want to miss anything, she arrived at the address on the invitation just after "seven of the clock."

Completely covered in her hooded black robe, gloved and booted in black and her face and hair made visible by the golden wig and holographic mask, glittering and sparkling with every step, she was, in the crowd of elaborately garbed and/or half-naked maskers, more invisible than she had ever been before. She was sweltering by the time she arrived at the address on her invitation, the mirror concealed in a portfolio-sized black bag she carried close to her robe.

The address belonged to a three-story building with the vast numbers of tall windows and the two wrought-iron balconies that were a trademark of French Quarter architecture.

A doorman dressed in a gray suit with a rat's mask and tail, ushered her inside. The rest of the staff of what seemed to be an exclusive historic hotel were also masked and garbed. She wondered if most of the hotels hosting the costume balls did this. The staff in her hotel remained stolidly in the day-to-day uniform of modernity and conformity.

Even more amazing, in this twilight hour, the entire lobby was lit only by candlelight from the wall sconces, candelabrum, and some quite impressive candle-bearing chandeliers. The air carried some flowery perfume—gardenia, maybe?

Another rat looked at her invitation and ushered her into a ballroom.

She *had* been expecting the usual Holiday Inn sort of ballroom—a large room with a folding fiberglass curtain that could be pulled across the center to make two smaller meeting rooms. An area of parquet floor for dancing, the rest of the floor covered with utilitarian carpet and furnished with institutional tables and chairs perhaps covered with white cloths. Sometimes they had one of those prismatic balls above the dance floor, the kind you used to see in roller rinks, and later, discos.

But if the room she entered had ever looked like that, the decorations committee of the Krewe of Melusine was to be commended on the transformation.

This truly looked like the ballroom from Cinderella as it never had been done but should have. The lighting was supplied by candles, just as it was in the lobby. Crystal and silver chandeliers reflected the light from the flames flickering within them. The light and shadow played across a floor that seemed to be a solid sheet of lavender-veined white marble. A patterned carpet, which looked as if with only a little help it could be airborne, padded the steps under her dancing boots.

Beyond the marble dance floor, tall doors opened onto a courtyard where concealed colored lights played on the waters of a splashing fountain with a mermaid at its center. What looked like ancient cypress trees and weeping willows and a couple of palms were lit with what the invisible woman hoped were not thousands of tiny candles—Christmas tree lights, more likely, in purple, green, and gold.

The room was edged, not with the conventional round tables and hotel chairs, but with great groaning sideboards filled with all sorts of things to eat and drink. The centerpiece of each table was an ice sculpture, the largest of which was a replica of the Melusine-themed float-boat with the mermaids.

She took all this in while peeking past the herald, closed the door softly, and repaired to the ladies room to finish her costume. It felt odd to actually have to go into a separate room for privacy after having, for such a long time, more privacy than she had ever needed or wanted.

When she returned, the herald glanced at her, blew a real trumpet, and announced, "The Magic Mirror from Snow White has arrived."

The ballroom was considerably more crowded than it had been when she ducked into the bathroom. On each step was at least one masker—sometimes a couple, sometimes more, filing down to a reception line that was now in place. She would have to run the gauntlet. Oh dear. Somehow she thought these things were much less formal than this.

The band began playing in the background, heavy drums and jingles, saxophone slithering through with a melody. Perhaps out of deference to the reception line, no singer had as yet taken the stage.

The invisible woman descended behind Rapunzel and the prince, who was covered with a thorny vine. On his other side walked a woman wearing a tiara, a brief sheer set of baby doll pajamas the invisible woman thought she had seen in a Frederick's of Hollywood ad, and carrying a spinning wheel. Rapunzel, the prince, sleeping beauty. A threesome? That didn't bother her somehow. Not nearly as much as trying to see through her mask and over the mirror so that she did not tread on or trip over the long yellow braid that formed a train to Rapunzel's costume. As the trio turned to face the reception line, she saw that Sleeping Beauty was a man. She wasn't sure about the other two.

Fortunately, nobody could see from her invisible and masked face if she was surprised or not. The guide had warned that cross-dressing for males particularly was a Mardi Gras institution.

First in the reception line was Snow White. Next to her—him actually—were seven very little men—children rather than dwarves, from the look of them though their eyes seemed very old, and some of them, she was fairly sure, were girls. One of them spoke up, laying a proprietary hand on Snow White's pale arm. "Oh, darlin' look," the little man said in a high, overly sweetened feminine drawl. "If it isn't the magic mirror! You must check and see if you're the fairest of them all!"

Snow White flashed teeth—fangs—at the child and said, "How very droll you are this evenin', Dopey, isn't it?"

The invisible woman was still taking in the fangs when the Snow White smile was flashed at her. "Thanks, mirror. That's real cute but I'm gonna have to pass. You understand, don't you?"

"Maybe she doesn't, darlin'," said the next tall person in line. This was interesting. A woman dressed as a man in drag. Overly made up and coifed but the décolletage in the gown was deep and genuine. "Never mind that little bitch, honey, you just come over here and tell Queenie who is the fairest of them all. My, that's a cute costume! Made it yourself?"

The invisible woman, unsure if she could make herself heard, nodded.

"Oh, you are soooo mysterious! I just love it. And you're new too—not that I can see you, but I can just feel that you are. I know you're going to have so much fun with us. You just run along now. Red Ridin' Hood, honey, would you get Ms. Mirror here some punch? I don't think she can manage with her—uh—reflectin' side in front of her like that."

Little Red Riding Hood turned a red-hooded head to her—and revealed a human face in the process of growing a snout and extra hair. "Never mind," the invisible woman squeaked aloud for the first time in years. "I can manage!"

"Oh lookee there!" squealed the first of the seven dwarves. "Look at all those gorgeous gals!"

Descending the steps in plumed tiaras and a variety of dancing costumes—everything from ballroom and tango through Irish step dancing—came twelve pseudo maidens, at least half of whom were male. Behind them came a fellow in a Confederate officer's uniform with a cloak draped over his arm.

Little Red Riding—wolf? said, "Well, if it isn't the Twelve Dancin' Princesses!" He had a nice deep voice.

While he was looking at the princesses, the invisible woman looked more closely at his increasingly wolfish face. If it was makeup, it was the best makeup job she had ever seen. You couldn't even simulate that with a computer. Looking at the princesses, he licked his chops, running a long pink tongue over a long mouth full of long teeth and—what big ears he had!

A werewolf. And the fangs on Snow White. They could be dental appliances of course. The dwarves, grinning up at the princesses, had fangs, too. Oh dear. And she had thought Anne Rice was writing fiction! But here they were, all around her, the creatures of the night Rice referred to. The fangs weren't part of their costumes. The fangs were the real deal.

That was how they'd seen her.

She turned to head to the ladies room again and take off her costume and run away. Except—what good would that do? They had *seen* her. At the parade, where she was as invisible as usual. Some one among them at least *had* seen her and somehow found out her name. Well, sure. The Krewe of Melusine looked like it was largely composed of vampires and werewolves and the like. They had their ways of finding out stuff, according to Rice and Bram Stoker and bad movies from the forties. Maybe, as creatures of the night, they did as much eavesdropping as invisible people.

Slowly, she made her way toward the punch table. She was very hot and very dry in this outfit, in spite of the ballroom air conditioning that was also wasting energy by trying to cool the courtyard. She took a glass of punch and drained it, took another, and sipped.

A hand touched her sleeve and she jumped, sloshing wine onto the marble floor. "Would you care to dance?" a masculine voice inquired.

It was the Confederate officer. Now that he was closer, she saw that around the domino mask from which showed deep brown eyes, his face was rather badly scarred—seamed, as if he had been cut up at some point and clumsily stitched back together. He was very tall. And his smile didn't have any fangs in it.

"Yes," she said. "But I'll have to shift my costume."

"You have a lovely voice," he said. "It matches your costume. Silvery and rippling."

She was completely taken aback. If this was southern charm, it worked. Especially since his remark was the most graceful compliment she had been paid since she was young and slender and visible.

"Thank you," she said, shifting her mirror to her back and hoping he was so tall he would not see that her neck was invisible in the shadows of the black robe. "I don't quite understand your costume, though. It doesn't look like a fairy-tale character to me. Who are you supposed to be?"

"Why, honey, I'm the old soldier who returns from the war and answers the king's challenge to find out where his twelve daughters go every night to wear out their shoes."

"Oh," she said. "Of course. I just never thought of him as being a Civil War veteran."

"My own little interpretation," he said with a smile. "Now then, this is your first Mardi Gras, I take it?"

"Oh, yes. And it was very kind of the Krewe of Melusine to invite me.

"Nonsense," he said gallantly. "Having you here is our pleasure entirely."

"New blood?" she couldn't help asking. Would all those fangs sink into her at some point during the night? Or maybe somebody would offer her immortality and a cozy coffin. And here she was without a smidge of her native earth!

"Now, then, no need to talk like that," he said.

"I didn't mean to be gauche," she apologized. Miss Manners didn't cover these situations, nor Emily Post. How was she supposed to know what to say? She felt giddy and rather girlish. Maybe it was the punch.

Probably her situation was dangerous. Here she was, on her own, unknown in a strange city, having fallen in with vampires, werewolves—and whatever her dancing partner was. Why had they invited her to fall in with them, she wondered? More to the point, were they all going to fall on her?

She decided to fish a little, and really, now that she had found her voice, and the "old soldier" seemed to like it, she found it a pleasure to talk and be heard. "Have you known these people long?" she asked. "The rest of the Krewe of Melusine, I mean?"

"Oh, for ages and ages," he said, with a smile that was appealingly bashful if a bit grotesque. "They're a fine bunch of characters."

"Ummm," she said. She decided not to press but go about sussing out the situation more indirectly. "Is the mermaid symbol the Melusine you are the Krewe of?"

"She's not exactly a mermaid," he said. "In fact, a lot of the French nobility—and some of the folks here—claim descent from her. She was supposed to be half fairy and half human. Her father was what the social workers these days would call an abuser, and Melusine managed to lock him up in a cave. Her mama punished her by makin' her a serpent from the waist down for part of every day. This didn't keep the girl from marryin' the Count of Poitiers, and they were real happy and had a mess of kids until he broke his promise to her and peeked at her while she was takin' a bath. Our own Count DeBase', that's Snow White to you, darlin', claims descent from her through his mother's line, and Louis Garou, Red Ridin' Hood, is related to her from the wrong side of the blanket. She's sort of the patron ancestress for all of the—well, if you were bein' politically correct, you'd probably say differently gifted, breathing challenged, in touch with their inner beast, folks on the Krewe."

She looked back at the emblem of the Krewe of Melusine and saw that the long mermaid's tail was indeed serpentine and had no fishy fork at the end. She nodded and turned her mask back to her partner.

"And what's your story?" she asked.

"Me, I don't normally come to this kinda thing but the Count is bound and determined to improve our civic image. He even sent a couple of the boys over to get interviewed by a lady writer. Then he and Louie got this notion that we would become the Krewe of Melusine and enter into the festivities this year. Raise our profile. Only none of them, after all the years they've lived, has learned come'ere from sick'em about practical matters. Me, I've got a carpenter's hands and I'm good at buildin' things, so I decided, even though I thought I'd feel silly in fancy dress, to go along with it, help 'em build the float and such."

He did have carpenter's hands—rough and callused, though he had evidently tried to soften them with lotion, and there were more scars at the wrists. Was he maybe a bipolar personality and had become so depressed at one time that he had attempted suicide? She hoped not! His eyes were wonderful, soft and deep and humorous at the same time. They seemed wise. Plus he was tall and he liked her voice and for such a big fellow, he danced divinely. No doubt it was idiotic, but she felt safe in his long arms. She asked quickly, "And are you glad?"

"It's the smartest thing I've ever done," he said. "I knew that the minute I saw you standin' in the front of the crowd, catchin' throws like a little girl." His arms tightened, drawing her to him. "Nobody else was lookin' so I knew they either had to be blind or you were invisible. I followed you. I'm sorry, I know stalkin's got a bad name these days, but I didn't mean any harm. I just wanted to know who you were so I could get you invited here, meet you, get to know you so maybe you'd be—less alarmed, seein' us lookin' so ridiculous in our masks and costumes."

Her breath left in a rush of belief. "Then it wasn't the vamp—the Count and the others who wanted me to come?"

"Not at first, darlin', no. They're kinda self-absorbed, if you know what I mean. But I bet they're gonna be as impressed as I am once they take notice. I just love your gumption. Not many ladies when they turn invisible start havin' fun the way you do. And I can just tell you're not narrow-minded or anything. You're still here, after all." His close embrace graphically demonstrated just how interested he was. When she was twenty, this might have seemed coarse or gross and annoyed her. But maybe not from someone she liked. And she liked this big fellow, even if he was a little on the seamy side.

"And you can see me?" she asked. "Even without the costume?"

He gave her a cheerful leer. "You bet I can, sugar."

"Well," she said, more boldly than she had ever dared even at the pinnacle of her youth and beauty, since in those days the men had to make all the moves. "I am so glad you invited me. It's nice to be a part of things, when I'm such a stranger here—everywhere, actually. It was very sweet of you to take such pains to impress me. I admit, at one point, this would have all been a little too—unconventional for me. But I'm unconventional now myself."

He gave her another little reassuring hug.

"The only thing is, I've had too much of crowds already, and I'm not used to being stared at." For she had begun to notice that all over the room people were staring at them.

"That's not you, honey. It's just that everybody who isn't one of the Count's kind is admirin' their costumes in your costume." Another leer. "You could just sorta slip out of it and into somethin' more comfortable and we could get outta here if you like."

She laughed and put on a Miss Scarlett voice. "Why, Sir, what makes you think I'm that kinda girl?"

He put his finger to his lips, his eyes twinkling, and helped adjust her mirror so that it was once more in the front of her costume. Then, taking a step back from her, he plucked up the cloak he had been carrying over his arm and swung it over his shoulders, adjusting the hood. In the mirror, one moment he was there, the next moment he was gone.

"Now how did you do *that*?" she asked.

"Don't you remember your fairy tales, darlin'? When the old soldier took on the case of the disappearin' princesses, he first got him a cloak of invisibility so he could tail 'em without bein' spotted. I do a little detective work myself, so I find this comes in real handy. It is also how I know what kinda girl you are."

"Oops," she said, again in the Miss Scarlett voice. "But that is so unfair. You have the advantage of me! I don't even know your name."

"Names are not all that important among kindred spirits, darlin'! Ms. Vanessa," he said, still smiling visibly—to her. "But you can call me Lamont."

She gasped appreciatively. "Lamont *Cranston*, the Shadow who used invisibility to fight crime?"

"Oh, no, darlin', he'd be way too old for you by now. My given name is actually Montmorte but close enough. And I—acquired—many of the original Shadow's traits after he disappeared last time. Includin' bein' able to make myself invisible with the help of this cape, which I got for savin' a poor old bag lady from a street gang, and a taste for crime fightin'. Say now, you bein' invisible yourself and all, I don't suppose you would want to try your hand at crime fightin' too." His big earnest scarred face looked down at her hopefully.

She thought of all of the violence she had fled from in the dark, glad that she could not be seen but feeling guilty for not helping the victims. "Could be. It's crossed my mind to tell you the truth, though so far all I've managed to do is keep out of trouble. Speaking of trouble, for an alleged good guy, don't you keep sort of questionable company?"

He smiled. "These folks took me in when I was barely a few days old, darlin', when even the folks who gave me life didn't want me. The Count and Louie and their friends are like family to me. And surely you've read Carl Jung, darlin'? Even us shadows got ourselves a dark side."

"Just how dark is that?" she asked, intrigued in spite of herself. Her heart was pounding. This was the kind of man she had longed for—powerful, intelligent, charming, complex, articulate—and a man of many parts.

He led her to one of the tall floor-standing candlabras and helped her take off the mirror, mask, and wig. All around them the masked dancers swirled. He pulled up the folds of the voluminous cloak and gazed into her eyes. It was so nice that he was even gazing at the right place. "Let me put it this way, Vanessa, honey, while I am on the other side of the crime-fightin' fence from the Count or Louie, I *do* have my little— kinks. You and me, I knew it the first time I saw you, we're two of a kind. And I just happen to know that out there under that big old cypress, right near that cool, splashing fountain, there is a little patch of soft grass just big enough."

It was an outrageous idea, something she would never have considered before, even with football heroes or movie stars, had she known any. On the other hand, she was glad it wasn't just another career opportunity. The night was warm and perfumed, and the courtyard was cool and not *quite* as public as the ballroom. The music had begun in earnest, with a throbbing, primitive beat. And now, well, she was invisible. And he was, too. No one would see, or know, but him. It was a uniquely intimate situation. And intensely erotic. Stealth, danger, romance. She felt as if she were seventeen again. Very much in the mood for some serious sexual *divertissement* as a prelude to her new line of work, she played with the buttons on his uniform. "We-ell," she said in the Miss Scarlett drawl, "I suppose if I'm going to help you fight crime, it's high time I reacquainted myself with the evil that lurks in the hearts of men."

He wrapped her in the cloak and kissed her, saying, "And women, dearheart. This shadow *knows*."

FAREWELL TO THE FLESH

John Helfers

Seth watched in bemusement as the black-robed figure next to him raised a gleaming dagger over the unconscious woman on the stone slab.

Chanting in a low monotone, the hooded form held the dagger aloft while his other hand gripped a golden, gem-encrusted cross, held upside down, over the woman spread-eagled on the stone, the ropes binding her wrists attached to large iron rings set in the rock.

Upon seeing the cross, the group of the similarly clad cult members standing in a circle around the sacrificial table bowed low, their chants mingling with their leader's. Seth also bowed, following their example, but he only mouthed the simple lines, a small part of his mind registering the cultists' mispronunciation of some of the ancient phrases. *Amateurs,* he thought, his eyes locked on the priceless cross the cult leader was gesturing with.

"Nyarlhotep, I ask that you come forth from the spirit world and take your rightful place in this vessel, which has been consecrated for you. Arise, Nyarlhotep, and begin preparing this realm for passage into the next world, the coming of the cleansing, the purification of the holy, and the destruction of those who would oppose you."

Like me, Seth thought. He had been on the cultists' trail for a few weeks now, ever since they had "acquired" the cross, and had followed them to their lair primarily to find out what they were up to. After following them to the cemetery, it had been child's play to snatch one and masquerade in his robes for the evening's ceremonies. He was rather disappointed to learn that they were garden-variety satanic worshippers attempting to summon some kind of ancient overlord to grant them dark powers over the rest of humanity. Seth would have sighed at the ridiculousness of it all, if he still breathed. *Stupid amateurs*, he corrected himself.

The cultists were now swaying back and forth, and their leader's voice, degenerating into a frenzied intonation of ancient incantations, had reached a fever pitch. Still holding the cross over his head, he plunged the dagger down toward the woman's chest.

Then Seth moved.

Faster than anyone could see, he rose to his feet, stepped toward the cult leader, and redirected the dagger away from the woman and into the man's stomach. There was a moment of shocked silence as everyone in the room sensed that something had gone very, very wrong.

Seth's hood had fallen from his head after he had gotten up, and as he looked into the leader's shocked eyes, he smiled, letting the light from the two torches that illuminated the chamber fall upon his elongated canines.

"Not tonight," he whispered, twisting the blade in his victim's abdomen as he plucked the cross from the man's trembling hand. Without a sound, the cultist slipped quietly to the floor, too surprised to even moan, and he passed into unconsciousness.

Seth didn't look back, but glided to the torches at the far end of the room and smothered both of them with his robe, plunging the chamber into complete darkness.

The next sixty seconds were a frenzy of crazed noise. Screams and scrabbling of the remaining cultists, trying to find their way out of the sacrificial room that had suddenly become a deathtrap, punctuated the heavy thuds of bodies being thrown against stone walls, thick wet sounds of torn flesh and snapping bone, and the gurgles and moans of the dying.

When the minute had passed, Seth walked to the door, mindful of the newly made mess on the floor, unbolted it, and threw it open. Moonlight flooded the room, illuminating the carnage. The silver light revealed a large pentagram drawn inside a circle around the stone coffer, with several parts erased by the smears of blood that covered the floor.

Seth paused by the door for a moment, looking outside to see if the commotion had attracted any attention. *Not likely, given where we are,* he thought. The odor of the nearby ocean was so pervasive that he didn't need to breathe to smell it.

He examined the cross in his hand, inspecting it for damage. Finding none, he tucked it into a pocket of his suit and walked back to where the head cultist lay, surrounded by a widening pool of his own blood. Kneeling beside the body, Seth removed the dagger from its temporary sheath and leaned down to drink his fill.

When he was finished, he looked at the knife, turning it over in his hand. It was a *kris,* or wavy blade, forged out of a dull gray metal. The handle appeared to be carved into the shape of a merman-like creature with scales covering its entire body. Its outstretched arms formed the guard, with scaled hands at each end, and its head, with its bulbous eyes and gaping, fang-filled mouth appeared to be swallowing the base of the blade. Although Seth didn't remember wiping the dagger off, the blade was clean, as if the knife hadn't even been used.

It wasn't immediately familiar, which was strange in itself. Usually Seth knew any kind of artifact on sight, but this one was foreign to him. *I wonder if Giancarlo knows anything about this,* he thought. Holding the knife gave him an unusual feeling, as if there was another presence in the room. Shaking his head, Seth chided himself for his nervousness. *It isn't every day that I find a unidentifiable piece of artwork, that's all.*

He used the dagger to cut the ropes that bound the girl to the stone slab, slinging her body over his shoulder. She moaned as he hoisted her up, and he checked to make sure that she hadn't woken. He could feel the warm blood coursing through her, smell the nearness of it, the vitality of it even more potent than the lake of spilled liquid in the bloody chamber, and, although he had just fed, the hunger pangs stirred feebly in him, the all-consuming need always making its presence known. Seth knew this would happen, and he was able to ignore the incessant thirst with relative ease.

Carrying his load to the door, Seth stopped and took one last look behind him. "When bad cultists go worse," he said, shaking his head and exiting, closing the door behind him.

Outside, Seth looked around, checking the cemetery for signs of life. He glanced back at the mausoleum he'd just left and was gratified to find no signs of disturbance. *Given the state of this place, it'll be several days, perhaps even a week or two, before these guys are found,* he thought. Shifting the girl to a more comfortable position, he carried her across the cemetery to his rented Lincoln Town Car. He opened the door and set her down in the front seat, tossing the dagger on the floor. He then walked to the large van the cultists had driven here, opened the driver side door, and scanned the car's interior, finding a woman's black leather purse on the passenger seat. He grabbed it, making sure there was nothing else there to connect her to the bloodbath in the mausoleum, then closed and locked the van's doors. Walking back to the car, he got in and drove away.

Once out of the cemetery, he got onto Highway 90 and accelerated east, toward the distant city. Driving through the low marshlands and the thicker swamps, Seth headed for the bright light that hung over the buildings that formed the low skyline. Streetlights, bonfires, spotlights, flashlights, headlights, and anything else that would repel the night were bouncing off the clouds of the overcast night and giving the city a glowing halo, a halo that Seth knew this particular place did nothing to deserve.

From here he could hear the noise as well as if he were standing on the corner of Bourbon Street listening to the jazz go down. Parades, parties, and block-long celebrations weren't uncommon as the laid-back people of Louisiana shook off their easygoing attitude, partied like there was going to be no tomorrow, and lit up the night with their festivities. And of course, since it was the year of the millennium, New Orleans was welcoming the next thousand years with the *carnivale* to end all carnivals.

He grinned. *I love New Orleans in February,* he thought. *The exuberance, the decadence, the intensity of it all. That, and it's one of the few times I can roam a city freely, without having to worry about keeping my guard up. After all, there are enough fake vampires roaming around, what's one more, even if I am real?*

A low moan from the passenger seat attracted Seth's attention. He looked over at the woman slumped next to him, her blonde hair hanging over her face. *Ah yes, what to do with you?* he thought, reaching for her purse with one hand. A quick flip of her pocketbook revealed that the woman Seth had rescued was Diana Corgan, and that she lived in the French Quarter.

Which will be impossible to drive to for the next week or so, he thought. *Better to take her to the church. I'm sure the good father can put her up for the evening.* He skirted around the city to the south side, about a kilometer away from the docks, and pulled into the parking lot of a large church. He drove around to the back of the building and parked the car near a pair of double doors lit by a single light bulb. Just outside the church doors, Seth paused for a moment, listening to the loud celebrations, the blare of trumpets, and cheers of the crowds watching parades, the constant reminder of the humanity surrounding him. *Ah, Mardi Gras,* he thought.

With the cross in his hand, and the still-unconscious woman over his shoulder, Seth entered the church.

The small entryway he found himself in was dark, but a dim glow led him into the main chapel. The cavernous room was lit by dozens of candles surrounding the altar, where a lone priest knelt, deep in prayer. Seth made no noise as he crossed the room to the first row of pews and gently set the woman down. He stood in the aisle beside her and waited for the priest to finish.

After a few seconds the shorter man raised his head, kissed the cross on his rosary, and got to his feet. When he turned around, he started at seeing the tall, pale man standing in the aisle of the church.

"Don't you ever knock? I didn't like it the first time you did that, and I don't like it now," the priest said, fingering his rosary as he slowly walked closer.

"I know, Father," Seth said, "Please forgive me. I meant no offense." Seth usually disliked priests, primarily because of their opinion of him, but Father Giancarlo was different. He still believed in the power of his faith, and he didn't try to bluster and threaten Seth every time the vampire accepted a Church assignment. The fact that each had saved the other's life fourteen years ago, the last time Seth had been down south, had only cemented their friendship. The arrangement suited both men just fine, and whenever Seth was in town, he always tried to visit his old friend.

"Besides, I had a very good evening, so I hardly think you can blame me for using a little levity to spice up the night," Seth said, holding up the cross so the reflected candlelight twinkled as it dangled on its chain.

"The Cross of Coronado," the priest breathed. "Finally back to its rightful owners after more than fifty years of searching." He reached out to reverently cradle the cross in his hands. "I suppose I do not want to know how you recovered this?"

Seth smiled, his lips closed. "You're too young. Let's just say that there's one less group of cultists running around tonight."

"I don't suppose I can get you to take confession for what you've done?" the priest asked.

Seth smiled, again not showing his teeth. It was an old joke between them, with Father Giancarlo often saying that it was the one thing that would assure him canonization. Although they had often discussed history in past visits, Seth had never mentioned his past deeds, and the priest had never asked. "Father, I've been around since the Church tried to excommunicate Queen Elizabeth, the First. I'm afraid the list of my misdeeds would cause you to expire of old age before we got halfway through."

Father Giancarlo grunted. "When I heard you had come to New Orleans to investigate this matter personally, I almost didn't believe it. But here you are. Although I agree with what you are doing, I cannot condone it. Nor, by the same token, can I stop you. By the way, what name are you using this time?"

When Seth told him, he nodded. "The ancient Egyptian god of adversity, eh? It suits you."

Since Seth had been walking the earth for more than six centuries, he had created several identities for himself to aid in his unique line of work. His passion for recovering and protecting art had taken him to all corners of the world, and he was known to many people under many different names. The last time he had been in America was when he had saved the statue of Sitting Bull from what he had thought was a group of racist skinheads. They had turned out to be vampire hunters who had baited a trap for him. After disposing of them, he'd been hunting the rest of the group for the past year, but had come back when he had stumbled onto the lead for the cross. Now that his obligation was over, he would probably resume his search.

"Who's this?" Father Giancarlo asked, motioning to the young woman sleeping on the bench.

"That was going to be the cultists' sacrifice for the evening. I was hoping you might be able to watch over her after I . . . speak with her."

"I will take care of her. Do you wish to be left alone?" the priest asked.

"I don't see why it would matter. This will give you something to talk to your superiors about. Just watch," Seth said as he leaned close to the unconscious woman. "Diana, open your eyes."

The young woman's eyes snapped open, and she lifted her head and sat up straighter on the bench. Her gaze was not focused on either Seth or Father Giancarlo, but on a point far off in the distance, at something only she could see. She appeared relaxed and calm, almost as if she might have been attending church, if this had been Sunday.

"Diana, listen to me. You have been out all night enjoying yourself during Mardi Gras. You will go directly home, where you will fall asleep and not awaken until noon tomorrow. You will not remember anything that happened tonight. When you awaken tomorrow, you will assume that you had too much to drink and passed out at home. The instant this man wakes you, you will thank him, get up and go to the cab outside this building, and instruct the driver to take you home. Sleep now," Seth said. He straightened and looked at Father Giancarlo. "There is one more thing."

The priest sighed and shook his head. "With you, there always is. What is it?"

Seth produced the dagger and held it out. "I would like any information you have as to where this weapon comes from."

Father Giancarlo took the strange knife and examined it closely. "This is interesting. Where did you acquire this?"

"Like I said, the cultists were going to sacrifice the girl, and this was the dagger they were going to use."

"There seems to be a lot of this kind of black magic and sacrificing going on, especially during Mardi Gras. In the past few years it seems that every crackpot claiming he's seen visions of Satan or what-have-you has started his own little church of fanatics." The priest held the dagger up to the light. "The merman motif would fit a number of old South Pacific polytheistic religions that often believed in the existence of a 'water god,'" Father Giancarlo said, "but they died out or were converted long before metalworking was known to them. What sacrificial weapons have been found were always made from stone or wood. I'll check the church's databases and see if we can come up with anything. I'll let you know what I turn up. Can I still reach you at the same number?"

"I'll get your message," Seth said. "Right now it's time for me to go."

"Understood, my friend," the stocky priest said. "The Church and I owe you another debt, as usual."

"Your friendship is payment enough for me," Seth said with a smile. He offered his hand, and the two men shook. "Go with God, Father."

"I always do," Father Giancarlo said. "I'll call a cab for our sleeping friend here."

"When it arrives, just wake her, she'll do the rest on her own. I'll be seeing you," Seth said as he headed for the back door. "Let me know what you find."

"Of course . . ." the priest barely said before his unusual companion was gone. "May the Lord keep and protect you as well, my friend," he whispered, but only the statue of the Virgin Mary heard him in the now-silent cathedral.

SETH AWOKE THE NEXT night with a strange desire to experience the nightlife of New Orleans. Outside, the party was in full swing, as usual, and the cheerful music and celebrating voices combined to produce a melancholy effect in him.

As much as I have experienced, and as long as I have survived, sometimes I still do not think that I have lived one-tenth as much as a single person out there. I wonder if they ever stop to think about just what it is they have, and whether they appreciate it. Probably not during this week, and especially not in this city, he thought while showering. Although his body didn't sweat or exude any kind of oil, Seth enjoyed some of the rituals of humanity, feeling that these simple experiences gave him a little more kinship with them. He also liked to thumb his nose at some of the myths regarding his kind. *Can't cross running water, my ass.*

The hunger hit him just as he was toweling off, the need coursing through his body, reminding him, as it did every night, of the price he was paying for the endless days to come. *And yet I feel it is worth it,* he thought as he staggered into his hotel bedroom, heading for the large locked cooler that was plugged into the wall. Opening it revealed the one thing he never traveled without, his own portable blood supply. Seth reached for one of the long plastic pouches and slit it open, pouring the unlife-sustaining contents down his throat. *Some fearsome predator of the night I look like now,* he thought while he drained the bag, then took another. Only after that one was dry did the hunger agony abate somewhat, but Seth knew that he couldn't be around a lot of people tonight, in case the hunger came upon him again.

With so much prey available, I might not be able to stop myself, he thought. *Better to spend my night alone, for safety. Again.*

Replacing the empty blood bags in the chest, Seth dressed and picked up his cell phone to check his messages.

"Seth, this is Marten. I've wrapped up our business in Istanbul and will be heading back by the time you hear this. None of the leads panned out. I'll have a report ready for you when you get back."

Seth smiled. Marten was his number-two man, his contact between himself and many top people in the art world. Their paths had crossed several years ago in Italy, when Marten had been cat-burglaring for wealthy collectors who simply had to have original works of art for their private enjoyment. Seth had been hired to stop whoever had been stealing the priceless works. Seth had won that one, and, instead of turning Marten over to the authorities, had made him a very lucrative offer instead, one that, in effect, couldn't be turned down. Over the years Marten had become more and more indispensable to Seth, serving as his eyes and ears during daylight. They had been in the Middle East together, but Seth had come back to America when the Church had contacted them. He played the second message.

"Seth, this is Father Giancarlo. I need to speak to you as soon as possible about that dagger you found. Come to the church after dark, and tell no one about this." The time stamp on the message told Seth that Giancarlo had called at about 3:00 P.M.

That sounds like something to take my mind off my troubles, Seth thought. He drained another blood bag to ward off the thirst for a while longer, grabbed his keys, and headed out the door.

DRIVING OVER IN HIS car, Seth mused on the apparent oddity of where he was going. *A vampire going to a priest, in a church, no less.* He shook his head at the false superstitions regarding his kind. *Holy water, crosses, the sacrament, garlic, all nonsense.* Vampires still had a few vulnerabilities, such as sunlight, a stake through the heart, and the need for blood. *Despite what the movies claim, we have fewer weaknesses than anybody thinks. But, the more misinformation that is spread about us, the better.* He pulled into the church parking lot, got out of his car, and headed inside.

As soon as Seth walked into the church, he knew something was wrong. It was too quiet, as if when the doors had shut behind him, they had cut off all sound in the church.

He stood there a moment, every sense alert, and it was then that the smell registered. A familiar scent hung in the air, a thick coppery odor that the vampire knew intimately. Seth was in the foyer before the main hall, and he strode forward without pausing, pushing the entry doors open and stepping inside.

At first glance, all seemed to be in order. The candles in the vestry were flickering, their soft golden light holding the darkness at bay. The holy water font burbled quietly in the corner, recirculating the blessed liquid for the faithful to anoint themselves with. Moonlight drifted down though the large stained-glass window at the other end of the church, painting the carpeted floor in a wash of silver and multicolored light.

But the scene above the altar at the far end of the cathedral made Seth stop dead in his tracks. The beautifully carved gilded cross suspended from the ceiling was coated in blood, which slowly oozed down its sides to create a puddle on the floor. The altar itself was also splotched with crimson, as if someone had been held there while being bled. But it was the figure hanging above that caused Seth's hands to clench into helpless fists and a snarl to escape his lips.

On the cross hung the body of Father Giancarlo, upside down, his arms dangling limply. Each leg had been stretched to an end of the crosspiece and nailed there. His throat looked like it had been ripped out, but Seth couldn't tell for certain, because his chest had been torn open, leaving a raw, eviscerated mess from his stomach to his neck. His once-immaculate shirt was soaked with congealing blood, a red collar instead of a white one. His eyes were still open and staring, a shocked look on his normally calm face.

Before Seth could take a step forward, he felt the cold metal circle of what was undoubtedly a gun muzzle press into the back of his neck. A low voice to his right started to ask, "Tell me why—"

Seth snapped. His right arm blurred upwards, striking the man's wrist with enough force to send the pistol flying straight up. Swiveling to face his attacker, his left hand, already curled into a fist, slammed into the man's solar plexus, causing his body to shake as if he had been suddenly electrocuted.

Seth grabbed the man by the throat and lifted him effortlessly into the air with his left hand. Without looking, he reached out with his right hand, caught the pistol as it fell, and put to the man's temple.

"—I shouldn't kill you right now?" Seth growled. "Believe me, if you had anything to do with my friend's death, you won't be alive long enough to hear the answer."

"But if you kill him, I won't help you find out who killed my brother," a new voice said from the front of the church.

For a moment there was almost complete silence, broken only by the gasping sounds coming from the man Seth was holding in the air. He looked over toward the grisly tableau to see a tall woman with cappuccino skin dressed in a long cashmere overcoat standing in front of the altar. She was flanked by two even taller men, both dressed in immaculate suits and expensive leather overcoats. Seth's keen eye also noticed the slight bulges under their arms.

"Ramon is my personal assistant. Killing him will not get our relationship off to the best start," the woman said.

"As I recall, he was the one who put the gun to my head. I don't like being threatened," Seth said.

The woman motioned for her guards to stay where they were, then started walking down the aisle toward Seth. "If you are who I think you are, I know you had nothing to do with Batiste's death. My brother spoke very highly of you, Seth."

"I knew Father Giancarlo for over fourteen years, and he never mentioned having a sister," Seth said, turning to face her. He still held Ramon a foot off the ground, oblivious to the small choking noises the man was making.

"Our mother married again after Batiste's father died," the woman said while coming closer. "Her first husband was pure Italian, her second was a *mulatto* French Creole. I am the result of the latter. Although my brother loves—loved me very much, he could not talk about me often, for fear of jeopardizing his position in the Catholic Church. You see, I am a *mambo*, a voodoo priestess. There were those in the Church who felt my brother already conspired too close with—unnatural things. I had no wish to add fuel to their fire."

"Oh? Then why the hired muscle? I wouldn't think bullets would help you against spirits. Or priests, for that matter," Seth said.

"My . . . family is responsible for much of the illegal activity that goes on in New Orleans. I am not involved in that aspect of my family's business, but rival houses would try to use me for their own ends. Perhaps you've heard of the Giancarlo house in Italy. We're quite notorious over there."

Seth hid his smile. *As a matter of fact, I have,* he thought. It had been at the patriarchal head of the Giancarlo family's mansion where he had found Marten and recovered several dozen paintings they had stolen. He was well aware of their reputation both in Europe and the United States. Seth had suspected his friend's history, but, like Father Giancarlo, had never brought it up. *That's probably why he never spoke about his past. Another thing we had in common,* Seth thought.

"Do you think you could put Ramon down now? I don't like that shade of purple he's turning. If you still need a hostage, I am close enough now. Although after watching you in action, I have no doubt you could kill all three of my guards before I could reach the door."

Seth regarded her for a moment. Close up, she looked to be about thirty-five, with a emerald-eyed gaze intent enough to rival his own. Abruptly, Seth released Ramon, who fell to the ground, his hands massaging his throat. The scowl on his face was directed at his former captor, who ignored him.

"So why did you come here?" he asked.

The woman didn't answer for a moment, her eyes looking down at Seth's chest. He followed her gaze to the pistol in his hand. "Oh," he said, letting it dangle by the trigger guard and holding it out to Ramon, who gingerly retrieved it. "Well?"

"I'm assuming it was for the same reason you're here. Occasionally my brother would consult me for information on some of the more—esoteric items the Church would find during their work. I found a message on my answering machine this afternoon about a sacrificial dagger he had been researching. He asked me to stop by tonight, as he had also wanted to introduce me to a friend. I assume he meant you."

"Some reception," Seth said.

"Well, when we walked in and discovered that," she said, waving at the scene behind her, "we weren't really trusting anybody anymore. I'm sorry."

"About what happened to me or about your brother?" Seth asked.

The woman's eyes flashed as she glared at him. "Don't patronize me. It tears me apart to see my brother desecrated like this. I respected his choice, just as he respected mine. When his killers are found and justice is done, then my grieving will begin. But for now, my only thoughts are to find whoever did this, and destroy them."

Seth nodded. "I'm sorry. Believe me, we both want the same thing, and I won't rest until I find those responsible."

"Whomever it was, they were obviously here for a reason," the woman said. "The dagger is gone. I've looked everywhere for it, with no luck."

"But how did they know? No one knew I was coming here. The cultists I took it from were all dead, I made sure of it," Seth said.

"Are you sure that was all of them? Did anyone see you coming or going?" the woman asked him.

"No, I was alone, except for . . . her," Seth answered.

"Who?"

"The cultists' sacrifice. A woman," Seth said. "If the cultists did manage to track me to here, then they may go after her again."

"It's possible they have her already. You'd better make sure she's all right. I have several leads of my own to check up on. You have a number where I can reach you?"

Seth handed over a card with a phone number printed on it, nothing more. "You can reach me at this number for the next three days. What about you?"

The green-eyed woman rattled off a string of numbers that Seth immediately committed to memory. "What do I call you?" he asked.

"Dominique," was her answer. "Call me when you've located her."

"Of course. One thing I have to do first." Seth said. He ran toward the altar and cross, right past the two bodyguards. Springing onto the marble platform, he leaped straight into the air, landing lightly on the crosspiece of the cross. As gently as possible, he removed Father Giancarlo's body from the cross and, holding it in his arms, jumped to the ground.

Seth walked toward the bodyguards and addressed the one nearest to him. "Give me your coat."

"What for?" the bodyguard asked. "He's dead already."

Seth smiled, baring his fangs at the man. "Care to join him?"

The man's eyes widened, but he still looked over at Dominique, who nodded slightly. With a shrug, he wriggled out of his overcoat and dropped it on the floor in front of him.

Seth tenderly wrapped Father Giancarlo's body in the coat, making sure his eyes were closed before covering his face. "*In pace requiescat,* my friend."

Seth rose and turned to Dominique. "I have no doubt that you will see to his burial. When you leave, make sure no one else comes in," he said, then ran out of the church to his car, heading for the home of Diana Corgan.

THE STREETS OF NEW ORLEANS were packed with partygoers, the city disgorging thousands of people into the clogged avenues for celebration, parades, bands, and just having a good time. All of which made traveling even remotely close to the city nearly impossible. Seth had to bite back his frustration at his snail's-paced approach to the neighborhood where Diana Corgan lived.

After an hour's travel, he finally inched his way into the French Quarter, pulling up to a massive house that looked like it had been split up into several apartments. Seth recalled Diana's apartment number from her driver's license, then left his car sitting in the street, trusting the carnival to flow around it.

He slipped through the deafening crowd, dodging well-wishers, drunken revelers, and endless offers to join the merriment, and headed up the stairs to the entrance. Once inside, the noise abated somewhat, but the pulsating throb of the celebration followed him up the stairwell to Diana Corgan's third-floor apartment.

When he reached the landing, the first thing he noticed was the open door with a faded number 2 on it. He tried to listen to see if anyone was inside, but couldn't make out anything. The noise from the street below swallowed any sounds from the apartment.

Seth edged over to the wall next to the doorway, looking through it at the part of the room he could see. What appeared to be a living room was decorated in thrift-shop modern, with an easy chair, coffee table, and part of a couch that had all seen better days visible in the room. Through an archway on the far side, Seth saw a small room that looked to be part of the kitchen. A door beside it was closed.

Seth reached out and pushed the door open all the way, listening to it thud into the wall. He stepped inside, scanning the rest of the living room. Finding nothing, he headed for the closed door. As he approached, he noted another familiar smell in the air, along with two distinct perfumes, one of which he had smelled before. He listened at the door, then, hearing nothing, pushed the door open.

The scene that greeted him could have been a twin of the one in the church, only this time the body was lying on a bed. This one was a young woman with short brown hair and a gaping red hole where her chest used to be. *It's not Diana,* Seth thought in relief. Looking around, he found no signs of a struggle. *Of course that doesn't mean anything,* he thought. *Perhaps she was taken by surprise. But where's Diana?*

The answer to that question was nowhere in the rest of the apartment. The familiar perfume smell was stronger in the living room, but when Seth tried tracing it, he lost the scent in the hallway. He went back to the apartment, looked around one final time, then pulled out his digital phone and dialed Dominique's number.

"Yes," her cool voice answered.

"They've already been here," Seth said. "Her roommate's dead, and Diana's nowhere to be found."

"If they already have her, then I know where to find them. Meet us at the cemetery you found her at last night."

"Of course, they'll try to complete the ceremony. Why do they still need her?"

"Because you let the ceremony go on for as long as you did, now it can only be completed with her as the vessel," Dominique said. "A mistake we won't let happen again."

"You've got that right," Seth said, ignoring the dig. "I'll see you there."

DURING HIS DRIVE TO the cemetery, Seth thought about what had happened the previous night. *I suppose what she said might be true. I don't know as much about magic as Dominique does. But whatever they were up to, it can't be any good. Assuming they could have actually pulled their little ritual off in the first place.*

By the time Seth pulled up to the cemetery, it was just before midnight. The cultists' van was still parked where it had been the night before. The cemetery, a place where Seth had confidently walked last night, was now layered in a thick gray fog that obscured the dozens of mausoleums dotting the landscape. Strangely, the murky vapor only extended to the stone wall of the cemetery and did not spill onto the road.

As Seth got out of his car, he felt a peculiar energy in the fog, a palpable power radiating from the unusual mist in the graveyard. As he approached, the fog seemed to solidify before him, completely blocking any view of the building beyond it. Seth shook his head, stepped forward, and vaulted the fence.

The fog engulfed him. Seth had no idea where he was in relation to anything around him. A quick glance behind him confirmed that he could no longer see the road or his car. Seth took a step forward, then another. The fog coalesced on his clothes and face, soaking him with cold droplets of water. Seth kept walking forward, waiting for something to happen.

When the fog moved, it almost took him by surprise. Gray tendrils of water vapor pushed against his face, pouring into him through his nose and mouth. Seth didn't struggle or fight, he just stood there, feeling the now condensed water streaming into his lungs. After a few minutes, the liquid filled his body completely.

Seth went limp, and the fog lowered him gently to the grass. It then began to dissipate, breaking up and vanishing into the night as if it never existed. Seth lay motionless and watched until every trace of the unnatural vapor had disappeared, then rolled to his hands and knees and began expelling the water from his body. *Once again, being a vampire does have its advantages, such as not having to breathe,* Seth thought as he spat the water out.

When he was done, he looked up and spotted the mausoleum he had been at the night before. His heightened senses picked up the low sound of voices across the graveyard, and he headed toward it.

He hadn't gone more than a few yards when he saw the familiar shape of the marble building looming in the night before him. The voices were louder now, and Seth could see shadows and flickering light in the entryway to the mausoleum. Seth crept to the door and looked inside.

Once again, the players from last night had resumed their familiar roles. Diana Corgan, her eyes wild and staring, lay bound once again on the stone table. Above her, dagger in one hand, cross in another, was the cult leader from the previous evening. His face was now an ashen gray, and he moved stiffly, like a puppet whose controller hadn't mastered the strings yet. *He was dead, I know he was, and I didn't turn him into a vampire,* Seth thought. *And anyway, why is he here, but the rest of the bodies aren't?*

However, an even bigger surprise was seeing Dominique and her two looming bodyguards standing next to the cult leader, watching him prepare for the ritual.

I might have known, Seth thought, gauging the distance from himself to Dominique. The torchlight cast flickering shadows that would easily hide his approach. Glancing over at the small group clustered around the stone altar one last time, Seth slipped noiselessly into the tomb.

He flitted from the door to behind one of the bodyguards in the space of a single heartbeat. Grabbing the taller man's head, Seth twisted it with all his strength, breaking the man's neck in a single movement. As the bodyguard started to collapse, Seth moved to the second man and crushed his throat with a single swift blow. By the time the first man had hit the floor, Seth had grabbed Dominique by the neck and prepared to end her life as well. At least, that's what he tried to do.

As he laid his clawed fingers on her skin, his hand felt like it had grabbed the sun. Snarling in pain, he pulled his arm back, recoiling from the shock of the burn. He steeled himself to try to seize her again, but before he could, he felt a cold hand encircle his neck in a vise-like grip and lift him off the ground. Seth tore at the imprisoning fingers, trying to free himself, but they might as well have been forged of solid, unyielding steel. In answer to his efforts, the hand simply increased its grip, cracking Seth's neck vertebrae. Suddenly his body went limp, unable to move, only this time he wasn't faking it. His head remained upright, held there by the implacable hand clutching his neck.

"So glad you could join us, Seth." Dominique's icy voice held a note of triumph. "I took the precaution of upgrading my bodyguards and my personal *gris* to something that could handle you should you actually appear here. It's too bad about Ramon, but I have no doubt he'll still serve me, even better than before.

"I'm very pleased the fog didn't kill you. It only confirmed my suspicions of what you really are."

Seth's mouth opened but no sound came out. Dominique noticed and spoke to the thing holding him. "Ramon, loosen your hold on his neck so he may speak."

Behind her, the cultist continued his chant, speaking, and then answering himself in a language long dead:

"Ia! Ia! Ia! Fthaghn fealth nostro carneilgn dosum
Y'targh vorbelg hah'thelth nutarngh esqis
Sothoth-Yog cyrnlea sulnabis queth'nas pax
Apsoh noxtra pacuon daggheth yan'noth es risciven!"

Seth tried his throat once again and found it in working order. "Surely you don't believe in all this crap."

Dominique smiled. "Of course, and soon you will, too. Just before my resurrected servant there completes his sacrifice, this time without interruption, I will step in and summon one of the elder gods to this plane. I have you to thank for making this all possible."

Seth thought frantically, trying to buy time until he could figure out a way to get free. "Why? Why here and now?"

"Mardi Gras is the largest, longest nonsecular celebration on the continent. Do you know how much spiritual energy is being given off in this city? The celebration, the revelry, the fucking, the fighting. All of that, a psychic explosion on the megaton scale, if you will, that before was just going to waste, but now, channeled through our young victim here, it will be used to power the opening of the gate across the dimensional universe, where Nyarlhotep will feel the vortex opening and come to me."

Dominique held up the Cross of Coronado, its gems winking in the torchlight. "How fitting that an artifact of my brother's pitiful religion provided the final key to unlocking the gate to the Old One's power. Two thousand years ago, a god supposedly walked this earth. Tonight, on this anniversary of his arrival, a new supreme being will come forth to supplant him."

Great, New Orleans rings in the millennium by unwittingly summoning the ultimate party crasher, Seth thought. "But if you already had the girl, why go to the trouble of luring me here?" he asked.

"We didn't have the body, the other group of cultists did," Dominique said. "I had investigated this scene today at my brother's request, where I noticed that the pentagram had been partially erased, which meant that some of Nyarlhotep's power had escaped and reanimated whatever inert matter it found, such as the cult's high priest. I knew that it would want the ceremony completed, and that the zombie would eventually come back here. As for you, your body, once properly prepared, will make a most suitable vessel for the avatar of Nyarlhotep to reign upon this world." Dominique's eyes shone with the fever of the insane. "I would love to tell you more, but my time is almost at hand. Bring him inside the circle at my command," she told her mindless zombie.

By now the marble tomb throbbed with otherworldly energy. Dominique removed her robe, revealing her brown skin covered only by a loincloth. Unholy ritual markings covered her breasts, arms, and stomach. "Prepare the sacrifice," she told the high priest.

The gray-skinned cultist had thrown back his hood, revealing dull watery eyes and a thin line of yellow drool hanging from a corner of his mouth. He used the dagger to slit Diana's blouse open, then carved an upside-down cross on her chest, the blood welling out to form the holy symbol in crimson. The priest quickly backed out of the summoning circle and stood next to Dominique.

Immediately the air above the bound woman seemed to solidify, thickening and coalescing into a swirling cloud of noxious smell and impenetrable solid blackness. In the middle of this cloud was a bright blue pinpoint of light that began to grow larger.

As soon as she saw it, Dominique took the dagger from the cultist's hand and, shouldering him aside, held it ready. The cultist staggered away from the stone slab and stood listlessly, staring at nothing.

The point of light was now basketball-sized, and a cold wind was rising inside the mausoleum, causing the torches to flicker, their light insignificant next to the unearthly illumination in the center of the room. Seth felt that same strange presence he had noticed when he had held the dagger the night before, only this time it was much stronger.

His spinal cord had regenerated, but Seth didn't know how that was going to help him. Dominique's damned zombie was holding him by the back of his neck, making it impossible to get the leverage to do any significant damage. *Besides, I couldn't even pry open his hand, even with my strength. What good would a punch do?*

Dominique began the final stage of the summoning chant. *"Ia! Ia! Ia-ka! Nyarlhotep nyarlop kaz'yeth vezuan ftheagh ust'yre!"*

The pinpoint of light suddenly expanded, throwing out bright blue beams that anchored themselves to twelve equidistant points around the stone slab. The wind was howling now, an eldritch scream that nearly drove all coherent thought from Seth's mind. He watched in wonder as the blue light became a pulsing, crackling ball that hovered in the air over the altar and the now mercifully unconscious Diana Corgan.

Seth watched in horror, the first time he had experienced that emotion in decades, as a huge, obscenely twisted shadow fell over the blue light. Writhing, slime covered tentacles slowly pushed out of the blue rift that had been torn between this world and some other unspeakably grotesque dimension, tentatively exploring the new realm they suddenly found access to. Seth knew that whatever those tentacles was connected to was about to poke its head, or whatever passed for it, through the portal.

If I don't do something right now, I'm going to see the rest of this thing, and that will be all she wrote for me, N'awlins, everything, he thought. Summoning up all of his remaining mental faculties, he directed them at the zombie holding him with all his strength. Usually he preferred to talk to whomever he was trying to control, but in dire emergencies he could expend the majority of his power in a single mental command that would almost automatically be obeyed.

But not this time. When Seth tried to enter the zombie's mind, he felt a solid wall of mental shielding protecting the creature. *Dominique's defenses. Now we're in serious trouble.*

The tentacles gripped the edges of the glowing blue portal and started pushing on it, enlarging it so the rest of its unearthly body could begin coming through. A gout of foul-smelling ichor spurted from the portal to land, smoking and hissing, on the stone floor of the mausoleum. The hideously distended head of whatever nightmarish monstrosity Dominique had conjured up was about to emerge from its extradimensional womb on the other side of the universe.

One more chance, Seth thought. With all of his remaining strength, he sought to control the cultist who was standing, slack-jawed, beside Dominique. With an effort, he pushed his way into the man's mind, finding it an empty shell. Seth could feel the immense power of the entity that had given the man his unnatural life screech in outrage as he gained control. *I hope this works,* he thought, as he gave the man one command with all of his strength.

Just as Dominique turned to command the zombie to bring Seth to her, the cultist jerked, then lurched forward and pushed her as hard as he could. Dominique staggered forward, through the protective circle, and squarely into the blue portal that had now grown to envelop the entire stone altar. Her agonized scream as the blue beams lanced through her knifed into Seth's ears like a scalpel sliding through his brain. The blue light immediately started to recede, and the tentacles, sensing something had gone wrong, jerked back inside, the last two wrapping around Dominique and lifting her, still screaming, through the blue portal with them. The blue light shrank to a pinpoint again, then vanished.

At once, everything was still and quiet again. Seth fell to the floor, twisting and rolling to come up on his feet and face whatever it was that had held him.

Collapsed in a boneless heap was the bodyguard whose neck he had broken, his hand still outstretched in a pincer grip. Seth looked around to see the other bodyguard and the cultist, both dead as well. Of Dominique, Diana Corgan, or the thing from beyond this world, there was no sign.

Seth got up after a minute, feeling his neck vertebrae stretch and pop as they finished regenerating themselves. He walked over to the cultist, took the golden cross out of his hand, and held it for a moment, shaking his head.

"You've been bought dearly tonight," he said, wrapping the cross's chain around his hand. He slowly walked around the summoning circle, looking for the sacrificial dagger, but could find no trace of it.

"I hope it's with Dominique in whatever hell she finds herself in," he said. Leaving the mausoleum, Seth ran back to his car, got a container of gasoline, and liberally soaked the three remaining bodies. A lighter found in one of the bodyguard's pockets set them all ablaze. He would call it in to the police later. Much later.

As Seth walked to his car, he stopped for a moment, fancying he could hear the party still going on in New Orleans. He looked over at the bright lights of the distant city and thought again of the thousands of innocent people there, living their lives, unaware of what they had, and how easily it could be taken from them.

They'll never know how close it all came to ending tonight. No one deserves to know that, he thought. *But I will. Tonight, and forever.*

How I envy you, Father Giancarlo.

I already wish I could forget.

Songs of Leaving

Peter Crowther

And I saw the dead, great and small alike . . .
Revelation 20:12

T he final ships go up reaching for the stars in the closing days of what is to be the last winter of the world.

They ride interlocking plumes of power and steam like anxious fingers of smoky fire, colored sunset orange, and cornfield yellow in the still afternoon. And each of them belches out a tumultuous roar, a hymn of steam and gasoline, a cadence of harmony and discordance, a syncopated symphony of regret and anticipation.

A song of leaving.

They have already left from Islamabad and Jerusalem, these ships—or ships like them . . . like them in intent if not in appearance—and from the arid wastes outside of Beijing and the heat-shimmering flats of Florida; from the snow-covered tundra throughout Siberia and the scorched plains of Kenya. From a thousand thousand places, the ships have lifted into the sky in these tired days, with the distant horizon darkened not only by their sheer number but also by the approaching asteroid.

The towering silver points of the final ships rise to hit the clouds and then puncture them, pulling them down and around their midriffs, bellies bulging with the almost-last people of Earth, their pinpoint faces turned to the grimy windows, acceleration pulling at muscle, sinew, and flesh as they watch the cities and the meadows fall behind, and the endless gray ribbons of highway and the veiny drifts of water drop down and down until they are at first partially obscured by the clouds and then completely obliterated by swirling whiteness.

On the ground, silent faces—some alone, some huddled in groups—also watch as the last ships dwindle in the azure blue, growing smaller until they are no longer ships but merely glittering shadows, and then distant needles and then, at last, merely the tiniest specks in an otherwise clear sky.

And then they are gone.

Ahead of the ships lie the domed cities of the Moon and Mars. Beyond those, a series of space-borne stations littering the heavens, some finished and some still under preparation. A colossal paper chase of metal and plastic, stepping stones of rivet and cable, leading humanity's survivors across the airless void and on toward untold adventures and undreamed-of destinies. The ships will touch down and their passengers and crews will consolidate and plan their next steps, always looking with one eye to the darkness before them and the other to the ghost of the doomed planet they have left behind. Only some of them will survive the journey. But that's something they do not think about.

Back on Earth the silence rushes in to remove the memory of the ships' engines, runs along the worn-down pathways of a million forests and the dusty streets of a million towns, replacing

their throaty roar with the sound of the wind through the trees
and the creak of swinging store signs.

THE ASTEROID WAS FIRST noticed by amateur astronomer Julio
Shennanen through the $199.95 telescope bought as a thirtieth-
birthday present by his brother Manuel from the *Keep Watching
the Skies* store on Bleecker Street and erected in Julio's back yard
in the Brooklyn suburb of Park Slope.

Julio, who was a native of New Orleans, had moved north
when his wife Carmen had gotten herself a job as a child-minder
for a wealthy couple in a penthouse apartment overlooking Central Park. Initially referred to as "Shennanen's Folly" by a skepti-
cal skygazing fraternity, the object reported as a shadow over
Alpha Centauri turned out to be a whole lot more substantial
and a whole lot nearer when it could be viewed by something
costing a little more than a week's grocery bill. It turned out to
be a whole lot more menacing, too.

At the request of its discoverer, the object was renamed
"Fat Tuesday," ostensibly because that was the day on which it
was first spotted (and because, at roughly the size of the entire
Eastern seaboard, it was big). But the underlying reason was an
acknowledgment of Julio's hometown—inasmuch as "Fat Tuesday" was a literal translation of "Mardi Gras," the name now
regarded as the entire celebration but originally intended as
referring only to the final day . . . a day of feasting. It was
also—and perhaps more significantly—a recognition on Shennanen's part, even in those early days of the object's arrival in
our planetary skies, that the Carnival's days were numbered . . .
the Carnival being Earth and all who lived upon it. A kind of
"lucky" cosmic coming-together of events for would-be word-
smiths with nothing better to do with their long New York
evenings than stargaze.

But there was nothing "lucky" about the appearance of
Fat Tuesday, particularly where Julio Shennanen was concerned. By that time, the writing was on the wall for the world,
and there were some in the world who held Shennanen

responsible—sad and bitter folks who had spent a lifetime blaming others for anything that happened to them. And so it was that, on the evening of the anniversary of his discovery, the computer programming sky watcher was shot and killed outside his home, with Carmen looking on from the bedroom window. When Julio's screaming wife ran out to help him, she got a bullet in her back for her trouble.

In a letter of pasted newspaper copy sent to the *New York Times,* the assassin said that he (or she—nobody ever found out) was committed to ridding the world of this blight on humanity (Shennanen) and, in so doing, remove the threat of Fat Tuesday. (Though quite how those two items could be connected was beyond all but those who sent fifty-dollar bills to P.O. Box addresses posted up on TV screens at the end of an afternoon session of down-home "back to basics" sermonizing on cable.)

The assassin was never caught—at least, not by the authorities—and the threat to others in the scientific community remained. Despite the fact that the media and pretty much everyone she spoke to or heard from condemned the action with vigor, a now wheelchair-bound Carmen Shennanen left the excesses of New York State and returned to the Big Easy, where she disappeared into an anonymity worthy of the FBI informant protection program and one that even Julio's brother Manuel could not pierce.

MEANWHILE, FAT TUESDAY BLUNDERS on.

According to one pundit, the asteroid is on course to "kiss" the Earth in the early afternoon of February 8, 2007, just seventeen months after its first sighting. "The particularly bad news is that this is going to be no platonic peck on the cheek," NASA's resident expert in "heavenly affairs," professor Jerry Mizzalier, goes on to tell Oprah Winfrey in a show interview whose transmission is debated for a full week before eventual release to a waiting and increasingly despondent world. "It'll be the full enchilada," Mizzalier continues, "a big smackeroo on the lips and the tongue right down the throat."

"And then?" Oprah asks in an uncharacteristically trembling voice.

Mizzalier's shrugged response says it all: The kiss is just the foreplay. After that, mankind gets fucked. Big Time.

WHEN YOU PUT YOUR mind to it, you can do a lot in nine months.

Throughout 2006 and into the January of Earth's final year, all potential solutions were considered while, at the same time, work continued feverishly on the construction of spaceships that would, if all else failed, carry the seed of humanity—and as many of its fellow planetary inhabitants as could be realistically mustered in so short a time—to the stars.

The alternatives were running out fast. Nuclear missiles failed to have any effect. "It's kind of like trying to blow up an elephant with a .45," Jerry Mizzalier explained colorfully to Dan Rather. "You may get lucky and dislodge a nickel-sized chunk of meat, but that's about all." That was Mizzalier's last TV appearance. Two days later, he told the *Washington Post* he was going down to the Keys to make his peace with God—"And maybe do a little fishing on the side."

Four attempts at landing a hand-picked crew of demolition experts *a la* the *Armageddon* and *Deep Impact* movies of the late 1990s got no nearer to Fat Tuesday than a few hundred miles. It seemed that either real-life Bruce Willises and Robert Duvalls were somewhat thinner on the ground than their celluloid counterparts . . . or moviemakers and screenwriters had simply got it wrong (hard as that was for many to accept).

Perhaps not quite so colorful as Jerry Mizzalier but no less succinct was the nonagenarian British astronomer Patrick Moore's verdict on BBC television's *Newsnight*. "One should liken it to a game of snooker," the monocled scientist explained to Jeremy Paxman, with a characteristic pinwheeling flourish of his arms, "with Earth sitting defenseless in the middle of the table, right in the path of the white ball."

On the other side of the Atlantic a couple of days later, Colorado physicist W. Martin Parmenter picked up the analogy on a special edition of *The Jerry Springer Show* when, along with other luminaries of the scientific establishment, he was invited to hypothesize the outcome of "the Big Kiss." "I don't know diddly about snooker," Parmenter said laconically, "but if we switch to the game I play, then we're the eight ball on a table in a pool hall in Denver . . . and we're about to get hit full on with enough force to drop us—or what's left of us—in the corner pocket on a table in a cellar barroom in Mexico City."

The disappearance of Springer from the airwaves following the show was openly considered by many to be the single silver lining in the approaching dark cloud that was Fat Tuesday . . . that and the appearance of an advertising board carried by a barefoot man down the full length of Broadway, his handiwork proclaiming, in hand-scrawled letters that were a mix of caps and lower case, "It's official—Fat Tuesday is a load of balls."

By the time of Earth's last autumn, with the browning leaves bidding a fond and final farewell, all continuing attempts to avert the inevitable catastrophe were cosmetic at best. The real energy was now being channeled worldwide into the construction of spaceships, huge gleaming monoliths that grew quickly on hastily prepared launchpads around the globe. That not all of these vehicles would survive the trip was accepted, as was the inescapable fact that, statistically speaking—particularly considering the haste and the resulting corner-cutting of their translation from blueprint to steel and wire and circuit board—many of the ships would not even make it off the ground. But it was a risk that an escape-mad humanity receiving its quota of "lottery" tickets ("Life's a lottery," ran the impassioned ad campaign, "so make sure of your tickets today.") was more than prepared to take.

WHEN THE LAST SHIP to successfully depart the green hills of Earth lifts to relative safety above the planet's atmosphere on February 4, 2007—a Tuesday, appropriately enough—the tally of successes against failures (for anyone remaining on Earth who might be interested) is an impressive 3.718 to one.

And then they are gone.

Small ships, sleek pointy-nosed, sliver-shaped missiles bearing ten- or twelve-strong crews snuggled amongst carefully secured boxes of artifacts and flags and religious ornamentation, and huge-bellied blunderbusses carrying cryogenically frozen embryos of the Earth's animal and insect populations and thin trays of seeds containing all manner of florae and fauna . . . all have disappeared over the months and weeks and days, up into the sky and far away. Now all that are left are the unlucky ones, the ones whose lottery tickets haven't paid off.

There are billions of them in mountains and valleys and towns and cities, all the distant off-the-beaten-track communities from China to Scotland, from the wine-growing regions of France to the sidewalk cafes of Vienna, all of them paradoxically breathing a sigh of relief as the last gleaming means of escape passes behind the clouds—in much the same way as the terminally ill patient relaxes when all the fit-and-well visitors depart the hospital and leave the slowly dying to get on with the job in peace and quiet. "Misery loves company" is the way it's often described.

But the truth of the matter is that, in these final hours, there is little sign of misery.

Movies and literature which, in the last half of the previous century, foretold of anarchy and chaos in the face of humanity's end, couldn't have got it more wrong. With the last spaceship now a memory of chances missed and debts now to be paid, a strange calm falls across the cities and towns and villages of Earth.

What little looting there has been has been dealt with swiftly and without mercy. A do-it-yourself system of law and order has grown throughout the winter months, bringing with it an acceptable face of vigilantism in which people are openly but unemotionally intolerant of any among their number who fail to live up to the dignity now expected of the last remnants of the species.

Because, after all, what use is a new video recorder? Or precious jewelry? And anyway, most storekeepers simply leave their stores open and go home. So stuff is there for the taking, but most people leave it be: gleaming Chevys and Cadillacs sitting in unmanned showrooms; the very latest fashions from Gucci and Versace adorning silent mannequins in the windows of stores, whose doors lie carelessly and casually ajar; and rare first issues—in mint condition, no less—of silver- and golden-age DC comic-books, their impossibly costumed super heroes staring off the covers regretting that there's nothing even Krypton's first son can do to avert the disaster spiraling closer with every passing minute.

Everywhere is quiet.

People stay home, make love gently, and talk feverishly, trying to pack all the thoughts and hopes and love they thought they had left into the few hours that remain. Sons and daughters return home like it's Thanksgiving or Christmas. In between their conversations, minds idly drift to thoughts of what it will be like when the end finally comes: wondering what it will be like, sitting in a fifteen-story apartment building and seeing a wave of water thundering toward the window blotting out the blood-red sky . . . wondering what it will feel like to have your midwestern home blown up from around you while you crouch with your family behind the sofa or, if you have one, in the cellar listening to the sound of Earth breaking up. Consequently, most folks don't leave potential talk- or love-making-time empty.

The last ship has gone.

Fat Tuesday's kiss is now accurately scheduled for 2:17 P.M. on Saturday.

On Wednesday, the Earth gives up its dead.

"HEY."

THE BOY TURNS around and looks at the man standing out on the street by the white picket-fence gate. "Hey yourself," he says, shielding his eyes against the sun's glare. It's almost mid-day and the California heat is stifling but, even so, the street is busy with people.

The boy's name is William Freeman—his friends call him Billy; his parents, Will. He is twelve years old and suddenly acutely aware that, as far as he had been concerned, the street had been pretty much deserted the last time he looked. And that was only a few minutes earlier.

"You must be Will," the man says, beaming a big smile and resting a liver-spotted hand on the gatepost as he looks William up and down.

William nods. The man must be a friend of his mom and dad, someone who's maybe been out of town for a while and has come back to more familiar surroundings for when the asteroid hits. Right now, though, William is more concerned with a tall thin man standing across the street with his back to them. This new man's hands are resting on his hips and he's shaking his head staring up at Mr. and Mrs. Manders's place, seeming to take a lot of interest in the new glass conservatory Mr. Manders tacked on a couple of summers back.

"Don't you want to know who I am?" the old man at William's gate asks in a voice bearing more than a hint of amusement.

When William turns back to the man, he can see the distant shape of Fat Tuesday over to the east, hanging on the horizon like a party lantern. "Who are you?" he asks, wondering if it was his imagination or does the man suddenly seem a mite familiar.

The screen door squeaks open behind him, whines shut, and clatters twice. William turns and sees his mother walking across the lawn, picking her steps real careful, like she was walking on thin ice. Her left hand is up to her mouth, her right holding a hank of hair at the side of her head. She's staring—with a mixture of frown and wide-eyed amazement—not at William but over his shoulder. William looks back at the old man.

"Hello, Pooch," the man says.

"Daddy?"

GEORGE CHINNERY WAS THE first to make contact. It had to be *some*body and, as luck would have it, it was George.

George slipped away to new adventures in the spring of 1998, leaving behind him a breathless cardiac arrest team, a callous flat green line on a bedside monitor, and a weeping daughter. William had been almost four years old but still young enough to forget quickly.

Forget and accept . . . or maybe the two were the same thing.

But while George was the first, over in the quiet suburb of Hawthorne, an area in the sprawling Californian conurbation that was famous for producing one of the last century's most enduring musical acts, the others quickly followed.

HILLARY AND SAM ARNOLD sit on the bed in their son's room.

Around them are strewn the collected ephemera that is all that remains of little Joseph Arnold: comic books, a *Millennium Falcon* toy spaceship—that looks nothing like the huge ships that have so recently left Hillary and Sam and the rest of the Earth far behind them—and a few favorite pieces of clothing that Hillary just hasn't had the heart to throw out when the tumor took their little boy away.

There are no tears. The tears dried up years ago. Now there is only a grim and quiet resignation that sometimes fades right into the background . . . only to return when they least expect it, usually in the mornings when, on waking, the imminence of Fat Tuesday—or even its very existence—seems for just a fraction of a second to be the remnants of a very bad dream. Only it isn't a dream at all.

"You want me to get some pills or something?" Sam Arnold asks his wife in a voice that is just above a whisper. He runs his hand down her back.

She shakes her head and folds the sleeves of little Joseph's sweater, laying the garment gently on her son's pillow.

"Jack Mason says old man Phillips—you know? down on Times Square?—he's giving them away to any that wants them. Wouldn't take me—"

"I couldn't bring myself to do that," Hillary tells her husband, turning to look at his face, seeing the darkness beneath his eyes. She recognizes that darkness: It isn't fear. It's the helplessness he feels at being unable to do anything for those he cares about. Since the death of Joseph and their decision not to try replace him, that "those" is just her.

He runs his hand up to her neck and gently kneads the skin between her hairline and the collar of her housedress. "It wouldn't hurt," he says. "Jack says old man Phillips said—"

"How do they know?" Hillary says in a tired voice. "And, anyway, it's not the hurt I'm bothered about."

"Then what is it?"

She shrugs and looks up at the window, imagining the cold skeletal trees of Central Park just a couple of blocks away. "No idea." She moves closer to him on the bed and wraps her arms around him, smelling his musk of fading cologne and skin mingled with cigarette smoke. "I had the dream again last night," she whispers.

"Little Joe?"

Hillary nods. "He said he was coming for us."

Sam pushes her back gently, holding her at arms' length. "Is *that* why you don't want me to get the pills?"

Hillary's eyes search her husband's face for some indication of an answer to his question. "I don't know," she says at last. "Maybe."

"Oh, honey," he says, "I wish it could—"

The knock on the apartment door sounds like a rifle crack in the stillness of the New York afternoon. And yet, for all that, it is a small knock . . . a delicate knock. And outside the window there seems to be some kind of commotion and lots of shouting . . . like a parade, maybe.

THE NEWS TRAVELED FAST, spreading like wildfire fueled by the wind of the approaching asteroid. Dead people were coming back to life . . . kind of.

It sounded comic-book-crazy, but it was true.

Telephones the world over buzzed and hummed with the news: sons and fathers, daughters and mothers, uncles and aunts and sisters and brothers . . . they were all coming back, sauntering down paths and knocking on doors, drifting into backyards and onto porches, peering through once-familiar kitchen windows, and smiling never-forgotten smiles.

At first, the people who heard the news thought it might be some by-product of the asteroid . . . like something dreamed up by George Romero and Stephen King, a plague of flesh-eating cadavers shambling the highways and byways of the doomed world in a final devastating flourish of death and destruction. But then their own doorbells and buzzers sounded or their own windows rattled with a distantly familiar tapping, or mailboxes clattered open to allow long-ago special calls in long-ago special voices that had lived on only in dreams and wishful memories. Sure, it just had to be something to do with Fat Tuesday, but the animated corpses seemed to possess not only no malice, evil intentions, or appetite for human skin and cartilage but also no idea of how they had gotten there.

They came in droves, huge processions of men, women, and children, some young and some old, some no more than babes in arms carried by another of their number, and all of them marveling at the things they passed by, each of them making their way to a familiar place and to familiar faces.

They came into towns and cities, along arterial blacktops empty of cars and trucks, and along the narrow roads that are the blue veins connecting communities. And a few came by other means . . .

THE MISSISSIPPI RIVER IS almost twenty-five hundred miles long, drifting and winding from a stream you could step across in northern Minnesota and washing miles wide through the country's heartland and down into the Gulf of Mexico.

If you counted the Missouri—which feeds into the Mississippi from the Rockies just north of Saint Louis—and the Ohio, which gets in on the act around Cairo, Illinois, and the Red, the Arkansas, the Tensas, and the Yazoo . . . you'd be talking about getting on for four thousand miles of river system. Only the Nile and the Amazon are longer.

The Mississippi and its tributaries drain almost one and a quarter million miles, including all or part of thirty-one states and some thirteen thousand square miles of Canada. Through Prairie du Chien in Wisconsin it drifts, where French fur traders exchanged goods and services with the Winnebego; down through Cave-In-Rock, Illinois, and into Vicksburg, with its vast Civil War battlefield where, on a still night, you might just hear the cries of Southerners still withstanding General's Grant's forty-seven-day siege; and on down to Hannibal, boyhood home of Sam Clemens, who took the *nom de plume* of the riverboat captains' calls for measuring the water's depth— "Mark Twain!"

So many places along that drift of water, so many swirls and eddies, you could imagine many things getting out into that watery flow to sail along.

So maybe you could imagine this: a huge, gaudily painted floating palace pulled from the secret depths of the river somewhere where nobody has ever been, a pair of enormous paddle wheels rucking up the frothy water, its saloons decked out in gilt and scarlet and velvet, bright white paneling and the sound of banjo-picking . . . sailing slowly, drifting between the West Bank and Algiers, drifting under the Huey P. Long Bridge upriver near Harahan, and then settling, just a stone's throw from the Moonwalk promenade of the French Quarter where, on an evening in the dog days of the world, a saxophone's lilting refrain merged into the sound of accordions and the smell of tobacco and the whoops and cries of people making the most of their unearned death sentence.

And as the riverboat nears the side, it sounds its horn, a mournful but somehow strangely exultant wail that breaks through the sounds of sometimes reluctant and sometimes forced revelry, causing it to stop, not all at once but itself like a wave, a wave of silence washing through the port of New Orleans where Mardi Gras is in full swing, a true "farewell to the flesh." And there they are, hanging from the sides of the riverboat in all manner of clothing, old and young alike, hanging onto railings and wainscoting, leaning against funnel and gate, waving for all their worth to folks in the crowds that soon gather around the moorings.

At the front of the throng of hand-holding, beer-drinking revelers sits a woman in a wheelchair, frowning in a mixture of disbelief and an excitement she thought she would never feel again. For now, in this magical short final era of the history of Earthbound humanity, a new ability holds sway . . . an ability known only to children, the mythical race that knows the power of the darkness and the light alike, that knows the real power of acceptance without reason.

"The dead are here!"

The cry moves through the crowds like the wind itself, touching every one of them as they recognize faces on the riverboat, return smiles and waves, anxiously waiting for the boat to dock so that they may all be reunited.

Then, "There's another one!" someone calls.

And there, up the river, is another boat just like the first one, paddle wheels thrashing the surf of the old Mississippi, churning it up like watery thunder. And behind that one, itself bedecked with a hundred or a thousand waving bodies, comes another, letting out its steamboat whistle cry . . . only this one doesn't sound mournful at all: this one sounds like the biggest cheer that ever was . . . until the boat behind it, just coming around the bend now, pulls fully into view and lets rip. Now *that's* the *biggest* cheer that ever was . . . at least for a minute or two, a deep-throated calliope wheeze that sets folks to holding their ears and laughing and crying all at the same time.

They hear the clarion call out in the plantations surrounding New Orleans, plantations with names such as Rosedown and Destrehan, where the *garconnieres* are already filling with old familiar faces . . . work-clothed men in overalls wading through the cotton plants or the rice, indigo, hemp, tobacco, sorghum, corn, peanuts, potatoes, and sugar, beaming grins big enough to crack the whole face wide open, or appearing from around majestic live oaks bedecked in Spanish moss and from behind centuries-old camellias and azaleas, the watery sunshine dappling them like fireflies.

As the ships reach the dock, one by one the people jump and drop and sometimes just walk right off. Their clothes are sometimes yesterday's fashions and sometimes straight out of the turn of the century, a mix of zoot suits and linen jackets, lettered sweaters, and gingham dresses, and all kinds of uniform—army, navy, air force . . . and many of them stylistically different, too. But all of them touch down on the riverside walkway beaming big smiles, their eyes scanning the crowds trying to pick out the faces they've come to see. And every time one of the waiters greets one of the visitors —be the newcomer old or young—their first word is often their name followed by a query.

"Poppa?"

"Sandy, is it really you?"

"Son? Welcome home . . . we're real proud of you."

And then come the questions . . . lots of questions. But the answer is always the same: "I don't know . . . I just don't know."

In the massing, thrusting, pushing throng of people, some searching and some who have already found each other, a wheelchair threads its way to the water's edge where the big paddleboat sits, its deckboards creaking and its funnel hissing softly. The woman in the chair searches the faces and the bodies, ignoring the good-natured jostling as she watches the arms outstretch, thinking each time that the arms are for her but then realizing that the clothes are wrong or the color of the skin is wrong or—

"Carmen. Over here!"

She feels emotion well up in her stomach, feels a tingle down her legs that she hasn't felt for what seems like a lifetime, and she feels the tell-tale tickle of a tear on her cheek. "Julio?"

Her eyes scan the knees and legs that surround her as she struggles to lift herself from the chair that has become her home, and amidst the mustaches and the sideburns, the long-tail coats and the swirling crinoline, she sees him.

And he sees her.

IT'S SATURDAY MORNING.

JUST another Saturday morning, to look at the folks strolling the streets of New Orleans. But if you sneaked and looked into the French Quarter—not that you'd need to sneak: you can hear the hullabaloo clear across town—you'd think that maybe the Saturday-night partying has started just a little sooner than usual. Either that, or the Friday-night session is going on past its usual cutoff time.

But then it isn't just another Saturday morning. In fact, it isn't just any morning at all: It's the last day of the world, and the songs of leaving it all behind fill the air like the scent of summer jasmine, thick and wistful.

The light is soft, like a late fall afternoon, with Fat Tuesday now sitting squarely between the sun and the ground, plummeting on to keep its scheduled appointment at 2:17 EST. Just a little over four hours from now.

All of the farewells have been said—most of them many times during the past three days. But there's been a lot of greetings, too.

Now the dead walk and sit alongside the living, chewing the fat, tapping a foot to the music that seems to wash around everything like the early morning mist that sometimes spills over from the river.

Over on Bourbon Street, Fats Domino and Mac Rebbenack are duetting on a couple of Steinway Grandes rolled out into the street from Jeff Dickerson's instrument store, while Alvin "Shine" Robinson powers up and down the fretboard on the Earl King favorite, "Let the Good Times Roll," while Robert Parker's sax wails and whines. The crowd cheers at every bum note that spills out—they've been cheering since well before dawn—as long as the constantly changing band has been playing (and drinking . . . so you can forgive the musicians a lot). Truth to tell, you can forgive anyone pretty much anything this morning.

In the audience, watching Fats and the good Doctor hammer the ivories, are Professor Longhair and Lloyd Price, Huey "Piano" Smith and Joe Tex, Ernie K. Doe, and Lee Dorsey. They'll all get a turn on the instruments and many of them already have. And if and when folks fancy a little oration between the music, former governor Huey Long is all set to bend their ears for one last time . . . though right now, just like everyone else, he seems content to whoop and laugh and slap his leg, spurred on by Democratic congressman John Breaux, the pair of them having given up trying to talk over the music.

The truth is, it's impossible to figure out who's dead and who's alive. Some of these folks you recognize straight off, and you wonder to yourself . . . wonder as you grab another bottle of beer from a passing waiter . . . you wonder just which is which. Not that it matters.

Sitting at one of the tables outside *Cafe du Monde,* at the corner of Decatur and Saint Ann, working their way through a plate of *beignets* and their third cup of *cafe au lait* while listening to Allen Toussaint play a little boogie-woogie on an old stand-up wooden piano, are Anne Rice, William Faulkner, Ellen Datlow, and British publisher John Jarrold (who, in all his years in the business, has never missed a convention in the Big Easy). Meanwhile, leaning against the front wall chatting to the driver of a horse-drawn cab, Jack Kerouac and Allen Ginsburg seem to be sharing a joke with Truman Capote and John Kennedy Toole . . . with Kerouac holding up a copy of Toole's Pulitzer Prize-winning *A Confederacy of Dunces* and shaking his head. Toole just shrugs and allows a slow trickle of water into his glass of absinthe, watching with satisfaction as the liquid turns a bright yellow.

On the riverfront round back of Cafe du Monde, hookers provide final—and occasionally first—sensuous experiences to men and boys on the steps and amidst the foliage, the sound of their anxious enjoyment permeating the already filled air.

A shoeshine boy stops Julio Shennanen—"A high five for the shine and just your thanks for the time," he says, holding his right hand in the air, fingers stretched out like twigs. "Gotta have clean shoes to meet your maker."

"I'm fine, but thanks," Julio says.

"How 'bout you, missie?" the man asks, a grin from ear to ear exposing bridgework gaps you could suck pickles through. "Polish up them wheels so fine you could make the sun put on his glasses."

Carmen laughs and claps her hands. "No, really," she tells him, reaching out to touch his arm. "We're both fine. Thanks."

The man shrugs and tells them to have a good day, and then he shakes his head and chuckles as he walks off. Alongside him, in the bushes next to a telescope overlooking the river, a tall, red-headed woman is sitting astride a young barefoot man. Carmen and Julio can see only the woman's back and the man's feet poking out from beneath her long skirts, and, just for a couple of seconds, they watch the woman moving slowly up and down and they listen to her voice, soothing and encouraging.

Carmen looks up at Julio and feels new strength from his smile.

"Wheel me over to the steps," she says, nodding to the gap in the railings overlooking the river. "Then you can get me out of this damned chair so's I can sit on land again."

Julio does as she asks.

The two of them sitting on the steps, Carmen looks up at the black hole that is Fat Tuesday. "You know," she says, closing one eye and squinting, "if you look at it just right, you can almost believe you could reach out your hand and feel it." She reaches up with her left arm to demonstrate, feeling around with her hand.

Without turning around to look at him, Carmen asks her husband, "How close do you think it is?"

"Close," comes the reply.

For a few seconds, Carmen doesn't say anything. Then, "You know," she says, "I think I'd like to go swimming."

There are already folks in the water, swimming slowly out in the middle of the river but she thinks that maybe Julio will say she shouldn't do that. Instead, he stands up and takes off his shirt and pants, dropping them into a neat pile beside her. Then he takes off his shorts.

Firecrackers light up the now dark sky and a chorus of cheers and trumpets sound above the already cacophonous din.

"You want me to help you?" he asks.

Carmen's mouth is wide open in a mixture of shock and excitement . . . the kind of excitement that comes only when you think you're doing something naughty. "Maybe with my pants and hose," she says, giggling as she unbuttons her blouse. "And then you can take me down to the water."

"Take you down to the water?" Julio says. "Heck, you can just fall in." And he gives her a push before diving in after her.

Carmen hits the Mississippi in momentary panic, sinking immediately beneath the surface, staring up through the swirling water at the dark shape that looms overhead. Then she sees another shape, the thin brown outline of her husband, cut into the water alongside her and she feels his arms wrap themselves around her and lift her gently to the surface.

She emerges spluttering and shakes her head. "You damned fool," she says, "I could have drowned."

For a second, neither of them does or says anything, they just float there, Julio paddling with his feet and keeping them straight with his left arm treading water. Then they both burst into hysterics.

"I wonder . . . I wonder what time it is," Carmen says as she allows her husband to turn her over onto her back and swim, pulling her with him.

There's a wind in the air now, a strong wind.

More fireworks light up the sky, turning the darkness into a daylight of sorts. The glow of the fireworks momentarily illuminates the surface of Fat Tuesday and she sees, suddenly, that it looks just like the ground out back of their house in Brooklyn. No more mysterious than that.

Somewhere over in the town, they can hear Dr. John playing "Such a Night."

"Who cares," Julio says, "we've got eternity . . . and we've got the river."

Carmen nods and squeezes Julio's hand. "Amen to that," she says.

"The great Mississippi, the majestic, the magnificent Mississippi, rolling its mile-wide tide along, shining in the sun."
Mark Twain, *Life on the Mississippi*

SKELETON KREWE

Nancy Holder

*C*arnivale.

Carnivorous.

The putting on of the flesh. The farewell to same.

At Mardi Gras in the French Quarter, the flesh was abundant. A cannibal would see paradise. Rolls of flesh; sunburned, tanned, pale, luminescent chalk. Moving flesh, at rest, drunk to unconsciousness. Laughing flesh.

Hidden flesh. Fabulous demons, sea sprites, chorus girls. Costumes, glittery and exotic. Mardi Gras: the revels of Fat Tuesday, uncontrolled feast before self-induced famine. Joy, and grief.

Few kept Lent anymore as it should be kept. For those who did, years of inbreeding had transformed it: Gone was the essence of sacrifice. In the twentieth century, it had become a positive, proactive act: giving up bad moods, tempers, unhealthy relationships.

On Canal Street, Saint Charles, the putting on of masks. The deep and real interior soul sought to devour, feared being devoured. Fat Tuesday, before it had to do with the pagan rituals of Christianity, had been the rite of sacrifice in its purest form: death. To keep the gods happy, you gave them your best, your brightest, your least expendable. The fiery bonfire. The cold ash.

In the twentieth century, it was hookers cruising, and pick-pockets stealing. It was women flashing their fleshy bodies and men screaming for more. Lust, suppressed rape.

On the first Mardi Gras of the millennium, magick no longer worked.

Jeanine knew a lot about magick. She had practiced it on herself. She had learned the essential truth: If you believed, you could make yourself breathe and walk and talk, even though you hovered between this world and the next. That was the message of the new century. That there was so little of you left that your heart shrank inside your chest, and yet it still beat.

Sunken eyes, sunken chest, sunken lung sacs: You could transform your own body into spiritual ether—transubstantiation in its purest form—and yet, live and move and have your being upon the earth.

The hospital authorities had released her because her insurance had run out. She knew it, even though they insisted that she was ready to "try it again."

Now, five-foot-five and not even one hundred pounds, she was faint with hunger and nauseous at the thought of food. She lurched down the streets of New Orleans in a transcendent miasma. She was here to gorge. She was here to revel in the putting on of flesh. For Lent, she would give up her brinkmanship. She would eat.

The parade was due to start in minutes. Crowds jammed and jangled the streets of the French Quarter. From the Cafe du Monde, tourists wolfed beignets by the handfuls. The air was sticky and sweet with moist powdered sugar. Men with round bellies guzzled beer from enormous paper cups. Three women with bleached hair, cigarettes planted like cue sticks between their fingers, swilled straight Scotch from a flat, square bottle. Their laughter was rich and diseased.

Shrimp on a stick; foot-long po' boy sandwiches. Hunks of garlic bread and oversized egg rolls. Enervated by the prospect of a spectacle, the oversized men and women around Jeanine gorged themselves. Their anticipation so distressed them that they tried to stuff it back down. She covered her mouth, revolted. The dry heaves, so familiar to her, rolled through her. Nothing came up, of course. Her body was pure and perfect; there was nothing to lose.

Painstakingly, with superior dedication, she had divested her spirit of all but the thinnest cloak of flesh. She was the closest thing to an angelic entity on the face of the earth. Or in New Orleans, at least. Sluggish and slow not because she was almost dead from starvation, but because the spirit is a gossamer thing. Flesh weighed it down; angel wings could not lift the revolting mass that was a human body.

Thanks to her inadequate hospital care, Jeanine understood that there might be an alternate point of view about her appearance. As she staggered down the street, people stared at her, then looked away. She was twenty-three, but a nurse had told her, frankly, that she looked like a forty-year-old heroin addict. Her hair had fallen out and was growing back very slowly. She had no breasts. Her arms were like sticks.

"Are you all right?" one of the whiskey-voiced women asked her suddenly. The woman touched Jeanine on the shoulder. Jeanine almost heard her bones shattering.

"I'm fine," Jeanine insisted. "I'm here to see the parade."

"Oh." The woman smiled. "It's really something, isn't it? I come to Mardi Gras every year. But this is special. A new century!"

"This is my first time," Jeanine told her. She was weary. She wanted to sit down. She wasn't used to speaking to anyone. The woman had a halter top on, and her stomach rolled over the waistband of her pants. Her breasts jiggled.

Jeanine felt sick.

"I saw a poster in the mall," Jeanine told her. "I'm from the Midwest. Missouri. I had to go somewhere . . ." She knew that didn't make sense to the woman, but it was what her therapist had told her to do. *Take a vacation. Clear out the cobwebs.*

Get some more insurance.

In the distance, a whisper of Dixieland jazz saved her. The woman was distracted; her eyes lit up.

"It's starting," she announced. She wheeled away from Jeanine. As she turned, her cigarette almost singed the hair on Jeanine's arm. If it had so much as touched her, it would have burnt a hole clear through. "It'll be great," she slurred.

Jeanine didn't want to watch the parade with the woman. It was the first of all the parades in the first Mardi Gras of the new century. It was a milestone. It was something no one who knew her had thought she would live to see.

The jazz volume increased, if slightly. Around her, everyone began to devour their food more quickly. For a moment, she wondered if food was not allowed during the parade. But that didn't make sense.

Then, as a wave of nausea overtook her, she had a vision of slitting their throats so they could cram the food in faster. But the full pleasure lay in the fullness of the food as it lay inside the mouth. The texture and mass as it slid down the throat.

She closed her eyes. She truly couldn't tell if she was sickened or intrigued by the memory of food.

Over the chatter of the throng, the steady throb of a drum echoed against her rib cage. She listened carefully for her heartbeat. During her long hospital stay, her heart had stopped several times. The therapist had been alarmed when she had spoken about it in clinical terms. *I didn't ingest quite enough calories. But I've reworked my calculations.*

Your heart stopped. You almost died.

I miscalculated.

Months were added to her stay. In that time, she learned to say, "I'm making friends with food again." It worked. They believed her.

Then she wondered why she cared if she was in the hospital or not. Why it was important to be released. In the hospital, no one stared at her gossamer frame.

The music swelled. The crowd shouted.

Around her, the people grew. Standing on tiptoe, stretching their necks, they rose into the air like kites. She, the closest thing among them to an angel, was too tired to fly. She wondered if she had miscalculated. She had eaten a piece of bread for breakfast. For lunch . . . she couldn't remember. Perhaps she had forgotten lunch along with the memory of it.

It was dark on Canal Street, save for golden light spilling from wrought-iron balconies. On the balconies, women bared their breasts and men hooted and shouted. The way of all flesh.

"Here they come!" the drunken woman cried.

The throng erupted into wild cheers. Jeanine was knocked forward by someone standing behind her. She stumbled and swayed.

Then the first float appeared. The long, oval base was a depiction of a cemetery. New Orleans folk buried their dead above the soggy, sunken ground, in ornate tombs. Women dressed like angels, spray painted all white, posed on top of the tiny buildings. Arms outstretched, hands folded in repose. Faces still and solemn and sad. Though the float swayed, not one of them moved.

My sisters, Jeanine thought. Her nearly weightless hands wanted to rise to her sides, like wings.

As the float lumbered forward, the Dixieland jazz slowed to a funeral dirge. The horns blurred; the drums snared. Jeanine remembered when she had been a music teacher. It seemed amazing to her now that she had bothered. *All flesh is grass.*

She had insisted to her therapist that many of the great thinkers fasted. Saints starved in the name of God. Gandhi went on a hunger strike.

"So you consider your anorexia a means to get closer to God?"

And of course, the way they had asked it clearly meant that she was even more insane. So she had denied her faith, denied the truth.

I am making friends with food.

The float was a stone city of the dead. Gothic arches, Grecian temples, even a pyramid. The center of the float featured a hexagonal building covered with weeping Grecian maidens. It was surrounded by miniature stone palaces, the cobwebbed crypts of illustrious families and wealthy merchants. Malaria and disease had claimed so many on the delta. Families spent an inordinate amount of time burying their loved ones; they spent the time there in style.

The cemeteries of New Orleans were world-famous. The occasional tourist was robbed or murdered, adding to their legend. The fact that the dead could not be buried below ground fascinated people.

As Jeanine looked on, the tombs began to open. Slowly, the occupants stick-walked forth: men and women too substantial to be dead, wearing skeleton costumes and mouldering grave clothes. Hideous makeup transformed their features into skulls trailing strips of rotting flesh. The crowd thrilled.

Someone shouted, "Throw me something, mister!"

It was the chant of New Orleans Mardi Gras. During the three weeks of the season, float occupants threw plastic beads, cups, and favors to the spectators. The dazzling, prized junk shimmered in daylight, in night light; hands stretched eagerly up and out, like fans at a baseball game straining for the fly ball.

"Throw me something, mister!" the drunken blonde woman shouted.

A mummer's drum sounded out a heartbeat. The costumed dead began to step-march in a slow, mechanical procession. Their eyes were the most authentic part of their regalia: they looked dull and blank, blind and drained.

Jeanine had looked like that when they admitted her into the hospital.

More dead emerged from the tombs. They carried *flambeaux*, the traditional Mardi Gras torches.

All the other sources of light along Canal Street went out, all at once. The onlookers were divided in their reaction: some gasped, entranced; others were startled.

The jazz band music died away.

A child began to cry.

On the floating graveyard, the dead stopped moving. They stood as still as the white angels atop the tombs.

The float crawled to a standstill.

Eerily silent, the crowd stood, straining to see. The drunken woman whispered to Jeanine, "This is weird."

In the center of the float, the door to the hexagonal tomb slowly opened. Jeanine heard the scrape of metal on stone. She took a dizzying breath and, like the rest, waited.

Fog rolled out and covered the floor of the float, which was covered with leaves and dead branches, mottled grass and stones. Dead flowers were strewn across the tiny alleys between the tombs. It looked like no graveyard in particular, and all graveyards.

The door creaked open. A figure emerged. It was clothed in black robes. Its head was shrouded in a black hood. In one end of the cloak—rather than a hand—it held a scythe. It glided like a shadow and drifted over the leaves and branches without disturbing a single one.

The spectators broke out into pleased applause. Still, the skeletons and angels did not move.

Its feet aren't touching the ground, Jeanine thought. *It's weightless.*

She tried to take a breath. Her rib cage was too heavy. The air settled around her shoulders like a weighty cloak.

The figure stopped. It turned.

It looked straight at Jeanine. She couldn't see its face, and yet she met its gaze, felt their eyes lock. She was ice cold.

"Oooh, how creepy," the drunken blonde said. She shivered with theatrical delight. "These guys are going to win a prize."

A drum beat slowly. Its cadence was measured; Jeanine anticipated each rhythmic count. The figure stared; the drum beat.

It was her heart. Sluggish, slow. Her heavy heart.

Sometimes we stop eating because we feel weighed down by our cares, the hospital psychologist had told her. *Do you think that makes sense?*

The drum beat more slowly. The rhythm was slightly off. Jeanine had no notion of the passage of time, but the crowd was becoming restive. The anxiety level in the air was high. Behind her, a man laughed and said, "Okay. That's pretty good." His voice was loaded with anxiety.

The blonde lit a cigarette. "This isn't funny anymore," she said. "They're holding up the show."

Sometimes we stop eating because we feel like the god, Atlas, holding the world on our shoulders. Does that make sense?

"I wish they'd turn the lights back on," another man said. "I'm hungry. I want to go get something to eat."

"Yeah, I'm starving," the blonde woman whined.

Sometimes we stop eating because we have stopped liking ourselves. We're trying to diminish our presence in the world. Do you think that might be the case with you?

"Mommy, you promised we could have ice cream," a little girl with curly blonde hair said. "Let's go get ice cream."

It doesn't matter what I think.

Now she stared at the figure and felt a curious lightening. *It matters what I want.*

She said, in a loud, clear voice, "Throw me something, mister."

Around the figure, the costumed dead swiveled their heads to look at Jeanine. The nearest, a woman, by the contours of her black body suit, painted with fluorescent, white bones, inclined her head.

She placed her right hand over her left forearm.

She began to peel back the sleeve.

And the hair and skin beneath it.

And the flesh, and the muscle.

As the crowd shrieked, she tore her flesh until she hit bone. Then she tossed the lumps to the crowd.

On the float, a dead man tore the desiccated strips of flesh from his face and flung them at the onlookers.

"Makeup," a man said. His voice was shrill.

To the slow, deadly drumbeat, the dead ripped open their costumes and dug their fingernails into their chests, their thighs, their necks. Large pieces of their bodies arced into the sky. Blood flowed like rain.

The crowd was electrified. As one being, they ran screaming, as the dead hurled their bodies at them.

The robed figure continued to stare at Jeanine.

She continued to stare back.

"Throw me something, mister," she whispered.

It tossed her the scythe.

It weighed nothing.

She looked down at her heavy, burdensome flesh. At her legs. At her arms. Her tongue. Her nose.

She took one hand and, as the figure looked on approvingly, tore off her clothes. She held the scythe with both hands.

She remembered that she had been a music teacher in a church. And this had happened once before.

She remembered the verse she had cried as she cut down the wicked. Revelation 3:1-2:

> "I know your works; you have the name of being alive, and you are dead. Awake, and strengthen that which remains and is on the point of death."

She was hungry. So terribly hungry. She had been starving to death.

Did that make sense?

She ran after the escapees, as the figures on the float stared after, unmoving. The little blonde girl with curly hair was sprawled on the ground, shrieking.

The drumbeat faltered. Jeanine fell within a yard of the little girl. Jeanine knew what was happening, and so, as her chest seized, she crawled toward the girl.

She raised the scythe.

The girl screamed.

And then suddenly, Jeanine floated from the earth. The scythe clattered to the sidewalk. Jeanine's legs fell next, and then her arms; her torso, her head.

She lifted her arms in ecstatic joy. "Behold the lamb of God, which taketh away the weight of the world," she whispered.

She looked down on the robed figure, as it looked up to her. It stretched out its cloaked arms. And then, though its face was cast in shadow, she knew it to be James, her love, her darling.

James Cavanaugh had been the pastor of her church, and she had sustained him in his battles against Satan for nearly seven years. A handsome man, not minding that she was plain—

"God made you plain so no man would choose you, except for me. I and I alone saw the beauty of your soul, Jeanine."

He was the man in whose shadow she had flourished, never mind that he had brought her forth into the sun. It was her soul he had loved, locked in a prison of flesh.

He was the man for whom she had cut down the righteous and the wicked. For he was the man who had died, slowly, of a terrible disease he had not chosen to contract. Never mind the evil gossip, even at his funeral. *For the blood is the death*—a transfusion, a mistake; the wages of sin were in that blood, and they tainted and murdered him—

The body is corrupt, the flesh, an abomination. The spirit within must be released, as his was, at all costs—

"Does that make sense to you?" she shrieked.

She soared high into the night clouds and looked down at the chaos. All over the French Quarter, and beyond, the tombs were opening. The stones were rolling back. The dead were lumbering forth.

"Oh, Babylon," she wept, exultant.

The screams of the wicked lifted her higher.

All flesh is grass.

DOWN IN DARKEST DIXIE WHERE THE DEAD DON'T DANCE

Gary A. Braunbeck

"Art thou pale for weariness
Of climbing Heaven, and gazing on the earth,
Wandering companionless
Among the stars that have a different birth,—
And ever changing, like a joyless eye
That finds no object worth its constancy?"
—Percy Bysshe Shelley, "To the Moon"

The ghosts of New Orleans are restless tonight.

The first to show himself is Bernard de Marigny, the colorful Creole character who named many of the city streets—Elysian Fields, Pleasure, Duels, Piety, and Desire; the next to materialize, wielding a sword that spilled the blood of many an unsuspecting seaman, is none other than Dominique You, the pirate captain who served under Jean Lafitte; following his dramatic entrance back into the world, still accompanied by his battalion of soldiers, is Pierre Gustav Toutant, New Orleans' most famous Civil War soldier, still weeping for all the fine men lost at Shiloh after he was forced to assume command when General Johnston fell to Union fire; next comes the dozens of nameless slaves who, at the hands of Delphine and Dr. Louis Lalaurie, were subjected to humiliation, torture, and hideous medical experimentation on the third floor of the *Maison Lalaurie* on Rue Royal; in their wake appears the ghost of Juliette Thibedeaux, an enslaved woman of mixed blood who fell in love with her Creole master and wished for the man to marry her and who, in order to prove her love, spent a cold December evening naked atop her master's house on Royal Street where she froze to death; after Juliette comes dozens, hundreds more, from Joseph Charbonnet who was beaten to death in the old Carrollton Jail to Ernestine Guesnow, murdered by her husband and then ground into sausage at the factory he owned.

From the jumbled maze-like paths of St. Louis No. 1 to the moss-draped, unmarked graves sprinkled throughout Holt Cemetery, from the *Vieux Carré* to the Metairie and all along Westbank, the ghosts begin assembling near the spot where, in 1768, the French residents of the city rebelled against the Spanish regime that had taken control of Nouvelle Orleans under the treaty of Fountainebleau, and here they wait for the arrival of the Capuchin priest Pere Dagobert who, in defiance of the Spanish governor and at great risk to his own life, performed secret religious services for the dead patriots of the uprising; when at last Father Dagobert appears to them, a tattered Bible clutched in his near-skeletal hands, his expression is anxious and tight.

"How's ba' you, Father? How's ya fam'ly n'nem dat followed you over?" asks Bernard de Marigny. "Ya come by to pass a good time with us tonight?"

"Not tonight, Bernard," replies the priest, turning his head in the direction of the music and laughter echoing from the French Quarter. "No, I'm afraid there will be no song or dance or celebrating for any of us this evening." The priest's eyes are wide but not with wonder.

"It don' madda much," says de Marigny, taking his place by Dagobert's side. "Ya be da one who buried a lot of us, we do what you say."

The priest says nothing for a moment, merely nods his head and stares in the direction of the merrymaking; eventually, after closing his eyes and breathing deep of the night air, he turns toward New Orleans' restless dead and says, "Company's coming."

Walking toward them are a woman and a little girl, both of them in the robes of the dead, both of them with haphazard stitches encircling their necks to mark the place where their decapitated heads were sloppily reattached to their bodies. The woman is crying, frightened, but the little girl, holding tight to her mother's hand, is not only calm but very, very happy to see the crowd of ghosts.

"Where 'bouts ya come from?" inquires the pirate Dominique You.

"I used to live in Ohio," says the little girl, "but me and my mommy, we're not alive anymore."

"Dat right, dat surely is," barks de Marigny.

Dagobert places a gentle hand on the little girl's shoulder. "What brings you to us this night, child?"

"There's a man and woman, bad people, Father. We gotta do *something*..."

Her fear is broken glass under the dead's feet.

Dagobert swallows. Once. Very hard. "Do you know their names, child?"

The little girl furrows her brow and thinks very hard for a moment, then says: "Laurie...?"

Dagobert feels a chill slither down his back. "Perhaps you mean... Dr. and Madame Lalaurie?"

"Uh-huh," says the little girl, nodding her head. "I can... I dunno... I guess I can feel them."

Dagobert turns back and looks at the faces of the slaves who died at the Lalaurie's hands, and he can see the memories of the whippings, of the burnings, of the countless humiliations they were subjected to; but most of all, he can see the memories of the agonized hours spent strapped to Dr. Lalaurie's operating table as he grafted genitals where noses should be and hacked off limbs simply because he enjoyed the way they screamed and—

—and Dagobert shakes away the thoughts.

"Father?" whispers de Marigny.

"The good doctor and his wife are among us once again," says the priest, and even he cannot hide his revulsion. "I think, Bernard, that this may be a very long and uneasy night."

And the ghosts of New Orleans grew even more restless . . .

DETECTIVE PETE RUSSELL THOUGHT of pain in its most mystifying expressions, of snipers in clock towers centering passersby in rifle scopes and the last sad whimper from the throats of crippled old men left bound and starving and neglected in putrescent beds and terrified two-year-olds methodically tortured to death by remorseless parents while neighbors who *knew* ignored the agonized shrieks, and he wondered if God's love was measurable only through the enjoyment. He seemed to take in the suffering of the innocent, but then remembered "Starry Night" and *The Heart Is a Lonely Hunter* and ". . . it was then that I carried you," and tenderness.

He leaned against the lacy iron rail on the balcony outside the second-floor room and stared down at the colorful Mardi Gras revelers cutting their noisy, joyous path through the *Vieux Carré*. *The ghosts of New Orleans are restless tonight,* he thought, *down here deep in darkest Dixie where dem dead doan dance, no-suh.*

He couldn't remember if that line came from a song or a poem or a nursery rhyme, then decided it didn't matter a damn.

Russell studied the bacchanal below and tried not to think about the body on the bed. The business end of the 9mm had been placed flush against the right eye, the trigger had been squeezed, and the gray matter inside the tabernacle of the skull had been introduced to its hollow-pointed celebrant. *Kyrie* (aim) to *Gloria* (squeeze) to the *Epistle:* "Do not let anyone have a claim on you, except the claim which binds us to love one another, which is all that the Law of God demands."

Bullshit and Amen—oh, by the way: Bang; you're dead.

The bullet had blown a hole the size of a grapefruit through the top of the head, decorating the wall with blood and viscera. So why did it look as if the body's chest was still rising and falling as if still capable of breath?

He lit a cigarette and searched for an answer among the throng of decadent, fantastic figures who moved along the cramped streets like clusters of cancer cells through a bloodstream.

The giant papier-mâché heads many of them wore were reminiscent of the stone monoliths on Easter Island—but where those ancient heads were solemn, inspiring awe, wonder, and even fear, those worn by the revelers were quirky and whimsical, inviting laughter and good cheer with their comically elongated noses and jaws and stiff, pointed horse's ears. Some carried banners that flapped in the wind, others had large bottles of wine cradled in bamboo baskets, a few held leather harnesses with sleigh bells above their heads, jingling and jangling as they twirled by through the blizzard of rainbow confetti, and one carried a well-used bodhran, using its thumbs to strike the goat-skin drum as krewe doubloons and multicolored potato chips bounced across its tightly stretched surface.

In the sputtering glow of their *flambeaux* torches, the figures looked diaphanous, mythic, otherworldly: A man with the head of a black hawk wearing a feathered headdress, a turtle with small antlers, a raven-headed woman in a golden flowing gown, a lion peering out from behind a visor in a suit of armor, a wolf in sparkling bandoleers, a mouse with angel's wings, a steerskull being wearing the uniform of a Spanish conquistador, an owl on a unicycle, a buffalo in a wheelchair, a rollerblading serpent; dressed in deerskin shirts and breechclouts and leggings, with *gris-gris* pouches and beaded necklaces, holding flutes and horn-pipes, trombones and ceremonial chimes, banjos and tambourines, their music and discordant singing was an intoxicated, exuberant chorale, holding every spirit in the spell of *Laissez les bon temps rouler!*

Russell shook his head, wondering how it was possible for anyone to be that happy.

He spotted the girl a few moments later. She was standing off to the side of the crowd, staring upward at the windows of the building that lined this side of the street. Twenty-four, twenty-five max, too-thin and pale-skinned, a Goth chick to the core, she was dressed in black leather and lace and silver metal from neck to ankle; her hose were fashionably torn and her lipstick was dark as a bruise, just like her eye makeup and fingernails. Around her neck hung a bright silver cross on a heavy chain, and around her wrists were black leather bracelets dotted with several small metal spikes. Her left biceps was tattooed with a coil of barbed wire that encircled the flesh there, and she sported a nose ring on the left side from which hung a thin chain that connected to another silver ring that dangled from her pierced left ear. She lit a cigarette and watched the partying masses move by, something distant in her eyes; Russell couldn't get a good enough look to tell if it was contempt, sadness, or anxiety.

"Are you sad, little girl?" he whispered.

For a moment she seemed to look right at him, as if hearing his question.

He wondered if she or anyone in the street below knew how physical evil and moral goodness intertwined like the strands of a double helix encoded into the DNA of the universe. Man was supposedly created to know wrong from right, to feel outrage at everything monstrous and evil, yet the scheme of creation itself was monstrous; the rule of life was get through the door and take that smack on the backside from the doctor's hand so you can be set adrift in a charnel-house cosmos packed from end to end with imploding stars and bloodstains inside chalk outlines.

And what then? A crapshoot: If you did manage to survive the agony of being born, there was always the chance you'd die from a fatal disease or be killed by a drunk driver or crushed by a falling building during an earthquake or drowned by your mother after she strapped you in good and tight and shoved the car into a lake, or you might be skinned alive or raped or tortured or beaten to a pulp or strangled or decapitated just for the fun of it, the thrill of it, the hell of it—So, whatta you wanna do tonight, Angie? Jeez, I dunno Marty, whatta you wanna do?

When he looked for her again, the Goth chick was gone, but in her place was a waist-high pile of small plastic baby dolls that glistened with drying wet sugar and icing; prizes found inside the traditional Gnawlins' king cake.

The way the dolls were stacked triggered something in his memory and he was suddenly too much aware of the beating of his heart—*thumpata-thumpata-thumpata-thumpata*—

—not his heart, not his heart at all, no, but some kind of secret beast pounding bloodied fists against a hidden door, Let me out! *Let me out so I can eat your fucking face!*

The pile of babies . . . oh, God—

—*the way he'd pounded his fists against the apartment door, knowing that something horrible was happening to the people on the other side, then, when the child screamed, he'd blown the lock off and kicked the door open and there stood the father over the pile of bodies, his wife and two daughters and the infant whose neck he'd snapped, and now he had the three-year-old boy against him and the knife seemed to come out of nowhere and before Russell could scream a warning or get off the first shot guided the blade across the kid's throat and*—

—stop it, stop it now—

—so he indulged for a moment in a flight of fancy that used to help him get through the bad ones way back when, before it seemed like they were *all* bad ones, before it had all become a cancer slowly devouring his mind, and closed his eyes and imagined that external reality existed nowhere else but inside his own head, which meant that nothing and no one outside the Iron Maiden of his flesh actually suffered. It used to work wonders early on in his career when even a simple shooting death seemed like the zenith of depravity, less so as the cases piled up and the perpetrated acts became more hideous and sickening; now it did nothing except reinforce how utterly meaningless and pathetically ineffective his every waking moment on the job and in his life had been.

A group of drunken musicians in top hats and tails yelled a four-count intro, then assaulted anyone in earshot with an off-key rendition of "Little Brown Jug" that was greeted by whoops and hollers and the *snappity-snappity-snap* of exploding firecrackers.

Russell clenched his teeth and snarled, "Let the good times roll, my ass."

"They're just having fun," said a voice behind him.

Russell whirled around and instinctively reached under his jacket for his weapon but the shoulder holster was empty and why shouldn't it be? His body on the bed was still clutching it.

The Goth chick laughed but there wasn't a lot of humor in it. "These bodies, they die easy; old habits, not so much, huh?"

Russell swallowed twice, very hard, and tried to gather what was left of his wits. The Goth chick was sitting on the edge of the bed, staring at his body. "It's kinda funny in a weird way, y'know? All my life I've had this thing about cops—not trusting them and all that? Now a cop's the only one who can see me and vice-versa." She reached out as if to touch the face of his body, then stopped, her hand suspended above his forehead. "Homicide Detective, weren't you?"

Russell nodded, "Fifteen years."

"What happened? No, wait, don't tell me . . ." She held both her hands over his body, moving them through the air as if patting him down during a search. "Jesus. They got pretty nasty toward the end, didn't they?"

"I guess."

"You *guess*?"

"For the last couple of years, it seems like they've all been pretty nasty."

"Was it any one of them in particular or . . . ?"

Russell shook his head. "Not really." He was only peripherally aware of the tears running down his face. "Mostly it was the way they all started to . . . jumble up in my memory."

"I didn't figure you for the melodramatic catharsis type, no; your spirit wasn't broken with one sudden blow; it bled to death in thousands of small scratches."

A large group of people began singing "If Ever I Cease to Love" from a bar across the street.

The Goth chick held her hands against her ears in mock-misery. "Oh, don't dey make wit' da *big* gumbo ya-ya! Give me headache, *suc au' lait!* . . ." Then she laughed.

"You finished with your Ragin' Cajun imitation?" snapped Russell.

"I thought it was pretty good," she replied, hands back on her lap.

"What's going on now? I mean . . . why are we able to be here talking like this?"

" 'Cause we're fresh, I guess."

"I don't follow."

The Goth chick lit another cigarette and smiled sadly. "I was a really good student—I mean, I know you wouldn't figure it to look at me, but I was. Especially in science and biology."

"I didn't ask for a résumé."

She shrugged. "What? You got someplace you need to be? Didn't think so. Okay, so here's what I was thinking: Death isn't instantaneous, right? The cells go down one by one and it takes a while before everything's finished. If a person wanted to, they could snatch a bunch of cells hours *after* somebody's checked out and grow them in cultures. Death's a fundamental function; its mechanisms operate with the same attention to detail, the same conditions for the advantage of organisms, and the same genetic information for guidance through the stages that most people equate with the physical act of living. So I've been asking myself, if it's such an intricate, integrated physiological process—at least in the primary, local stages—then how do you explain the permanent vanishing of consciousness? What happens to it? Does it just screech to a halt, become lost in humus, what? Nature doesn't work like that, you dig? It tends to find perpetual uses for its more elaborate systems. I mean, that still doesn't explain why you and I are talking to each other like this, but it gave me an idea. Maybe human consciousness is somehow severed at the filaments of its attachments and then absorbed back into the membrane of its origin. I think that's all we are right now: the severed consciousness of a single cell that hasn't died but is instead vanishing totally into its own progeny."

Russell snorted derisively. "We're *ghosts*, lady. That's all."

"Not quite yet, we're not."

"I don't have the slightest goddamn idea what you're talking about."

"Not all of our cells have died yet, and the ones that're still alive are *remembering* us. And as long as just *one* cell remembers us, we're tied to the corporeal in some form. But when those final cells finally give it up—" She snapped her black-nailed fingers. "*Then* we're ghosts."

"I'm guessing you weren't a big churchgoer."

She leaned against the headboard and crossed her arms over her chest. "Okay, smartass, let me ask you something: How is it you're able to smoke a cigarette still?"

Russell looked at the smoke he held between his fingers. When had he fired up another one?

"Don't remember doing that, do you?"

He shook his head.

"That's the trick. There's a thousand things we do without thinking about them—walking, eating, breathing, lighting a cigarette, picking up a pen. All done by rote. We explain it away by saying that we do it 'unconsciously,' but the truth is it's our *cells* that remember this stuff for us, that tell the rest of our body how to pull a pistol from its holster or add a little more sugar to the iced tea because it's not sweet enough. C'mon, Dirty Harry, look at your own body here—see the way the chest still rises and falls every so often. That's because those cells in you that are still alive haven't figured out yet that you're gone."

"So what?"

"So that's why I came to see you."

"To give me a lecture on biology and metaphysics?"

"Because it's going to be several hours before you become a ghost and cross over into the spirit world. In the meantime, you can move between the Land of the Dead and the World of the Living."

"Again: *So?*"

She sat up straight and—not looking at what she was doing—shoved her hand through a bluish-gray ripple in the atmosphere and pulled the gun from the body's hand, then tossed it to Russell; he watched it pass quickly through several other bluish-gray ripples and caught it without thinking.

"I want you to find my killers, Detective Russell. A man and a woman, both very elegant-looking Goths. I've been worm food for several hours but you've only been dead a couple of minutes. Right now we're just like electrons, able to travel from point to point without having to move through the space between, and I want to use that to my advantage. The people who killed me, who raped me *while* they were torturing me—until it just got too messy for the likes of even them—are still walking around this city . . . and their 'itch' hasn't quite been scratched to their satisfaction yet, if you read my meaning. I don't know how long I've got until the last of my cells check out and I become a permanent resident on the other side, but until then I can still *touch*, I can still *feel*, and I can still *manipulate* things on the physical level.

"I want you to help me find them so I can make the two of them suffer the way they made *me* suffer, understand?"

"What good would it do you?"

"What do you care, now?"

He thought about that one. "I guess part of me still clings to all that stuff the priests and nuns taught me when I was a good Catholic schoolboy—'Vengeance is mine,' sayeth the Lord and all that."

"Yeah, well, the Lord evidently stepped out for a smoke while those creeps were introducing my lower areas to the business end of a Leatherman tool, so I'll save Him the effort of exacting justice on my behalf."

"Why ask me for help, then? Why not just do it yourself?"

She sighed. "Know that guy you arrested back in '89? Killed his wife and little girl, then cut off their heads and stuck 'em in the freezer?"

Russell closed his eyes, trying not to remember how—

—the guy had jammed pinballs between the upper and lower rows of their teeth so their mouths would always be open because every once in a while he liked to take one of the heads out of the freezer and pleasure himself—

—he'd wanted to blow the sick fuck out of his socks because the guy acted like they were stomping all over his civil rights, what he did in the privacy of his home was his own business, and Russell had studied the guy's face and eyes and saw neither insanity

nor remorse there, the guy did it because he *liked* it and saw nothing wrong with his actions . . . and it hadn't helped when the medical examiner said that, based on histamine levels or something
like that in the muscle tissue, odds were both the wife and child
had still been alive when decapitated—looks like he did the wife
first—and oh, by the way, did you know that a severed head can
still see for about thirty seconds after it's been cut off? Yeah, that's
why the French always held up the heads of people executed on
the guillotine—wasn't just so the crowds could cheer, but because
the person's brain hadn't stopped receiving data yet, so they
could still look down and see their headless bodies and have just
enough time to realize they were dead and be scared as hell
before the final curtain fell, isn't that interesting?

Russell snapped open his eyes. ". . . yeah, I remember . . ."

"The wife was bad enough, but it was the kid that really got
to you, wasn't it?"

Tears again. ". . . yes . . ." *The terror that must have been in that
child's heart and mind as she cowered shrieking in the corner and
watched Daddy kill Mommy and then come after her . . .*

"Of all the death you've seen, it was always the kids that got
to you the worst, wasn't it?"

". . . hell, yes . . . it was like . . . toward the end . . . it was like
people were bringing kids into the world just so they'd have something to rape and beat and starve and mutilate and torture . . ."

She rose from the bed and walked toward him. "You'll help
me because of all those kids, Detective. You'll help because of all
the killers and torturers you never caught. You'll help because
you need to clear just one small corner of your conscience." She
took hold of his hand. "You'll help me because when those fuck-
ers left me lying there in the *Ex-Voto* room in the Saint Roch
Cemetery, when they walked away and left me under all those
replicas of hands and feet and handicapped childrens' braces
and that statue of Saint Lucy with eyeballs on a plate, they were
singing a little song." She moved closer to him; her breath
smelled like cloves. "Do you know what that song was, Detective?"
Her face was so close to his, their lips were nearly touching.

". . . no," whispered Russell, suddenly filled with her smells,
so rich and sultry and seemingly alive.

" 'Thank Heaven for Little Girls,' " she replied.

Russell pulled away from her. "Oh, God . . ."

"Yeah," she said, her eyes filling with rage. "I think they're going to finish off their night on the town with a child, Detective. That's why you'll help—because even if you don't care about justice for me, you won't leave this Earth knowing you could have prevented the death of another child."

Russell went back out onto the balcony and stood there in a space between fear and longing where his only companion was regret and thought about all the savagery he'd seen during his thirty-nine years on Earth. Good God—the human brain could detect one unit of mercaptan amid fifty billion units of air, and if the human ear were any more sensitive, it could easily hear the sound of air molecules colliding; the eye possessed tens of millions of electrical connections that could process two million simultaneous messages, yet could still focus on the light from a single photon; the nervous system was a wonder, capable of miraculous things, yet more often than not every fiber of an individual's being was geared toward destruction. Why? The evolution from paramecium to man had failed to solve the mystery, so what chance did he have to bring something as corporeal and therefore alien as this girl's killer to justice?—assuming there was such a thing. Matter was nothing more than energy that been brought to a screeching halt, and the human body was only matter, and the fundamental tendency of matter was toward total disorganization, a final state of utter randomness from which the cosmos would never recover, becoming more and more unthreaded with the passing of each moment while humanity flung itself headlong and uncaring into the void, recklessly scattering itself, impatient for the death of everything. So what if he *did* find the son-of-a-bitch who killed this girl and took him out before he could get his hands on a child? Somewhere out there was another son-of-a-bitch who *would* get his hands on a kid, or an old woman, or some unsuspecting Goth girl on her way home from a club, and drag them into basements or alleyways and split them open or burn them or twist their most sensitive parts with handyman's tools until their victims screamed enough to get them excited, and then . . . and then it would go on and on and on, a race sinking further into the pit of depravity, all the while forgetting that they possessed the ability to write music or formulate equations to explain the universe or cure diseases, create new languages and geometries and engines that could power crafts to explore space.

"Russell?" whispered the Goth girl.

"What?" he said, not turning to look back at her.

"Can I ask you a question?"

"Would it make any difference if I said no?"

She laughed, but only a little. "If humanity is as inherently evil as you seem to think it is, then how do you explain goodness? How do you explain love and a newborn's smile and a haunting tune you can't get out of your mind and the great way you feel when you smell fresh bread baking in your mother's kitchen?"

"I can't."

He felt her hand touch his shoulder. Though neither of them knew it, it was at this moment that the ghosts of New Orleans became restless and began to assemble.

Russell thought of pulling away from her but there was a heat in her palm and fingertips, a gentle warmth that had been missing from his life for as long as he could remember. "I'm not from around here, you know."

"Me neither," she said.

"I came down from Ohio. I was on medical leave."

"Where you injured in the line of duty?"

"No. Cops don't use words like *burnout* or *unstable* or *breakdown* when talking about their own. *Medical leave* is the term of preference."

"I'm sorry."

"It's a sorry world."

"You can make it a little less so before . . . before you have to . . ."

" 'Things will not be this way within reach of my arm.' That's something my partner and I used to say whenever we were assigned a really miserable case." He shrugged. "Sometimes a delusion is the best thing for you, especially when you *know* it's a delusion." He turned toward her and took hold of her torn-gloved hands. "What's your name?"

"You're gonna laugh."

"I won't, I promise."

"Saffron. My parents were a couple of old hippies."

Russell laughed.

"I knew you were going to do that," she said.

"Then you know what my answer is," he replied, jacking a fresh round into the chamber of his gun. "Let's go find those pieces of shit that did this to you."

"Why did you decide to help me?"

"Seems my schedule recently opened up—kind of like the top of my skull. C'mon, before I change my mind."

Saffron squeezed his hand and guided him toward a blue-gray ripple in the air; they stepped into it, dissolving bit by bit, until the room fell to silence, its only occupant on this plane the stilled, bloody corpse on the bed that clutched no weapon in its suicide hand.

Simultaneously, at the intersection of Decatur and North Peters Street, another blue-gray ripple appeared, unseen by the partying Mardi Gras attendants, and Saffron and Russell stepped through it. The smell of the Mississippi River hung heavy and damp and bitter in the air.

"Why here?"

"Because," said Saffron, "this is where I met them. There's a Goth club called the Crystal not too far from here. I was heading back to the room I'd rented in a shotgun hotel near Chartres. They were hanging around right here, smoking a joint. Even for the Goth world, these two looked pretty hardcore—elegant as hell, the wardrobe and jewelry they wore probably cost more than you make in six months, but they seemed friendly enough. The man had this gorgeous, jewel-handled dagger hanging from his belt, and the most beautiful leather shoulder bag—how was I supposed to know it was filled with surgical instruments? He smiled at me and offered me a couple of hits, then the woman— I'd've killed for the boots she was wearing—pulls out this flask filled with what she claimed was absinthe and we all took a sip." Saffron shuddered. "Christ, that was some serious stuff."

"Didn't your mother ever tell you not to take candy from strangers?"

"Up yours, cop. My parents were terrific people and raised me just fine, thanks very much. And if you'll look—" She gestured to her belt, where a small canister of pepper spray hung near her right hand, a sleek black stun gun near her left, "—I wasn't exactly defenseless. My mommy and daddy didn't sire no simpleton."

"So that's why you grew up to dress like some character out of an Anne Rice novel?"

Saffron glared at him. "Look, *cop*, let's you and me get something settled right now. Ever since those two yahoos in Colorado picked up their Tec-9s and did the Columbine Boogie, everybody thinks that all Goths are morbid, self-destructive, nihilistic schizoids who like to cornhole dead bodies and shoot heroin with shared needles and gather in the wee hours for a circle-jerk while they watch homemade snuff movies, and I get sick and tired of being labeled 'anti-social' just because I like to dress like this and go clubbing and listen to bands like Concrete Blonde, Attrition, the Sisters of Mercy, and Love Spirals Downwards! Christ—didn't you ever listen to Black Sabbath when you were in high school? Did everyone think you were gonna go postal on them because you thought 'Children of the Grave' rocked? Don't look at me that way! I'm not saying there aren't Goths who might fit that bill, but you name me any so-called subculture that doesn't attract its dregs. Goth culture is one of the few that embraces anyone who has an attraction for a darker aesthetic—Republicans, Anarchists, Christians—yeah, we got 'em!—Pacifists, certified public accountants, Goths don't judge. So what if we mix blackcurrent juice with vodka so we can act like we're vampires drinking blood—didn't you ever pretend at 'Monsters' when you were young? We read 'dangerous' magazine like *Carpe Noctem*—like you never took any shit for subscribing to *National Lampoon* in its glory days. There's nothing wrong with being attracted to things on the darker side and enjoy visiting there—why the fuck else do people go to horror movies or read Clive Barker and Stephen King? It's *fun*, period. Just because you're attracted to the darkness doesn't mean you're going to set up permanent residence in the neighborhood and build Torquemada's torture chamber to get your jollies, so I'd appreciate it if you'd get that condescending smirk off your face and quit making offensive remarks about a lifestyle that's given me a healthier sense of self-worth than a hundred summers at Bible camp! Think you can do that?"

Russell stared at her, then gave a slow nod of his head. "Would it do any good if I said I'm sorry?"

"It might."

"I'm sorry."

Saffron waved a hand in the air as if swatting away a mosquito. "Forgiven."

"Can I ask you something now? Would you please stop saying *cop* like it was some chunk of vomit you had to scrape off the bottoms of your shoes? I gave my life to the force and I'm still damned proud to have been a police officer. I never took a bribe, I never used excessive force—and believe me, there were times I'd've liked to!—and I never once ratted out a fellow officer."

"How noble of you. The years on the force must have left you with so many fond memories of a life well spent and—" Saffron's eyes grew wide and she suddenly covered her mouth with her hands. "Oh, *shit*! Oh, Pete, I'm . . . I'm so sorry, I didn't mean that, really, I'm sure you did a lot of good—"

Russell waved away his own mosquito. "Forget it. Like they say down here, 'It don madda none, no-how.' " He looked around the area for a moment and caught sight of a police car parked in front of a store. His detective's instincts still with him, Russell wandered over and watched as the officers assigned to guard the storefront began unrolling the yellow crime scene tape.

The store—a Goth shop called Gargoyle's—had recently been broken into.

"What is it?" said Saffron, looking at the shop. "Oh, man! That's the best Goth shop in the city! What's going on? A break-in?"

Russell slowly shook his head. "They wouldn't post officers out front and use the crime scene tape if it was just a burglary. Whoever broke in there killed someone—an employee or janitor is my guess. That's a murder scene—trust me, I've seen enough of them." He shook his head once more at the sick state of the world, then turned to his companion and said: "Okay, Saffron, what happened after the three of you toked it up here?"

Saffron pointed. "We started walking over to Canal. I was pretty buzzed at that point. It seemed to me that we were walking through water, you know? I could see it rippling as we passed through." She took a step forward and stuck her hand into one of the blue-gray ripples; it disappeared up to the knuckles, then reformed into a whole when she pulled it back. "I thought it was kind of cool, you know? Like moving through various dimensions of reality. I kept expecting to turn a corner and run into Rod Serling."

"Did you talk to them or remember anything they might have said?"

"Hell, I don't know."

"Think. You'd be surprised at what you can remember if you just concentrate."

She glared at him. "Please don't use that tone of voice with me."

"What tone?"

"Like you're talking to a three-year-old. I *told* you I can't remember anything that was said so stop getting all over me about it."

Russell rubbed his eyes. "Real hard case, aren't you? Live by your own rules—look where that got you—and don't take no shit from nobody, right? You are a rock, you are an island."

She started walking away from him. "I don't need this."

"Bullshit."

She whirled around. "Lay off!"

Russell threw up his hands. "Fine by me. I never asked for this, anyway—"

"No, you just took the chickenshit way out instead!"

"That supposed to hurt my feelings?"

"Fuck you! You're just like every other goddamn cop I ever ran into, you never turn it off, you're always suspicious of everything, always a Nosey Parker—"

" 'Nosey Parker'?"

"Something my mom used to say all the time whenever one of our nibby neighbors started asking about stuff that wasn't any of their business." This seemed to trigger something in her mind, and she looked off in the distance at something only she could see. "You know what I remember most about my childhood? Laundry days. Mom would wash and dry the loads, then lay out the shirts and slacks and things that needed to be ironed—oh, I *loved* to iron the clothes. You start out with this warm, wrinkled-up wad of material, you lay it out on the board and start moving the iron over it, and pretty soon you've got this clean, crisp, new-looking piece of clothing." Her eyes glistened. "I loved to iron because it was like making something new again. It was hardest on Dad's white shirts because you can see the smallest wrinkle on a white shirt. Like that guy tonight, his shirt was so *crisp* and smooth, it looked either brand-new or freshly ironed and I remember saying something about that and—" She stopped, mouth open, and looked over at Russell. "Oh, Jesus. I remember asking him how he kept his shirts so smooth and he said something about their servants doing that for them and then the woman, she suddenly looked really disgusted and said something about their useless, 'coon-ass' help—that really should've pissed me off, but I was too stoned to get on a soapbox about racial stuff—and then the man said, 'Watch your tongue, Delphine,' and I asked them where they lived and they started going on about their house on Royal Street and the awful changes that had been made there and—and you did that on purpose, didn't you?"

"Did what?"

Saffron walked toward him quickly, pointing a finger. "You got me mad on purpose because that way I'd remember something, right?"

Russell shrugged. "It's an old cop trick you use with witnesses who're too rattled to recall specific details. Make them focus on what they can't remember, then get them to think about something else for a minute. Seven times out of ten, if you distract them well enough, they remember things they thought they couldn't."

"Huh. You know, that's kinda cool." She grinned, then playfully smacked his upper arm. "You're pretty slick . . . I mean, you know, for someone who's a cop and all."

Russell grinned at her. "I got lucky. I figured anyone who excelled at science and biology wouldn't forget details that easily, even if they were pretty toasted." He shrugged. "If your aptitude for something is high enough, it becomes second nature. I know fingerprint experts who can trace whorl patterns in their sleep. You struck me as being too bright to not remember at least *one* bit of conversation. Thank God for laundry day, huh?"

They smiled at one another. It seemed both strange and natural.

"Come on," said Russell. "Let's head over by Royal Street and find their house."

They found another ripple in the atmosphere and moved into it—but not before Russell took one more look at the Gargoyle's crime scene. An occupational hazard.

They emerged from another ripple just in time to find themselves behind a crowd of tourists who were following a young bearded man dressed in a cape, tuxedo, and top hat. He carried a cane with a silver wolf's head that reminded Russell of the one used by the guy who used to play Barnabas on *Dark Shadows.*

"Next on our stop," intoned the tour guide in a mock-macabre voice, "is the infamous *Maison Lalaurie*, the scene of one of New Orleans' most unspeakable crimes."

Saffron giggled. "The 'Haunted New Orleans' tour. I thought about going on it but then decided it was silly."

The tour guide was still talking to his group. ". . . belonged to Dr. and Delphine Lalaurie, both of whom were, to the eyes of the world, cultured and refined leaders of New Orleans' society."

"Delphine," whispered Russell.

They followed the tour.

"But Madame Delphine, it was later discovered, had a dark side to her personality, oh, yes. She routinely starved and brutalized her slaves, whipping and torturing them. Furthermore, her staid physician husband committed ghoulish, experimental medical procedures on some slaves.

"The Lalauries were able to conceal their evil side from the public, although once Delphine had been fined for the 'accidental' death of a slave—a girl who fell off the rooftop while running in terror from her mistress. And upon more than one occasion a neighbor would complain of strange sounds coming from the house, including screams in the night."

"Sounds like a charming couple," whispered Saffron.

"Shh."

"Oh, you've got to be kidding me! You're not actually *interested* in this crap, are you?"

Russell looked at her. "You think ghost stories are crap?"

"Hell, yes, I mean who would ever believe in—oh, wait. Scratch that."

"So you see my point?"

She sighed. "Okay, okay, okay." He pointed toward the group. "Lead on, O Wise One."

They caught up with the tour group. The guide was really getting into his narrative now, once in a while even lapsing into a not-terrible Bela Lugosi. "One day, however, the Lalauries' hidden chamber of horrors was permanently revealed by a kitchen fire, perhaps started deliberately by a slave as a call for help. When the fire patrol and some neighbors came to the rescue, they discovered more than fire. They found a secret laboratory on the third floor where several unfortunate slaves were misused for bizarre 'medical' procedures. It was a true chamber of horrors. The authorities discovered some slaves dead, while others had been badly mutilated and intentionally deformed. In some cases the victims had suffered the deliberate and unnecessary amputation of limbs. Body parts and human organs were in disarray about the room, while some slaves were found still chained to the wall. The scene was horrific, grotesque.

"The firemen called the constables, who secured the area, taking the enslaved victims to the hospital. When the neighbors learned of the hideous nature of the crimes, they became enraged and demanded justice. However, Dr. and Madame Lalaurie escaped the angry mob of citizens that had formed around the house when news of the torture chamber spread. The Lalauries disappeared—although some Madame Lalaurie sightings appeared on the north shore of Lake Pontchartrain as well as in the city, and as far away as New York and even France. But the Lalauries were never brought to justice. And the once gracious *Maison Lalaurie* deteriorated, becoming the haunted house you now see before you."

Russell and Saffron both stared at the structure.

"Looks like every other house on the street," said Saffron. "I mean, it's falling apart but . . . I'll bet it was pretty in its day."

"Tell that to the third-floor guests."

"Then the ghosts began to appear," said the guide in a *Danse Macabre* sing-song voice. "Neighbors heard shrieks at night coming from the rundown house and some claimed to see apparitions. Visions of tortured slaves appeared on the balconies; some people claimed to see a white woman, perhaps Madame Lalaurie herself, with a whip in hand. Others claimed to have seen the ghost of the girl slave who had died after running from Delphine.

"Over the decades other horrible apparitions have been reported—butchered animals and visions of tormented slaves in chains. No one has been able to prove or disprove the validity of these sightings. And take care, my friends, for legend has it that on this night, the Night of Shrove Tuesday, between midnight and sunrise, the ghosts of New Orleans can enter this world and do as they please. Can you be certain that the person next to you isn't a ghost? How do you know that fellow over there isn't the hideous doctor, or that woman standing so near you—might it be Madame Lalaurie, come back to relive her foul acts? No, you can't be certain, not in this place, for perhaps Evil still dwells here in the House of Lalaurie!"

The crowd *oooh*'d and *ahhh*'d appropriately, then it was time for flashbulbs and video cameras to commemorate their fun and fascinating visit to this place of torture.

After the group moved on, Russell turned toward Saffron. "The woman, did she have a whip?"

"A cat o' nine tails. It was hanging from her belt."

Russell nodded. "So now we know who they are. You were murdered by a couple of ghosts."

"How is that possible? They were decked out in Goth gear!"

"My guess is they were the ones who broke into the Goth shop and killed whoever was in there." He chewed on his lower lip for a moment. "But how could they have *physically* done any of this? I mean, if what you were saying is right, that because all our cells haven't gone belly-up yet, we're still able to manipulate things in the living world, then there has to be some way that they can do it, as well."

"Maybe what the tour guide said isn't just crap. Maybe on this night the ghosts can enter the world of the living and do whatever they want."

Russell nodded his head. "That would explain how they were able to break into the shop and kill people. That would explain why two ghosts from the 1800s were decked out in Goth garb."

"That's important to you, isn't it?"

"What?"

"Answering all the questions, making sure there's no loose ends."

"There's always loose ends—and, yes, it's important to me. Whenever I finished a case that still had a couple of loose ends, it made me nuts. Oh, sure, I might have the killer, and the motive, and the weapon, and the timetable of events . . . but there was usually *something*, you know? A small detail that didn't quite fit in with things. I—oh, skip it."

"No. That's the first thing you've told me that even comes close to revealing the person inside the cop."

He considered that for a moment, remembered the way people used to complain that he'd never let anyone get close to him, looked once more at the house, then said: "I remember the way I used to love watching horror movies when I was a kid. This house looks like any one of a hundred that was in those movies. My dad, he worked at a factory, right, two until midnight every day except Sunday. On Friday nights Channel 10 used to run *Chiller Theater*—a double feature of great old horror movies. *Frankenstein, The Wolf Man, Murders in the Rue Morgue, Fiend Without a Face* . . . anyway, I got to stay up late on Friday nights so that when Dad came home, Mom would set up these TV trays in the living room and he and I would watch these movies together. I remember that any time there'd come a really scary part I'd scoot over next to him on the couch and say, 'Hold my stomach, Daddy,' and he'd press his big hand against my middle and it wouldn't be so scary then." He pulled in a deep breath, then lit a cigarette. "I miss him and Mom. I miss those Friday nights and those awful, *awful* TV dinners and *Chiller Theater*. I miss . . . a lot of things." He was suddenly aware of Saffron staring at him, and felt awkward, exposed. "Sorry. I didn't mean to—"

"That's okay," she said, taking hold of his hand. "I thought it was kind of sweet. I liked hearing it. Don't apologize. It obviously meant a lot to you."

"Yeah, it did. Then I grew up and the whole fucking world turned into *Chiller Theater* and being scared sort of lost its magic."

"I'm sorry, Pete. Really, I am."

"Thanks."

She hadn't let go of his hand yet. For some reason, Russell didn't mind that so much.

"I think I'm getting a bit fond of you, cop."

"Maybe I'm growing accustomed to your face, as well."

Saffron smiled. "We're having a movie moment, aren't we?"

"I guess."

Silence for a few seconds, then Russell said: "Is it over yet?"

Saffron let go of his hand. "Party pooper."

"Tell me what else you remember about your walk with the Lalauries."

"Like I said, we just started walking and . . . next thing I know, we're in Saint Roch No. 1, heading into the *Ex-Voto* room. We get in there and fire up another joint, then take a couple more little sips of the absinthe, then the guy starts feeling me up." She looked down at the ground, embarrassed. "The woman, she started kissing the back of my neck. I hate to admit it, but they got me pretty hot." She looked into Russell's eyes. "I'd never done anything like that before—you know, a threesome. But there was just something so . . . *erotic* about being in that place with them. Mostly it was just a lot of kissing and licking and nibbling on nipples until most of my clothes were off and I started to get a condom out of my purse. That's when the guy went ballistic on me."

Russell shook his head.

"What?" said Saffron.

"You were stupid to go with them, you know that, right?"

"So I was stupid—because of that I deserved to have my areoles and nipples sliced off and rammed down my throat?"

Russell started. "They mutilated you?"

Tears brimmed in Saffron's eyes. "Cutting off my breasts was one of the nicer things they did."

She hugged herself. "Oh God, Pete—I'm getting cold! Are you cold? Is it getting cold?" A single tear slipped down Saffron's cheek. "The last of my cells are starting to go down." Her face pleaded with him. "I think it's going to be soon now. I'm scared, Pete. I'm . . . *I'm so scared.*"

Instinctively, Russell put his arm around her and pulled her close to him. The department had unofficially reprimanded him several times for doing something like this, but he didn't care then and he didn't care now, so he held her with all the strength he had, hoping all the while that she couldn't tell how suddenly terrified he was of losing her company.

He kissed the top of her head and stroked her hair, surprised at the intimacy they were sharing, even more surprised when she took hold of his hand and kissed its palm—with both her soft lips and warm tears. There was nothing sexual about their embrace, that would have ruined it for both of them; it was, quite simply, a moment of untainted grace. In this silent communion both found a trace of lost empowerment, lost hope, lost dreams.

Saffron looked up at him. Tears had blended with her mascara to create several long, black streaks down her face. "God, how I must look."

"It's not so bad," whispered Russell, brushing at one of the streaks with his thumb; he succeeded only in creating a horizontal black streak that made her right cheek look like someone had drawn a tic-tac-toe board there. "I think I made it worse."

"Do I look too bad?"

"No worse than any other Goth freak."

Saffron laughed. "Hey, *pig*, I got my rights, back off! I'm tired of being hassled by the Man!" And with that she stood back and raised her right fist in the air, defiant.

Russell snorted a laugh. "You look like an extra from *Billy Jack Meets Dracula.*"

They both burst out laughing at that, then Saffron came into Russell's arms and they kissed; warmly and passionately. Russell pulled her into him again and rested his chin on the top of her head, overwhelmed and mystified by the depth of the sudden affection he felt for her, and it was then that Detective Pete Russell, a solitary and often lonely man who'd given his life over to the detection and apprehending of the worst of humanity, who had come to think that the universe was nothing more than an obscene slaughterhouse where the blood of the innocent flowed in rhythm with the echoes of their agonized screams, who until this moment believed he would never feel the kind of all-consuming *need* for another human being that the poets wrote about, realized that he *cared* about this woman, this Goth girl, this Saffron-daughter-of-old-hippies, and vowed to who- or whatever might be listening: *It will not be this way; for these last minutes on this earth, the world will not be this way within reach of my arm, not for her.*

And that's when he saw the old man coming toward him.

Wrapped in a morgue blanket but whipping it around his naked body like an elegant cape, the old man danced and twirled down the street, coming ever closer, until he was close enough to shout: "Why, hello, Detective Russell! Interesting night, isn't it?"

"Do I know you?" said Russell, nearly choking on the words.

Saffron turned around. "Who is that?"

Russell shook his head. "I'm not sure . . . I *think* I know his face but I—"

By this time the old man was right next to him. "Name's Harold Crider, son. I was one of your very first cases. My kid strapped me into my bed and left me there to rot. I'd been there so long that my skin was stuck to the sheets. My guts started to spill out when you rolled me over, remember?"

Russell shook his head. "Not really." This said with deep regret.

Crider slapped a hand on Russell's shoulder. "Well, that's okay, don't go beatin' yourself up over it any longer, you hear? Good Lord knows you seen more than your share of terrible sights."

"Wh-where did you come from?"

Crider cocked his head to the side like a grade-school teacher sizing up a slow student. "Why, from *you*, Detective. We all did. You been carryin' us around with you for so long ain't one of us thought we'd ever get out—but that bullet you put through your brain sure did the trick, yessir. Shot us out of your brain like we were cannonballs." Crider made a grand sweeping gesture with his arm. "We just wanted to . . . to see you again."

Russell and Saffron looked all around and saw—

—on rooftops and from alleyways, coming around corners and scurrying down fire escapes, climbing through broken warehouse windows and forcing open long-locked doors of boarded-up buildings, the ghosts of the victims from every murder case Russell had ever worked gathered around them, all smiling despite their still-existent wounds, all of them clambering to touch Russell or shake his hand—

—all of them speaking their thanks.

". . . really appreciate everything you did to find that guy who shot me, I'm really sorry you never caught him because it made you so sad . . ."

". . . was so great the way you tackled him in that alley after he cut my throat; I didn't shed a tear when they gassed his ass later . . ."

". . . and my mommy can't be mean to my little brother like she was to me 'cause you *caught* her . . ."

". . . forever in your debt, it takes a special kind of man to do what you did for the likes of me—I mean, who cares about some fag with AIDS who gets gunned down? But you gave a shit, Detective, and I love you for it . . ."

". . . it meant so much . . ."

". . . you were so upset when you saw my body, you were the only person who cried for me and that meant a lot . . ."

". . . never thought of us as corpses, you always thought of us as people . . ."

". . . didn't mean for you to feel so responsible . . ."

". . . you did everything you could . . ."

". . . you felt so angry for us . . ."

". . . so sad . . ."

". . . you did everything you could . . ."

". . . everything you could . . ."

". . . everything humanly possible . . ."

Crider held up his hand, silencing the ghosts who now lined both sides of the street for as far as Russell could see. "Okay, Detective, it's like this: We figure that, since you felt so bad for all of us, since you could never forget what was done to us even if you didn't remember our names or faces, and on account of you blaming yourself in a way, thinking you didn't do enough, thinking that what you did didn't mean a damn thing, that your whole life was pointless . . . well, we understand that's why you carried us around for all these years—no hard feelings there, so we figure that we *helped* you pull that trigger, in a way. And we owe you."

Russell shook his head. "You don't owe me a thing, any of you. I'm just sorry that—"

"None of that 'sorry' shit, son; you're way past that now. You were a fine man and a good cop and you deserve to end your career better than with your brains blowed out in a hotel room." Crider looked at Saffron. "Them two that killed you, they're on their way to Holt Cemetery with a three-year-old child they snatched from a crowd watching the Orpheus Parade, a little retarded boy wearin' a *Star Wars* T-shirt and a sailor's cap.

"We been with you so long, we'd kinda like to be in on your last arrest, if that's okay with the two of you."

Russell's throat was so tight and his eyes burned so hot that he could little more than nod. Saffron brushed away one of his tears, kissed his cheek, then faced Russell's ghosts and said, "We'd be honored. And thank you."

"Thank *you*," the ghosts replied.

"It wasn't for nothing," choked Russell into Saffron's ear. "All those years . . . all the bad dreams and people thinking I was a head-case and me wondering if there was still decency in the world . . . it meant something . . ." He was sobbing openly now. ". . . my *life* meant something . . ."

"Yes, it did," she whispered. "You bet your ass it did." Then she pulled his face up and kissed him hard on the mouth. "You sound like you were one helluva guy, Pete Russell."

"You know, even with mascara smeared all over your face, you're the most beautiful woman I've ever seen."

"*Now* you want to make with the warm and fuzzy? *Now*?"

Russell pulled himself up, took a deep breath, and removed his gun from its shoulder holster. "No; *now* I want to get my hands on those two before they—fuck it. Let's go."

They moved *en masse* through a large blue-gray ripple—

—and emerged in the heart of Holt Cemetery.

Where the restless ghosts of New Orleans were waiting for them.

The two crowds of ghosts approached one another. Bernard de Marigny and Father Dagobert stepped forward.

"Little girl," shouted de Marigny over his shoulder. "Dis here da man and woman you spoke about?"

The little girl and her mother made their way to the front of the crowd. Upon seeing Russell the girl broke into a smile and ran to him, throwing her arms around his legs. "I knew you'd come!"

Russell knelt down and with his index finger traced the sloppy stitching around her neck. "Oh, *Karen*. I'm so sorry about what your daddy did to you and your mother."

Karen smiled. "That's okay. Now that we got out of your head, we're having fun! I made a *whole bunch* of new friends, see?"

Russell looked up at the ghosts of New Orleans. "They look real nice, Karen. Are you happy now?"

"Oh, you bet! *Everybody's* happy here." Then she scrinched up her face as if forced to eat a vegetable on her plate that she found repulsive. "Not like over *there*." She pointed out toward the world of the living.

Russell looked over his shoulder and saw with a kind of x-ray vision past the vine-shrouded ruins of the cemetery gates to the world beyond. A world filled with vicious, selfish people who looked grotesque and deformed; they pushed, shoved, struck at each other, and knocked each other down, were hateful to their fellow man, each one of them trying to better the next and get to some unknown location not realizing that they were heading nowhere. It was a macabre sight, a cruel, pointless struggle of inhuman lunatics.

"I don't wanna be like that," said Karen.

"Me, neither," replied Russell.

"Russell?" said Saffron. It was less than a whisper.

She was starting to quickly fade. Russell leaped to his feet and reached for her but his hand passed through her body to grasp only emptiness.

"No!" he whispered, then cried: *"Goddammit, NO!"*

". . . Pete . . ."

He tried to grab hold of her hand once again but could not. He then turned to face the ghosts of New Orleans. "What can I do? Tell me—somebody *tell me!*"

Father Dagobert moved closer. "The last of her earthly body is dying away."

"No, Father, no!" Near panic, Russell grabbed the priest by his shirt and slowly pulled him closer. "Listen to me, Father—"

". . . so cold . . . so c-c-cold, Pete . . ."

"—I will not be without her by my side, do you understand? All my life I was alone and miserable and never thought I'd feel about anyone the way I feel about her. When it's time to pass over into your ranks, she and I will go together. Please tell me this can be done somehow, please show me that God or Who-ever's in charge of this fucking freak show isn't a sadist. Tell me. *Please, tell me.*"

Dagobert was visibly moved by Russell's plea. He reached up and gently removed the detective's hands from his shirt, smoothed down the ruffles, then held his Bible close to his chest. "You love her that much?"

Russell looked at Saffron's fading form and said, "Yes, yes, I think maybe I do."

"Russell?"

He turned back toward her. "I'm here, I'm right here."

"I've got an idea . . ."

He tried to hold her again but embraced only air. At least he could still hear her voice, at least he could still see her, though it was like looking at an image in a slowly developing photograph. "Tell me, Saffron. Whatever it is, I'll do it. Whatever it takes."

She was thinking aloud. ". . . keratinocytes and maybe . . . maybe 3T3 feeder layer . . . no, shit, that won't work . . . wait a sec . . ." Her now-translucent eyes found him. "So you love me, huh?"

"I do. Don't ask me why."

"I think I know how you can help me."

"*Tell me.*"

"You're not going to like it."

"I don't care. I'll do anything. *Anything.*"

And she told him exactly, *precisely* what he had to do.

Some of it turned his stomach but he dealt with it. "Are you sure that'll work?"

"Fuck no! But it's the best I can come up with."

Russell rose to his feet and looked into the ghost-crowd. "I need a knife, a *sharp* one."

The pirate Dominique You unsheathed his jewel-handled dagger and tossed it into Russell's waiting hands. "This will split anything, sir. On that you've my word."

"Best be on your way, son," said Harold Crider. "Them two you're after, they'll be here right soon."

Russell looked at Saffron. "I won't disappoint you. I swear it." He looked into the crowd. "I need someone to . . . to go with me. Someone who knows their way around the city."

It was Father Dagobert who stepped forward. "I'll accompany you, Detective, if you don't mind."

"Thanks, Father."

And they entered the blue-gray ripple—

—to emerge in the *Ex-Voto* room where Saffron's body lay, still undiscovered.

Russell swallowed back the bile he felt rising in his throat. The savagery inflicted on her was among the worst he'd ever seen.

"Lord save us," intoned Dagobert, making the Sign of the Cross over the body, then opening his Bible and quietly reading a prayer.

Russell knelt down next to the piece of bloody flesh and meat that was once the woman he now loved and began to touch it, then pulled back his hand, took a deep breath, and began his work.

Don't use any of the skin that isn't still attached to my body, Saffron had told him. *Cut away a section of my cheek, then cut that section in half lengthwise, top to bottom, got it?*

Feeling as if he were murdering a child, Russell wiped away the blood and viscera on her face until he found an unharmed section of cheek flesh, and did what he had to do. Once the section of flesh was split in half (Dominique was right, his dagger was *amazingly* sharp, making the delicate work simple, if no less sickening), Russell took a clear plastic evidence bag from his jacket pocket (another occupational hazard—he *always* had an evidence bag on his person), carefully slipped the two sections inside, then sealed it tight.

He looked at Father Dagobert. "You all right, Father?"

The priest shook his head. "That poor girl. The horrors she must have endured . . ." His gaze met Russell's. "She'll find peace with us . . . as will you, Detective."

"Blew my brains out, Father. From what I was taught, I bought myself a one-way ticket to Hell."

Dagobert put a hand on Russell's shoulder. "It doesn't quite work that way, Peter. Yes, it was a sin, but God is not so angry that He would turn away a soul for having been in *that much* pain. You've nothing to worry about, I promise."

"Do you know how to get to—"

"Yes. Come."

They exited the *Ex-Voto* room and entered the next rippled doorway—

—and emerged in the Burn Unit lab of the Department of Dermatology in the basement of the Tulane University Medical Center.

"Where's the goddamn refrigerator?" snapped Russell.

Dagobert pointed to the large silver doors in the wall opposite them. Russell ran over and grabbed the handle, pulled—

—and the doors wouldn't open.

He looked down and saw the short chain and secured padlock.

"Fuck!" He pulled out his gun and said to Dagobert: "Go over to the doors, Father, and watch for anyone. I'm gonna make a bit of noise."

The priest did as Russell told him. "There's no one about."

Russell took two steps back, aimed, and fired three shots in rapid succession at the lock—which blew open and clattered to the floor. Russell quickly yanked the chain from around the door handles and opened the refrigeration unit.

You'll be looking for Petri dishes with collagen-based growth mediums in them—just find one that looks like it's got yellow Jell-O in the bottom. Take the lid off, then put the two sections of my skin on top of the yellow stuff, all right? But make sure that the halves that face down are identical: the outer layer of skin on both halves should be facing you.

Done.

He froze. "Jesus . . . now what?"

Think, think, c'mon, you don't have time for this—

—he remembered the smell of her breath when she stood close to him in the hotel room, how close their lips were at that moment, how tempted he'd been to kiss her just to see what it felt like to share a moment of tenderness after you were dead—

—and he had it:

As soon as that's done, look around for some lactated Ringer's solution—okay, I've confused you. Look for a spray bottle—there should be several of them nearby, if not right on top of the refrigerator. Spray it all over my skin samples, then put the cover back on the Petri dish.

He found the solution, sprayed, and covered the dish.

"Now the incubator," he said to himself

"Someone's coming," said Dagobert.

Russell found the incubator and began to open the lid—

Put the dish on top of the incubator, not inside. If you put it inside it could be a while before anyone finds it and realizes it's not an authorized sample. The top of the incubator will be slightly warm. That little bit of warmth plus the growth medium in the dish should be enough to keep the cells alive for a few more hours. That's all you've got left, and I want to leave with you.

He put the dish on the incubator, then noticed that someone had set a pair of houseplants on top of the thing, as well. He moved the plants closer together in order to hide the dish.

"All done, Father."

The security guard shone his flashlight through the windows of the lab door as Dagobert and Russell slipped through the ripple—

—and stepped back onto the soil of the cemetery.

The ghosts all stared at Russell, silent.

Oh, please God, no, he thought.

A few seconds later, de Marigny laughed loudly. "Wha' ya waitin' for? Give dat little gal a kiss 'fore I do it fo' ya!"

Russell spun around and there was Saffron, kneeling on the ground and shuddering. He fell to his knees and pulled her to him.

"I g-guess th-this is the part where I thank you," she whispered.

"I thought I was going to lose you."

". . . just like a cop . . . won't let you get away no matter what."

He smiled and kissed her.

"Y-you done g-good, Pete."

"Smart girl, you're a very smart girl."

"Dean's list every quarter." She placed one of her hands against his cheek.

"I saw your body . . . Christ, I'm so, so, so sorry."

"You and me both." Then: "So I guess this means we're stuck with each other, huh?"

That's when the echo of the child's terrified scream reached them. Russell was on his feet immediately, his weapon in his hand. "Not within reach of my arm," he snarled through clenched teeth, then shouted: *"Not within reach of my arm!"*

Without thinking about it, he ran toward the scream, and the ghosts followed him.

Lighted torches illuminated the path through the cemetery. The ghosts passed ribbons and ravels of tissue and sparkle-tape that clung to ancient headstones and hand-carved, love-polished crucifixes on the outer walls of the above-ground tombs. Everything shone in the moon- and torchlight like marble jewelry cases, especially the stone angels spilling down the sides of the entryways, eyes bespeaking approval. Russell jumped over dead flowers and overturned statues, skidded around corners where the moss hanging from the monolithic oak trees turned the way into a jungle, and stomped through the thick vegetation that might have ensnared him had he still been a part of this world; at last he rounded the final corner and there, less than fifty feet away from him, stood the beasts with the child, who was laid out on an overturned headstone like a slab of meat on a butcher's block.

The man was taunting the Down Syndrome boy with something thin, shiny, and sharp, while the woman ran her hands over the child's face and chest, eventually working her way down to his belt buckle, which she began to loosen. The child's eyes looked downward at his sailor's cap on the ground, and when he tried to reach for it the woman made a fist and struck him hard in the stomach. The child's face turned red and he threw back his head to scream but the pain was too intense for any sound to escape him.

Ignoring the layers of blue-gray ripples that he passed through, Russell sprinted toward them screaming, *"Hands in the air and move away from the kid RIGHT THE FUCK NOW! Right now or I'll kill you where you stand!"* He slammed to a halt ten feet from them, the 9mm pointed directly at the man's head.

"Suc au 'lait!" cried de Marigny. Several dozen ghost slaves echoed his surprise.

"What?" shouted Russell.

"Dat be Madame and Dr. Lalaurie! Dey kill many, many of dere slaves, some of them in very nasty ways."

The murmur of the ghost slaves became more and more angry.

"Some evil never dies when it should," whispered Father Dagobert. "Those two should have joined the Devil in Hell over a hundred-and-fifty years ago."

It didn't matter a damn to Russell that the tour guide had been right, that the ghosts of New Orleans could affect the world of the living between midnight and sunrise—he just wanted them away from the child.

"Move!" he shouted at them.

Dr. Lalaurie smiled a hideous grin. "My, my, my—a white man avenging nigger slaves. Why bother yourself? They were little more than animals."

Russell gripped the wrist of the hand holding the gun to steady his shot. "You've got till three, then I shoot."

"Or is this about the *girl*? Ah, of course. You looked like a smart man to me, one who would not bother himself with the likes of those worthless, black-skinned dogs." He gestured with obvious distaste toward the ghost slaves.

Russell gritted his teeth: "One . . ."

Dr. Lalaurie parted his hands before him; in one he held a scalpel, in the other, a bone saw. "But I see that you're one of them, after all, aren't you? Merely a ghost, no threat to me or my wife."

". . . Two . . ."

"And this child! What use could a mongoloid moron like this be to the world? Best to use him for experimentation and wet, private pleasure, don't you—"

Madame Lalaurie made a sudden move, and in the second before she could bring the dagger down into the child's throat Russell squeezed off three rounds in quick succession that should have struck her in the chest, throat, and right eye and crumpled her dead to the ground.

But they passed right through her, winging off the stone pillars of a nearby crypt.

She pulled back the knife, looked at her husband, and laughed.

The child, unharmed, very still, very frightened, pulled in ragged, wheezing breaths.

"Why the hell didn't it work?" shouted Russell.

"Because your gun, like yourself, is still not fully a part of the World of the Dead."

Dr. and Madame Lalaurie, now realizing Russell was no threat to them, leaned back against the headstones and smiled hideously.

Russell threw down his gun and reached for the dagger Dominique You had given to him. "Then I guess we do it the messy way."

Dagobert grabbed hold of his arm. "I thought you wanted justice."

"I'll make do." He couldn't take his gaze from the Lalauries' arrogant expressions.

Delphine Lalaurie, her hand placed firmly on the child's chest, laughed.

It was then that Russell saw the first shadow move on the roof of the crypt behind the Lalauries; slowly at first, perhaps a nightbird fixing its nest, but then the moon- and torchlight revealed, albeit briefly, the taut sinewy muscles of a dark arm, and soon the ghost-slave on the roof was joined by another, then another, and then several more, all of them lined up and squatting, ready to pounce.

"They're waiting for you to give the word," whispered Dagobert.

Russell squeezed the handle of the dagger.

Neither of the fiends made a move to harm the child.

But for how long? wondered Russell.

Then: *Distract them.*

He walked toward them very, very slowly, arms parted before him so both of them could see the dagger in his hand.

"You can only kill us one at a time with that," said Delphine Lalaurie. "It matters not which of us you strike first—the other will make quick work of this—" She looked down at the boy. "—this piece of human shit."

"May I ask a question of you, Dr. Lalaurie?"

Happy that the balance of power had now shifted his way, Lalaurie nodded.

"Why did you do it? Any of it, *all* of it?"

"There's a tribe in Africa, Detective, called the Masai, and every so often they choose one of their elders, or a cripple, or some other useless member of the village like this child here, and they give them a huge party, then take them out into the jungle and leave them there for the hyenas to eat alive. It's their way of not only controlling the population but of thinning out those elements that might taint the purity of their tribal seed.

"Why do we do it? Because the world, from pole to pole, is a jungle, no different from the one where the Masai feed the hyenas. It's inhabited by various species of beasts, some which rut in caves and devour their young, others that wear tailored suits and dine on their rivals' broken businesses. All of these beasts have only one honest-to-God function, and that is to survive. There is no morality, no law, no imposed manmade dogma that will stand in the path of that survival. That humankind survives is the only morality there is. And for the White Race to survive, we must be superior, we must dominate all lesser creatures, and in order to ensure that, it is not only vital but necessary to destroy, to eliminate, to thin out and expunge any undesirable element that threatens to stop the march of progress. Now, you're a smart man, Detective, so let me ask a question of you: What possible use to the world—aside from medical experimentation—is this child or those ignorant slaves behind you?"

Russell shrugged. "I guess maybe you ought to ask them yourselves." He drew back his arm and tossed the dagger through the air; the first ghost slave reached out from the roof of the crypt and caught it in his hand as he simultaneously dropped to the ground directly behind Dr. Lalaurie; an instant later the others were on the ground and tackling the Lalauries, tearing away at the clothing and using the dagger to cut apart Delphine's whip, using the strips of leather and clothing to tie the Lalauries' hands and feet.

The ghost slaves pulled the murderers to their feet and then waited. The child had leaped from the headstone, grabbed his sailor's cap, and now huddled in the doorway of the crypt that was to have been his murder site.

Russell looked at Dagobert. "Now what?" Was it just him, or had the atmosphere in the cemetery suddenly gotten much warmer?

"After they disappeared, the late Judge William Radcliffe issued an order that, if ever the Lalauries were to return to this city, they were to be arrested and executed at once." The priest then turned toward the crowd and called, "Captain Pierre Gustav Toutant!"

Still dignified in the Civil War uniform he wore at the moment of his death, Toutant came forward. "Yes, Father?"

"Your men still have their weapons?"

"Yes, sir."

"Then I believe you have an execution to carry out, sir."

Toutant snapped his hand up in a sharp salute, clicked the heels of his boots together, then turned and called for his men to assemble front and center.

The dead of Shiloh came forward, each man readying his rifle for one final duty.

The Lalauries were marched over in front of one of the largest marble crypts in the cemetery and stood against its wall. The ghost slaves then stood along each side of the crypt, well out of firing range.

There was no place for the doctor and his socialite wife to run.

The dead of Shiloh lined up in two rows.

Toutant barked: "Company—ready!"

The first row of soldiers knelt down and aimed their rifles while the row behind them remained standing, then readied their own weapons.

Russell looked at Saffron. She was wiping sweat from her forehead.

"It isn't just me, is it?" he said.

"No—it's getting hot."

Toutant made a quick inspection of his men, then stood off to the left and pulled out his sword, holding it high above his head. "Company—take aim!"

The air itself seemed to be boiling over with heat.

Russell looked over at the Lalauries and saw that the air around them was glowing a deep red. Their clothes seemed to be smoldering.

The air was suddenly filled with the stink of sulfur and putrescence.

The first flame spiked up next to Delphine Lalaurie's feet, spread across the ground to her husband's, then began to encircle them as they rose ever higher.

Toutant, nerves of steel, brought his sword down and shouted, "Fire!"

The guns went off at the same time the flames around the Lalauries rose as high as their heads, and in the midst of the conflagration Russell saw a third figure rise up, a man three times the size of anyone he'd ever seen before, with coal-dark skin and eyes red as flowing blood. The figure released a deep and bone-chilling laugh. Its breath stank of slime and brimstone and the fungus from a cesspool. It pushed out its massive arms and lay a clawed hand atop the head of each Lalaurie, then lifted their charred but still moving forms above the flames.

Then it—and they—began to sink down as if caught in quicksand.

Russell could not take his eyes off the gigantic ram's horns that jutted forth from the figure's temples.

In a flash, it was over. A cool breeze wafted through the cemetery and the Lalauries were gone.

All was shocked silence for a moment; then, at last, Father Dagobert turned to Russell and said, "I never would have believed there would come a day I would be happy to lay eyes on the Devil." The priest shrugged. "Looks like I was wrong."

The child finally found its scream then, and other voices from elsewhere in the cemetery yelled back in panicked, urgent tones. The beams of several flashlights cut a new path through the darkness, and Russell stepped back, through one of the ripples, where the living could not see him.

Saffron put her arms around his waist.

All of the ghosts stood and watched as the tourists with their flashlights came around the corner with the police officer on horseback they'd gone after when first hearing the child's screams.

A little while later, amidst the dizzying, whirling visibar lights of police cars, the child's parents, in tears, fell to their knees and embraced their most precious little boy.

Russell allowed himself a tight-lipped grin.

"Think you'll be okay now, son?" asked Harold Crider. "Think you can move on in peace?"

Russell looked down at his fading flesh, then at Saffron. "I think maybe, yes."

A hand slapped him on the back, and de Marigny proclaimed loudly, "Dat's good. Dis heh war you been fightin', it over fo' ya now. Time to come 'long with us and pass a good time in a beddah place dan dis!"

"In a second," said Russell, taking hold of Saffron's hand. "The rest of you go on, we'll be right behind you."

The ghosts—those of New Orleans and those that had been within Russell's mind for most of his adult life—passed through a final ripple and disappeared.

"That *was* what I think it was, wasn't it?" Saffron whispered.

"That," replied Russell, "was justice. *Justice.*"

"Thank you," Saffron whispered.

He watched the police and paramedics swarm around the little boy and his mother and father, he studied the joy and relief on their faces, and then he thought about pain in its most mystifying expressions—but only for a moment. "My pleasure, miss; my very, very great pleasure."

She squeezed his hand. "C'mon, lover, dey be waitin' fo' us ober dere!"

"The Cajun thing doesn't really work for me."

"You need to get a sense of humor."

"I get a lot of complaints about that."

They turned, hand in hand, and walked toward the bluish-gray ripple.

"Never thought I'd end up with a cop," Saffron laughed. "Though you are kind of yummy."

"Think I planned on spending eternity with a Goth chick?"

"Aw," she said in mock pity, "you don't need to worry. I won't bite."

They passed through the ripple and vanished from the world of living; all that lingered—and it lingered only for a moment before being drowned out by the noise of emergency vehicle sirens—was the soft echo of Saffron's voice as she whispered: "That is, unless you want me to."

And the ghosts of New Orleans rested easy.

For Lucy, Jen, Steph, and all Goth Chicks everywhere: Black is so your color.

Authors' Biographies

Michelle West is the author of *The Sacred Hunter* duology and *The Broken Crown*, both published by DAW Books. She reviews books for the online column *First Contacts*, and less frequently for *The Magazine of Fantasy & Science Fiction*. Other short fiction by her appears in *Black Cats and Broken Mirrors*, *Elf Magic*, and *Olympus*.

Bruce Holland Rogers is no stranger to anthologies, having appeared in *Feline and Famous* and *Cat Crimes Takes a Vacation*. When he's not plotting feline felonies, he's writing excellent fantasy stories for such collections as *Enchanted Forests*, *The Fortune Teller*, and *Monster Brigade 3000*. Winner of numerous Nebula awards, including the 1998 short fiction award for his story in the anthology *Black Cats and Broken Mirrors*, his fiction is at once evocative and unforgettable.

Charles de Lint is a full-time writer and musician who makes his home in Ottawa, Canada, with his wife MaryAnn Harris, an artist and musician. His most recent work is a collection of his short fiction entitled *Moonlight and Vines*. For more information about his work, visit his Web site at www.cyberus.ca/~cdl.

Jane Lindskold, a full-time author and part-time cat wrangler, is the author of more than thirty short stories and several novels—including *Changer* and *Legends Walking*. She lives in Albuquerque, New Mexico, with her husband, archeologist Jim Moore. She is currently at work on another novel.

David Bischoff is active in many areas of the science fiction field, whether it be writing his own novels such as *The UFO Conspiracy* trilogy, collaborations with authors such as Harry Harrison, writing three *Bill the Galactic Hero* novels, or writing excellent media tie-in novelizations, such as *Aliens* and *Star Trek* novels. He has previously worked as an associate editor of *Amazing* magazine and as a staff member of NBC. His latest novel is *The Crow: Quoth the Crow*. He lives in Eugene, Oregon.

R. Davis lives in Wisconsin with his wife Monica and their two children, Morgan and Mason. He writes both poetry and fiction in a variety of styles and genres. His work can be viewed in numerous anthologies including *Black Cats and Broken Mirrors*, *Merlin*, and *Catfantastic V*. Current projects include more work than he can keep track of and trying to keep up with his extremely energetic children.

Elizabeth Ann Scarborough is the Nebula Award–winning author of *The Healer's War*, as well as twenty-two other novels and numerous short stories. Her most recent works are *The Godmother's Web* and *Lady in the Loch*, as well as an anthology she edited, *Past Lives, Present Tense*. She lives in a log cabin on the Washington coast with two lovely cats who find her useful for the inferior human DNA that granted her opposable thumbs for opening tuna cans. When she is not writing, she beads fanatically, and she is also the author/designer/publisher of a bead book of fairy-tale designs called *Beadtime Stories*.

John Helfers is a writer and editor living in Green Bay, Wisconsin. A graduate of the University of Wisconsin–Green Bay, he has fiction that appears in more than a dozen anthologies, including *Future Net*, *Once Upon a Crime*, *First to Fight*, and *Warrior Princesses*, among others. His first anthology project, *Black Cats and Broken Mirrors*, was published by DAW Books in 1998 and contains the 1999 Nebula Award–winning short story "Thirteen Ways to Water." Future projects include more anthologies as well as a novel in progress.

Peter Crowther is the editor or co-editor of nine anthologies and the co-author (with James Lovegrove) of the novel *Escardy Gap*. Since the early 1990s, he has sold some seventy short stories and poems to a wide variety of magazines and chapbooks on both sides of the Atlantic. He has also recently added two anthologies, *Forest Plains* and *Fugue on a G-String*, and a new chapbook—*Gandalph Cohen and the Land at the End of the Working Day*—to his credits. His review columns and critical essays on the fields of fantasy, horror, and science fiction appear regularly in *Interzone* and the *Hellnotes* Internet magazine. He was appointed to the board of trustees of the Horror Writers Association in 1997. He lives in Harrogate, England, with his wife and two sons.

Nancy Holder has published more than forty-one novels and more than two hundred short stories. She is a four-time Bram Stoker Award winner, including a Best Horror Novel of the Year award for *Dead in the Water*. Recent titles include *Sabrina, the Teenage Witch: Up, Up, and Away*, *The Logs of the Gambler's Star: Invasions*, and more than a dozen *Buffy the Vampire Slayer* titles.

Gary A. Braunbeck is the acclaimed author of the collection *Things Left Behind* (CD Publications), released in 1998 to unanimously excellent reviews and nominated for both the Bram Stoker Award and the International Horror Guild Award for Best Collection. He has written in the fields of horror, science fiction, mystery, suspense, fantasy, and western fiction, with more than 120 sales to his credit. His work has most recently appeared in *Legends: Tales from the Eternal Archives*, *The Best of Cemetery Dance*, *The Year's Best Fantasy and Horror*, and *Dark Whispers*. He is co-author (along with Steve Perry) of *Time Was: Isaac Asimov's I-Bots*, a science fiction adventure novel being praised for its depth of characterization. His fiction, to quote *Publisher's Weekly*, ". . . stirs the mind as it chills the marrow."

Copyrights